D1636157

RIDERS WEST

RIDERS WEST

ERNEST HAYCOX

Thorndike Press • Chivers Press
Thorndike, Maine USA   Bath, Avon, England

This Large Print edition is published by Thorndike Press, USA and by Chivers Press, England.

Published in 1995 in the U.S. by arrangement with the Golden West Literary Agency.

Published in 1995 in the U.K. by arrangement with the author's estate.

U.S.	Hardcover	0-7862-0481-8 (Western Series Edition)
U.K.	Hardcover	0-7451-2587-5 (Chivers Large Print)
U.K.	Softcover	0-7451-2591-3 (Camden Large Print)

The text of this Large Print edition is unabridged. Other aspects of the book may vary from the original edition.

Set in 16 pt. News Serif by Minnie B. Raven.

Printed in Great Britain on permanent paper.

British Library Cataloguing in Publication Data available

Library of Congress Cataloging in Publication Data

Haycox, Ernest, 1899–1950.
    Riders west / Ernest Haycox.
      p.   cm.
    ISBN 0-7862-0481-8 (lg. print : hc)
    1. Large type books. I. Title.
[PS3515.A9327R5 1995]
813'.52—dc20
                                95-13692

RIDERS WEST

1. "The Past Is Dead!"

Beyond the blurred car window the land lay dark and formless and unvarying — a flat emptiness across which the westbound train rushed hour after hour and yet seemed to make little progress. Occasionally the shape of a corral whipped by, less occasionally glimmering ranch lights reached forward from the remoteness of the prairie; but these were minute flaws to accent the loneliness of a world lost in its own immensity. When some restless passenger opened either vestibule door, the clacking assaults of iron on iron rushed in, and biting air currents turned the gauze gaslights of the coach redly dim. Cecile, a social and warmth-loving creature to her last plump fiber, made a small shuddering gesture.

"This is simply insane, Nan. It really is. You've got to change your mind in the next half-hour. Listen to me. You can't drop out of your own set — it will be so horribly dreary. If you must run, come on to the coast, where at least you'll meet your own kind of people."

Nan Avery answered with a falling inflection, with a queer lack of tone. "The past is quite dead,

7

Cecile. I buried it, laid on the flowers, and shed my tears." She sat relaxed, supple hands crossed in her lap, the neat military shoulders swaying in response to the motion of the car. Nothing, Cecile thought, could ever erase the smooth, fine regularity of Nan Avery's face. It was definite, it was proud, it was close to being beautiful. The mass of brushed copper hair heightened a whiteness of temple and brow; and had some odd disciplinary effect on the gray, straight-glancing eyes. All the Averys were like that, very direct and honest, very strict with themselves. What saved Nan from the otherwise Puritan sobriety of the tribe was a zest for living, a vital gayety that once had colored everything she did or said.

But she was not gay now. She sat there with an air of inner quiescence, as if all thinking and all hoping had ceased to be important; and in those expressive eyes was a foiled, faint bitterness. No strong character herself, Cecile felt a queer sense of desolation to see this swift surrender. For it was surrender; it was defeat. Even Cecile knew that after five miserable days on the train. Somewhat desperately she said:

"I actually can't bear the thought of leaving you. Nan, you'll come home after everything has settled and been forgotten."

"No," murmured Nan in the same detached manner. "I don't know what lies ahead. It doesn't matter. But I'll never go back."

"But why, of all places, should you choose to live out here?" cried Cecile.

Nan Avery's words were aloof, impartial — as if she were viewing herself from afar. "My life has been luxurious and easy. See what has come of it. Now I shall really find out if I'm any good!"

"Oh, you little fool, there is no blame on you!"

"But there is," said Nan softly. "My name has been dragged around the mud. However right or wrong it may be, people are talking. They always will." Then a small echo of hurt anger warmed her speech. "Can't you see what that does to me? It — it makes me feel like soiled linen! I hate it! I hate myself! I never expected it and never deserved it. But it happened, and so it must be my fault. Why should I try to find excuses? Well, it won't happen again. What's done is done, and I am through crying."

"You don't know anything about this country," brooded Cecile. "Nor anybody in it. You're stepping into a wilderness. Really you are. You might as well be dead as far as your friends are concerned."

"Just as I want it to be," said Nan indifferently; and her clouded glance turned to the vague landscape. A red-and-green light bloomed and vanished. The engine's whistle signal fled by in long, undulating ropes of sound.

The conductor came in to collect fares from a group of obvious cowhands at one end of the car,

9

and Cecile, always intensely interested in people, looked at the visible figures with a silent admiration. During the past two days the transcontinental had become a sort of accommodation local that collected and dropped travelers at each station. Sometimes it would be a woman, sometimes a family; but usually it was otherwise, for this clearly was a man's country. The coach was crowded with men now, of a type entirely new to her. They were tall or short and of all degrees of appearance, but certain particulars about them were inevitably uniform. For one thing, a characteristic slimness of body; for another, a similarity of boots, vests, and broad hats. When they walked they were awkward. When they sat they talked with a slurred briefness, and they used their hands freely to piece out phrases, Indian-like. Their faces were watchful, somehow deliberately wooden. Their eyes were more often than not blue, a blue turned almost green by the surrounding darkness of tanned skin. They moved about a great deal, played poker interminably, always were rolling cigarettes. The coach was a fog of smoke. Directly across the aisle a pair of them, more subdued than the rest, sat silently along the miles, and only when the end doors opened did they show interest — a momentary alertness that was quick and hard. Both had their saddles beside them, and both wore belts and guns. By now Cecile was accustomed to the weapons. More men wore them than didn't. She was thinking of the scratched scar on the face of the younger one when Nan broke a prolonged silence:

"You really don't know how glad I am to have you along. No, you don't, Cecile. It has kept me from remembering things I don't want to remember. But when I get off, you'll go on and I shan't ever see you again. After you reach the coast, take another route home. If you want to write, address the letter in care of the lawyer. Save for yourself, he is the only person who has the name of the town I'm going to. He will never tell." Then Nan bent forward and said soberly: "And you must never tell. I don't want the past to follow me. It is too hard to get rid of."

The conductor came along the aisle and paused. "We reach Trail in twenty minutes. I'll see about your luggage. Kind of sorry you have to put up with this smoke, but you can't do much with these fellows."

Nan's answer was limpidly cool: "I have observed that men like to make their own rules."

The conductor, appearing a little puzzled, went on. Cecile spoke: "You never used to be bitter, Nan. It isn't like you to be unkind."

"That, too," said Nan gently, "is part of the past. I shall not again trust a man, make allowances for him, ask favors of him."

"You'll soon forget that notion," said Cecile,

very positive. She could not let such heresy go unchallenged; for if she was not reflective, she had the wisdom of her own desires.

"No," contradicted Nan. "Now remember what I told you. Don't ever give anyone my address."

Cecile flushed. "I shan't."

But Nan, looking sharply at her friend, thought she had touched an otherwise frame of mind. So she said: "If you do, I'll of course have to move on. Beyond even your letters."

"Oh, Lord, Nan, I won't!"

"The break is complete," Nan observed, more to herself than to Cecile. "I am glad I had just enough courage to make it."

"But what will you do?" demanded Cecile forlornly.

"Does that matter?"

"I hate to leave you like this," worried Cecile.

Cold air poured into the car, and the lights dimmed again. A man hurried forward, stopped beside the pair across the aisle — a young and bulky man with a wide, loose mouth and a flattened nose. It was not possible to avoid hearing him speak.

"Get on at Green Springs, boys?"

"Howdy, Hugo. Yeah."

Hugo's glance swept the coach and fell on the women with a focused brightness. Cecile felt that she was being weighed, considered unimportant,

12

and dismissed from thought. The man's voice dropped to a lower pitch: "Dan Bellew is on this train."

That name had its instant effect. The younger of the pair stood up and looked to either end of the car. The other said: "When did he come aboard, Hugo?"

"At Big Mound."

"He's seen you?"

"Think so," answered Hugo.

The older one was obviously irritated. "He's always showin' up where he shouldn't be. I don't want him to see us."

"Get in the washroom," said Hugo.

The other rose. The older man murmured something Cecile, now frankly listening, didn't catch; then the two went along the aisle and disappeared into the washroom. Hugo sat down in the vacated section and hoisted his feet to the red plush seat. Nan was speaking again:

"When you get back home, Cecile, you'll probably meet Jamie Scarborough. There's no doubt he'll ask you about me. Tell him nothing. Absolutely nothing."

"You're sure?" asked Cecile.

"Well," amended Nan, "tell him this — tell him I don't want to see him or hear from him. And that there is absolutely no use trying to find me."

"That will hurt Jamie," observed Cecile.

"How about me?" answered Nan curtly.

Cecile started to speak and stopped. The inquisitive half of her mind was engaged in the affair across the aisle; and now she saw the rear vestibule door swing open before a high-built man. He stood in the opening for a while, visually searching the car. Then he came on and halted before the apparently indifferent Hugo, one hand idly resting on the arm of Cecile's seat. Over a long interval he said nothing — only looked down with a faint amusement that had no friendliness in it. He was, Cecile thought, cut in much the same pattern as the others; with a slimness of waist that strengthened his shoulders and a sense of solidity and deep-seated health about him. The flare of his hat accentuated all the angles of a rather broad face, sharpened the sweep of jawbones. His skin was ruddy and quite smooth, save for those finely etched weather wrinkles about the temples which seemed so universally stamped on these riding men. And that sense of inner amusement turned a broad, compressed mouth into a slightly skeptical curve. There was, Cecile said to herself, something just a little formidable about him. His continued silence disturbed her.

Quite apparently it also disturbed the reclining Hugo. His attitude of unawareness failed him. Turning his head, he looked up through half-closed eyes and casually spoke:

14

"Hello, Dan."

Dan Bellew's "Hello, Hugo," was equally casual. He pushed back the brim of his hat. "Traveling for your health?"

"A little business," muttered Hugo.

"Going to Trail?"

"Yeah."

"That's strange."

"What's strange about it?" demanded Hugo, on the defensive.

"Shouldn't think you'd find much business in a town you got run out of," mused Bellew. He had never taken his attention from the other, and that attitude of being sardonically entertained grew more obvious. It seemed to Cecile he was playing with this Hugo. Turning, she found Nan watching the scene, and she said to herself, "Nan's not too depressed to see a good-looking man."

"My business is my business," grunted Hugo.

"Would be if it was a legitimate business," observed Dan Bellew. "You wouldn't really try to fool me, would you, Hugo?"

"What do you want?" rapped out Hugo.

The lurking grin broke through Bellew's face, hard and sharp. "Just came in to tell you that you're not going to Trail."

"I think I am," contradicted Hugo flatly.

"You've been wrong before," drawled Bellew. "You're wrong again."

15

Hugo said nothing, but he was staring back at Bellew with a winkless attention. His body had gone still on the seat; his hands were idle beside him. The softness, the suavity of this quarrel astonished Cecile, who glanced at Nan in mute astonishment. Nan — and this was surprising, too — looked on with little signals of anger staining her cheeks. The conductor came down the aisle, stopped in front of Bellew and recognized him with a friendly nod.

Bellew said: "This man has made a slight mistake, Sam. He thought he was going to Trail, but he finds he isn't. He'd be pleased if you'd stop the train just long enough for him to get off."

It was, of course, rank insolence, and Cecile waited breathlessly for the conductor's explosion. Oddly, the latter's answer was mild to the point of being conciliatory: "Maybe he's got a different idea, Bellew."

"Hugo," stated Bellew gently, "seldom has ideas of much importance. Sorry to bother you, Sam. Please pull down on that bell cord."

The conductor was handling the situation gingerly. He looked now to the seated Hugo. Hugo abruptly rose. "You're puttin' me afoot on the prairie, Bellew?"

"My apologies."

Cecile could see no weakening of the deadlock. But the conductor apparently did, for he reached up and seized the bell cord. There was a swift reply from the engine's whistle ahead and an immediate shrilling of the applied brakes. All the other men in the car had turned silent and were watching with an absorbed, inscrutable interest. Hugo's countenance was dry of expression; nothing of his thinking showed through except for a brighter flare of light in his greenish eyes. He said, very briefly:

"All right — this time, Dan."

Something of Bellew's preoccupation left him. He stepped back a pace and waited for Hugo to precede him down the aisle. The door opened and let them out, and afterwards there was a moment's strange quiet as the train came to a full halt. Cecile heard feet strike the graveled road-bed; a man in a near-by seat murmured, "Told you so." Then the coaches lurched ahead under a wrenching application of power. The conductor returned to collect Nan's baggage. "Ten minutes to Trail," he warned her. Presently Dan Bellew came again into the coach and walked to the deserted section. For a little while he looked down, rolling a cigarette with an air of abstraction. Cecile wondered about that until the man abruptly reached over and lifted the skirts of the two saddles still lying there.

He seemed to find something of particular interest. Straightening, he studied the car, and when he lit the cigarette the matchlight glowed against a smooth, guarded face. Cecile was startled to hear Nan Avery speak in a clear anger:

"Arrogance in men is not a pretty thing to see."

Cecile swung to caution her friend, but she saw instantly that Nan had meant the observation to be heard. Nan sat straight, her chin up — sure sign of her temper — and she was directly meeting the surprised look of Dan Bellew. He had turned; he had withdrawn the cigarette from his mouth. His eyes, Cecile thought, confusedly, could be very bleak and unfriendly. They were now. She had the distressing feeling that he was stripping Nan's mind for his own cool satisfaction. Yet even as she thought so a sure gleam of humor replaced the severity of his glance.

"Little girls, especially strange little girls, should be seen and not heard," he said and walked away.

"Why didn't the other man fight back?" fumed Nan.

"You deserved what you got," said Cecile candidly.

"What right has he to put anybody off this train?" demanded Nan irritably. "It was outrageous. I hate men who use force like that."

"Must have been a reason," said Cecile practically. "He doesn't look like one to do anything without cause. Anyhow, why should you care?"

Nan caught a quick phrase on her tongue and turned to the window.

After a long period she spoke: "You're right.

I shouldn't mind it. Only, there is so little fairness in this world, especially among men."

Cecile was thinking, in half a panic, of other things. Through the window she saw the clustered lights of an advancing town. The train was again whistling for a stop, and some of the cowhands were collecting their effects. The conductor put his head into the coach and shouted, "Trail — Trail!" Nan's face was turned back to her, a sign of strain showing through the long-maintained composure.

"I guess this is the end, Cecile. Remember what I've told you. And be a good girl."

"It's so damn hard to see you go!" cried Cecile.

"Don't!" warned Nan. She rose and walked along the aisle. There were quite a few men in the vestibule, and the two women stood silent and constrained while the cars came to a sighing halt. The conductor swung down and held up his arm for Nan. One faint light seeped out of a station house — and that seemed to be all of the city of Trail, to which she had blindly bought a ticket. Behind her was the pressure of the men impatient to be off; but Cecile was clinging to her shoulder, and suddenly she turned and kissed the girl. Cecile, frankly crying, said:

"You little fool!"

"Nothing," said Nan in a small voice, "can be any worse than what was." Then she got down and stood uncertainly to one side. Cecile disappeared, the men filed out. Steam jets from the engine made sharp reports through the night, and the bell's ringing rolled resonantly across an emptiness that seemed to have no boundaries. The conductor waved his lantern in a full bright circle and swung up, the cars gathered momentum and slid by.

She saw Cecile's face pressed against a window, very dim; and presently there was only a line of faintly glimmering lights curving across the flat land westward.

She stood there in the darkness, with her luggage around her, ridden by a loneliness she could not help. The rest of the deposited passengers had gone off, and she was quite alone, smothered in the shadows. Small impressions came to her — the smell of sage and woodsmoke, the clatter of a telegraph key. Along the station wall was a sign that read: "See Townsite Jackson." But her mind was on that fast-fading red-and-green glow of the train; and as the lights grew dimmer and dimmer, so did her courage. Out there vanished the last of her old life, gone forever with nothing to replace it; and it was like a dark omen to think that her last view of Cecile had been blurred and uncertain. She found herself thinking desperately: "Why should this happen to me?" As much as she had prepared herself for this final break, the sweeping reaction of helplessness and regret was worse than she had ever imagined it could be; it carried her downward into an abyss from which there seemed no return.

She heard a shifting of weight on the gravel. That literally dragged her from her reflections. Turning, she found the tall shadow of a man standing by. When he spoke she instantly recognized — with a revival of resentment — the casual calm voice of Dan Bellew:

"Were you expecting someone to meet you?"

2. The Foreshadowed Tempest

"No," said Nan, pointedly brief.

"Then I'd better help you to the hotel."

It further irritated her that he refused to accept the implied dismissal. He was only an arm's length away, looking down from his height, immovably certain. She couldn't read his expression very well through the dark, but she believed he was smiling with that same faintly amused manner he had used on Hugo in the car. A critical inner voice told her she was being ungracious and a fool, yet her answer went curtly back to him: "I'm quite able to help myself."

He didn't hear it, or if he did he brushed it aside as being inconsequential. His body swung around to meet the arriving sound of some other person. A shadow, small and narrow, made a breach in the night, and a voice containing the surcharged weariness of the world drifted forward: "Wasn't sure you'd be on this train, Dan. Your horse is in front of Townsite's."

"Solano," said Bellew, "you lean against the wall over yonder for about ten minutes. If you see anybody walking up the track, come and tell me."

22

"Yeah," murmured Solano and backed away.

Bellew took possession of the luggage. "There is only one hotel," he explained, "and it's a pot-luck affair. Around the left side of the station."

Nan closed her lips against a quick, resenting answer and fell in step. He was, she decided, one of those dogged men against which irony made no impression; and she was too weary to argue. When they turned the corner of the station she saw the lights of the town run irregularly down one long street and halt against the farther darkness of the flats. There were a few tall trees growing up from the sidewalks, and the buildings she passed beside were all of weathered boards, set apart by narrow alleys. A rider loped out of the shadows and drew into a hitch rack, leaving a series of dust bombs behind him. He crossed in front of them, threw a musical "Howdy, Dan," over his shoulder, and pressed through the swinging doors of a saloon. Yellow radiance momentarily gushed out, and a confused murmuring of many voices rose — and died as the doors closed. They arrived at a square which seemingly centered the town, went over it and came up to a building identified by a faded sign on its porch arch: "TRAIL HOUSE — 1887 — Maj. Cleary." Bellew stepped aside, and thus Nan preceded him into a lobby gaunt beyond description. Behind a desk stood a cherubic man whose eyes were brilliant beads recessed in a pink round cushion; there was the air about him of having been waiting indefinitely for her.

"Customer for you, Cleary," said Bellew.

"Et supper?" asked Major Cleary in a ridiculously treble voice.

"Yes," said Nan. She was busy for a moment signing the register, one part of her mind wondering how she should thank a man she had no desire to thank. When she turned around she found Bellew had settled the problem for her; he had quietly retreated and stood now at the doorway. A woman's quick pleased exclamation raced in from the street: "Hello, Dan — I thought you'd be back this evening."

Cleary came about the counter and took Nan's luggage, saying, "Up these stairs, please." But Nan, faintly curious, remained still. Dan Bellew was smiling, and in another moment a girl walked into the lobby with a swift, boyish stride. She was very slim, not more than twenty. Her face was slightly olive and clearly modeled. Black hair clung loosely and carelessly to a restless little head, and two shining eyes seemed to gather all the light of the lobby lamps and throw it laughingly up to Bellew. "She's pretty," Nan found herself thinking, impartially. "Very pretty." The rest was obvious, for the very manner in which this girl took Bellew's arm and raised her shoulders was a frank, unconscious admission of what she thought.

Bellew was indolently speaking:

"I'm put out with you, Helen. Didn't meet me at the train. No girl of mine can neglect me like that."

Helen's laugh was exuberant, throaty. "Careful, Dan, careful. I'm apt to take you seriously."

Nan followed the heaving Major Cleary up the stairs, vexedly asking herself why she had spent the time looking on. Cleary went into a musty room, lit a lamp, and retreated. When the door closed behind him, Nan relaxed suddenly on the bed, bereft of all energy. She had hoped, distantly, for some glamour of the country to carry her through; but she saw nothing of it, felt nothing of it. Trail was a drab and common and flimsy cattle town on the prairie, and she sat in a room cheerless beyond words. A yellow mirror hung on the wall, a chair covered with dust sat in one corner. These articles and the iron bed on which she sat made up the furnishings. A shade flapped full length against an open window; and there was a hole — it looked like a bullet hole — through one partition. All this grated on her sense of neatness. But, studying her gloved fingertips, she quietly warned herself: "The trouble is not with the place. It is with me. I must not ask for too much." Tired and forlorn as she was, some restlessness would not let her sit still. She got up and went to the mirror, to see there the clouded

25

reflection of a person she scarcely knew. The image disturbed her, and she turned away, thinking: "I've got to keep moving or I'm lost." Abruptly she left the room and went down the stairs. Major Cleary was in a lobby chair, rocking himself to sleep.

"I want to talk with somebody about a house," she said uncertainly. "Something that will be outside of town."

"You'd want to see Townsite Jackson."

"Would you mind getting him for me?"

Cleary looked at her through nearly shut lids. "I doubt if he'd come," he said indifferently. "Better go see him."

"Where?"

Cleary's pipestem described a half-circle. "Catty-corner from here across the square. They's a building there with four doors — bank, post office, store, and land office. Any one of 'em will lead you to Townsite. Fact simply is, any business you may do will by and by take you to Townsite."

Nan said "Thank you" soberly and left the lobby. Certain shadowed forms loitered on the porch, and an idle talk died as she went down the steps and along the boardwalk. Men strolled casually from place to place, without hurry or apparent purpose. The air was sharper than it had been, and she caught the keen taint of burning wood and an intermingling dust scent. Water trickled pleasantly from a trough; a densely black stable's mouth yawned at her, through which traveled the patient stamp of stalled horses. There was, she thought slowly, an air of deep peace here, the peace following a hard day's work. The yellow dust settled beneath her shoes as she crossed the square and turned into the doorway of a starkly rectangular two-story building. Bright bracket lamps hung over a counter, but the long shelves of supplies ran into a dim background, and great mounds of sacked and boxed stuff made breastworks along the floor.

A man walked slowly from some other room.

"I'm looking for Mr. Jackson."

"I'm Townsite," said the man cheerfully.

He was, she decided, a rawboned General Grant; with the same square, closely bearded face, the same indomitable mouth. His eyes were a clear blue and patiently kind. Past middle age, he had the appearance of physical strength. She thought of all this while framing her request. It was more difficult than she had imagined, for she stood on wholly alien grounds, a transparent Easterner. Unconsciously she threw her shoulders back.

"This," she said, slowly, "is what I've come to see you about: I want some sort of a place, a house only large enough for myself with just a little ground around it. I want it away from town. The rest is entirely up to your judgment. Pick the

27

place, arrange for it. Select whatever I shall need. Tonight, if you please. In the morning I will be here with a check to pay for it — and ready to go.''

Townsite Jackson stood still while she spoke. And afterwards he studied her for a long interval with that same slow, judging scrutiny she had experienced at the hands of Dan Bellew. He was smiling, but behind that smile was a shadow of sympathy and regret.

"I'm always kind of sorry to spoil a fine dream," he told her gently. "Now let's consider this thing a little more fully."

Dan Bellew stood under the black shadows of a locust and idly talked to Helen Garcia. Then Solano came ambling out of an alley, and Helen walked away. "I saw nothin'," said Solano.

"We'll ride to the ranch in the morning," observed Dan. "So you better get your serious drinking done tonight." He crossed the street, all at once fallen into the indolent tempo of the town, and paused at the swinging doors of the Golden Bull. Viewing the crowd inside — and identifying each man with particular care — he stepped discreetly back into the shadows. The girl from the train was at that moment heading for Townsite's, and Dan watched the quick sure swing of her body with a silent approval. There was no doubt of her firm, independent mind; the incident on the coach had determined that. Dan chuckled soundlessly when he thought of the scene. It was somewhat strange that the outline of her features, the gray straightness of the glance, and even the still, angered clarity of her voice remained distinctly with him. Her display of temper had something to do with it, he reflected; yet beyond that was a clear-cut personality at once colorful and feminine. Meanwhile he searched the odd corners of Trail with a careful eye. Seeing nothing, he strolled down to the sheriff's office and went in.

Jubilee Hawk was at the moment assembling the parts of a rifle scattered along his desk. He looked up swiftly — all the muscles and nerves of this keenly edged young man were tuned to abrupt responses — and the oddly angular face relaxed from its concentration. He reared back, sorrel hair shining beneath the light, and reached for his pipe. Dan sat down, rolled a cigarette. It was, invariably, a ceremony between these two ancient friends who knew each other so well. Dan put his feet on the desk, struck a match, and idly surveyed the surrounding walls — Jubilee watching him through the smoke with an oblique, half-lidded interest. When Bellew did at last break the silence it was so casually as to suggest the continuation of a previous sentence:

"When there's carrion around, the buzzards circle down."

Jubilee nodded. "Election's only ten days off, if that's what you mean."

Dan looked across the table. "How'd you like to be an ex-sheriff?"

"May damn well be," grunted Jubilee. "And very soon. Neel St. Cloud is going to frame the election if he can. Once he gets Ruel Gasteen wearin' this star he'll have the best luck of his life. Ruel Gasteen will absolutely obey orders. St. Cloud knows that."

"How," went on Bellew idly, "would you like to be a dead sheriff?"

"Thought we'd get to the nigger in the woodpile pretty soon. Let's have it."

"I'm going to catch thunder for monkeying in your business," said Dan whimsically. "But anyhow, Hugo Lamont was on the train tonight."

"So?" Jubilee straightened. "I ran him out of here once by the slack of his britches."

"I knew that. Why do you suppose he wanted to come back?"

"Vote St. Cloud's ticket of course."

"No," answered Bellew. "No. If it was that, he'd wait until the last day. Only reason he'd venture into this town again would be to take a shot at you. He's got a score to settle."

"I can run him out again," was Jubilee's laconic observation.

Bellew smiled. "As I said, I'm going to get the devil for interfering. But I was afraid if he got here he'd broach you before I could put my warning in. So I stopped the train and set him off. If he's comin', it will be afoot. You're warned."

"I wish you'd quit goin' to trouble for me, Dan."

"I'm not sure there wasn't somebody else of interest on that train," added Bellew, very thoughtful. "Saw a couple of saddles in an empty section. You watch your step."

"Why should everybody have the sudden desire to make a target out of me?"

"St. Cloud isn't any too certain he'll win the election. If you got unfortunately killed in line of duty it would simplify matters for him. He's determined to put his whole ticket of scoundrels into office."

"He's a cool enough cucumber to figure all the angles."

"Never underestimate him," said Dan. "He has a first-rate mind. And when you harness a good head to crooked schemes, you've got a situation full of dynamite."

Silence came again, prolonged and studious. Jubilee ran a hand through his sorrel hair and appeared puzzled. "This is a rougher, tougher country than it used to be, Dan. More trouble, more suspicion, more thievin'."

"I've watched the grief gatherin' up for the last couple years," agreed Bellew. "The trouble is right over yonder in Smoky Draw, my lad. Neel

St. Cloud never used to be anything but a talking man. Then he got himself an idea. He's been working on it ever since.''

"What idea?"

"I don't know," was Bellew's slow answer. "I can't figure out a sensible story.''

"If it was a decent candidate runnin' against me," grumbled Jubilee, "I wouldn't mind losing. This job is nothing but sorrow — and gettin' worse. One of these days I may have to do something I don't want to do. Learned yesterday that Pete Garcia finally made up his mind to throw in openly with the crooks. He's moved to Smoky Draw. He's ridin' with St. Cloud's outfit.''

Bellew reared, showed a disappointed disgust. "That's something I halfways expected but hoped wouldn't happen.''

"He's plain no good. Don't see how one family can produce two such different kids. Helen's straight as a string. Pete's foolishness hurts her, Dan.''

"Of course it does. I've got to talk to that boy.''

"For more reasons than one," added Jubilee quietly, "it hurts her.''

Dan stared at his partner. "Well?''

But Jubilee got up, shaking his head. "I'll say no more. Shoot a game of pool?''

"No, I've got to see Townsite yet." Bellew also rose, openly disturbed. "All Helen ever got

32

out of that shiftless family of hers was a dirty deal. Now here is her brother gone haywire. I'm going to find Pete and make his ears ring."

"Do you no good. You've kept him on the safe side long as you ever will." Jubilee made a circle about the room, scowling at the floor. Presently he stopped in front of Dan. "You could go farther and do worse, Dan."

"Cut that out. Helen's just a kid."

"Nineteen. You're only twenty-six."

"What are you trying to do?" challenged Bellew. "Marry me off? Be sensible."

Jubilee grinned slowly, but his eyes remained sober. "Wanted to get a declaration. If you're not in the race, then the field's open to me."

"With my best love," drawled Bellew.

"Don't want yours. I'd want hers. That's no good, either. Hers is on another man."

Bellew was instantly interested. "Who is he?"

"Not sure," said Jubilee evasively and changed the subject. "While we're speakin' of being careful, you do same. If St. Cloud really takes to a hardware campaign, you'll be number one on his list. Don't forget that. You and him have been on the opposite ends of the teeterboard for a good many years."

Bellew, not paying much attention, went out, deeply engrossed with the affairs of Helen and Pete Garcia, somberly and acutely displeased. He could not remember when they had not brought their troubles to him. He couldn't recall when he hadn't fought for the both of them. With Pete it was only a question of keeping him out of too serious trouble, for the boy was a slack and shiftless Garcia. But Helen, and the thought brought a quick upswing of pleasure, was always full of pride, always indomitably at work. To see her was to see a flash of something bright across an otherwise gray scene.

"She's been a good soldier, with never any reward," grumbled Bellew. "She was made for something better than a slavey to a plain, no-'count family. I'm going to run Pete out of the country. If he wants to go to hell, he can do it beyond her sight."

His feet struck the edge of the walk, and he woke from his preoccupation to find he had unconsciously turned back to the Golden Bull. Recollecting he wanted to see Townsite, he started forward. A moment later he came to a full halt in the shadows, strangely puzzled. Something happened on the edge of his vision — happened swiftly and surreptitiously. That odd movement was enough to throw him instantly against his alert and wary self. Placing his shoulders against the saloon walls, he turned his eyes to the lower and blacker half of the town.

He saw, first, a man standing quite alone on the walk about fifty yards away. The fellow was drawn up against a porch post in an attitude of rigid attention, and his face was aimed on the sheriff's office diagonally across the street. This went on for perhaps half a minute; then the man lifted an arm in apparent signal. At once a second figure came from an alley near the sheriff's office and stepped along the boards, keeping well against the building walls. All this, Bellew thought with a narrower interest, was deliberate and premeditated; the man passed Jubilee's door, looked swiftly in, not breaking his stride. A little later he arrived directly opposite Bellew, whom he apparently didn't see.

Bellew flashed a glance back toward the first man, to discover instantly that one had faded out of the scene; and then this predatory maneuvering became clear to him. The second fellow halted near Townsite's, turned on his heels, and began to retrace his route. Bellew reached the dusty street in three long paces, coldly afraid he had come into action too late. His challenge broke across the quiet:

"Wait a minute."

It was, he realized, a bad place to be and a poor move to make. He stood aligned between the two — and the game was deadly serious. He recognized that before the echo of his order had quite died. The cruising man pulled to a sharp halt, evidently startled out of his set design. Taut and fine-drawn, Bellew saw the impact of that surprise congeal the man to a postured stillness — a

35

warning stillness that hit Bellew with a chilling effect. Thinking about the fellow somewhere behind him, and thinking of Jubilee off guard in the brightly illumined office, Bellew spoke again:

"Don't lose your head. Cut loose from your rope. Come over here."

There was a dimming of that lamp glow flooding from Townsite's door. Somebody stepped out — this much was on the remote area of Bellew's vision. A chair scraped a floor near by. The opposing man let out a long, gusty sigh and said, "You're in the way, Bellew." His whole body was released from the cramped immobility; he leaped aside. Bellew thought distantly: "The fool is drawing on me," and brushed the skirts of his coat away from his gun's butt. A swelling roar drove all the silence of the town up beyond the housetops, and those peaked roofs seemed to come crashing down. A snake-head of dust sprang in front of him, and a hard, fierce sense of pleasure flowed along his fibers from knowing he survived the shot. He brought his weapon swiftly forward and fired twice on the plaque-like silhouette ahead. There was a tumbling rush of bodies in the Golden Bull. Jubilee was in the play now, for Jubilee's metal order beat across the street to check somebody's advance: "Get back there, you!"

Bellew, motionless, said into space: "Careful,

36

Jubilee. There's another one." The figure before him swayed, called weakly, "That's it, I guess." Then fell and turned shapelessly still on the dust.

Bellew called again to Jubilee: "Watch for the other one." He walked forward, stood directly above the fallen gunman. The sleepiness of Trail was gone, and people were running up from all its quarters, to make a discreet gallery along the walks.

"Somebody get a lantern," he muttered.

Jubilee came back in long, unhurried strides. "I saw that other mug when I came out the door. He faded on the run. What've we got here?"

"I walked into it," said Bellew slowly. "But it was meant for you. Bring that lantern here."

The crowd stood back, cautious of sudden shots out of the dark. But one lantern made a gleaming, restless wake forward — that was Townsite Jackson coming up. He swung the light down against the prone body.

"Tom Addis," said Jubilee, surprised. "What in thunder was he sore about? This is queer."

"He and his partner were on that train," reflected Bellew. "They belonged to those saddles I saw. A nice trick. Use your head, Jubilee. He didn't have to be sore. He was obeying orders."

"Well," mused Jubilee, "here's the end of something."

"No," put in Townsite gravely, "the beginning of something."

"That's right," assented Bellew. Then he added a very quiet phrase: "I'm sorry for this poor lad."

Only Townsite and Jubilee heard that. Jubilee watched Bellew with a strangely blank expression. His arm fell lightly on Bellew's shoulder. "Might of been you, Dan."

Bellew stared at his partner, but looked quickly away. "Solano!"

Solano's exhausted voice came from a hidden alley. "Yeah."

"I thought I told you to keep an eye on the station."

"Wasn't nothing there," said Solano positively.

Nan Avery, leaving the store, stepped directly into the full shock of it. The sound of the shooting leaped at her, the wake of a passing bullet passed across her face. Not comprehending, she did the natural thing and shrank back against the wall. Looking around, she saw the two of them planted in the street, both motionless, both speechless; and then the sense of all this went through her, actually shaking her body. The nearer man sighed, a sound more horrible than anything in her experience. He said faintly, "That's it, I guess," and fell in a wheeling, dreadful motion. After that Bellew's rapid "Watch for the other one" identified him to her for the first time.

He came forward from the obscurity and stood

with his head slightly bowed. Townsite passed with the lantern, and then Nan observed Bellew's face rather clearly. It was very sober, very calm. Other men were talking, but she paid no attention to what they said. A bit of powder smoke drifted back and left a definite taste on her palate, strengthening her feeling of physical sickness. The fallen man never moved again; he lay sprawled there without dignity, without shape, one hand stretched out in a vain reaching. It was all so merciless, so savage. The slow conversation that went on seemed to have no sympathy in it, no regret. Looking up again to Bellew and vainly hoping to find the established coldness breaking into a more humane expression, all the bitter resentment at a heartless world swept through her and found an outlet. She straightened from the wall, calling directly to Bellew:

"You — you killer!"

His face came quickly up, but she saw it only in blurred outline. Wheeling, she ran confusedly across the square and into the hotel. Major Cleary still sat in his easy chair, though upright. When she passed him he said: "Who was it?" Halfway up the stairs she heard a woman's voice follow her, arresting and imperative. Going defensively about, she found the girl Helen framed in the doorway. The boyish body was straight with anger, the olive face pale — so pale that the deeply black eyes made a burning impression against it. The vivid lips parted.

"Until you know more about this country," said Helen, words rushing violently across the barren lobby, "and until you know more about Dan Bellew, keep your mouth shut!"

Major Cleary bawled out: "Get out of my place, Garcia!"

The girl turned impetuously on him. "You — you're no better than any other St. Cloud man! Why don't you tell people how you play his crooked game!" She looked back at Nan, stormy, shaken by her own feelings. Then she flung herself around and disappeared, the sound of her hurried steps striking into dead silence.

Nan pulled herself up the stairs. Soon in bed, she couldn't sleep. The images of what she had seen palpitated across the darkness in stark and terrifying distinctness, like a nightmare dream. Lying there, she had the sensation of the cruel weight of this land pressing down on her, smothering her.

3. The Charming Sinner

Dan Bellow walked through the thickening crowd and across the square to Townsite's store, feeling his nerves loosen and grow ragged. It was, he realized distantly, the inevitable after-punishment a man took for throwing his past and future into one debatable moment of time. All the sounds and sensations of the fight remained with him, and the last scene — of Tom Addis lying on the earth like a vagrant shadow — was etched in his mind with an intaglio sharpness. Thinking of it, his eyes assumed a somber, smoky coloration. Townsite and Jubilee noticed that the moment they followed Dan into the store.

Townsite, older and wiser, said nothing; he began a little chore of whittling plug tobacco for his pipe. But Jubilee, whose thoughts always ran parallel to those of his partner, cast a keen glance at Dan and broke the spell:

"He was free, white, and twenty-one. He had his plain choice, and he chose to make the fight. Forget it. Might of been you, Dan."

"I'm sorry for him," said Dan, profoundly regretful.

41

Townsite drawled: "A man always goes through these scraps twice. Durin' the shootin' and after the shootin'. Second time is hardest."

"I should have moved into the play sooner," said Dan, reviewing each step of the way. "I caught him too late, after he was set. He was in no frame of mind to back up. I'm sorry for that. It wasn't his personal fight — it was the fight of the man that ordered him to Trail." His temper rose and rubbed the words. "There's something else to put on Neel St. Cloud's record."

"You sure?" questioned Jubilee.

"Not the slightest doubt of his part in this," answered Bellew. "He's not sure he can muster the votes to put his thugs in office. So he's going to the gun."

Townsite removed his pipe, bent over the counter. "We can't let him, boys. It'll be a taste of raw meat for him and his kind. Once the wild ones climb the saddle, this valley will be bloody ground, I'm telling you."

Jubilee squatted on a sugar sack, shook tobacco in a brown paper. He threw back his angular, sorrel head and surveyed the others slantwise. "Well, first shot has been fired."

"There will be more," observed Bellew, very quiet. "The break's been made. It can't be stopped — not short of a decisive defeat for one side or the other."

Townsite's bearded face waggled slowly from

side to side. He muttered forebodingly: "I hate to think of the next ten days."

"Why just ten days?" asked Jubilee practically. "The election is only part of it. Doesn't matter who wins, the grief is going to go on."

There was a little silence. Heavy smoke folded across the yellow lamplight. Townsite's pipe wheezed. "I have lived here twenty-seven years. I put up the first cabin in this town. I helped drive in the first herd of Texas beef." Paused, Townsite stared at the others with a sudden angry energy. "I knew the fine men that made this range, and I'll be damned if I'll stand by and let the crooks make an outlaw strip of it!"

"I wish I could see what there was in it for St. Cloud," fretted Jubilee.

Bellew came to a stand. "Three years ago he had half a dozen cowhands up in Smoky Draw. Maybe three thousand head of stock. Today nobody knows how many riders are hiding back in that timber. I've checked twenty or better. As for the beef, it has grown out of all proportions to the natural increase."

"I know," agreed Jubilee. "But there's a limit to thievin'. What will political control of the county buy him?"

"I've told you before the man has a restless, fertile brain. He's got some plan."

"We're ruined if he does gain control," grumbled Townsite.

"Well —" began Jubilee.

Dan said "Careful," in a flat voice; and all three turned toward the doorway and toward the man framed in it. "Gasteen," muttered Dan, "you have a poor habit of eavesdropping."

Ruel Gasteen remained still. Beneath the shadowing brim of his hat lay features scarcely conforming with one another. A lantern jaw threw the lower lip beyond the upper and so created a plain impression of brutality. The man's skin was very dark, tightly bound across broad blunt bones; his eyes were secretively inset and somehow suggested the predatory. Inordinately long arms hung straight and motionless beside him.

"What do you want?" challenged Townsite.

Gasteen shifted. "If I was sheriff, Bellew," said he in a strange softness, "you'd be in jail for that shootin'."

"We'll wait till you are," countered Bellew evenly.

Gasteen nodded. "It will be my first official act — to put you there."

"Thanks for the warning."

Gasteen stepped backwards, out of sight, as discreetly as he had entered. The three presently heard his pony drumming down the street, northward.

"Gone to report the bad luck to St. Cloud," growled Townsite.

Bellew said, "Just so."

Townsite thought of something else. "By the way, that Eastern girl came to see me. Name's Nan Avery. She wanted me to get her a homestead somewhere beyond town."

Bellew displayed a quick interest. "You told her that was impossible, didn't you?"

"It did me no good," chuckled Townsite. "I talked to her like a beloved uncle. When I got through she went right on as if she hadn't heard. That girl has been accustomed to giving orders."

"You should have mentioned the danger of a woman living alone on the prairie."

"She waved that aside, too. The girl's got courage, Dan. And I think she's been in trouble. Anyhow, she was so downright about it I had to give in. As much as told me she'd go ahead anyhow if I didn't see fit to do the dickering for her."

"And she would," mused Bellew.

"Well," Townsite wanted to know, "where'll we put her?"

After a moment Dan said: "Tanner's old cabin."

Townsite was dubious. "Too close to St. Cloud's wild boys."

"I know. But Henry Mitchell's only half a mile from it, and I'm just west of the coulees a couple miles."

"All right," said Townsite. "Now I've got to arrange everything tonight. Guess she never heard about the values of procrastinatin'. Who'll show her up there?"

"It's on my way," said Dan. "I'm going home in the morning."

Both men looked oddly at him. Jubilee's question was faintly ironic: "After she gives you a lacin'?"

"She didn't understand," said Dan gently.

Townsite repeated his conviction: "She's been in trouble."

Dan nodded indifferently and left the place, obviously thinking of other things. He took his horse to the stable and afterwards headed for the Golden Bull, there locating Solano. "Go on home tonight," he told Solano. "Early in the morning take a broom and a hammer over to the Tanner cabin and clean it up."

Back in the store Townsite said: "The shootin' hurt him pretty hard."

Jubilee morosely assented. "A lot of things hurt him. What worries me is the future. You realize that Dan will sure be the chief target in this fight? You'll never organize the respectable ranchers under anybody else. St. Cloud knows it, too. His aim will be to get Dan out of the way."

When Nan came from the hotel next morning early, she had for a moment the sensation of definitely beginning another existence. A hard, bright sunlight washed the unlovely walls of

Trail to create crisp black and white contrasts. All the buildings stood before her with a gaunt angularity. In another hour it would be hot, but there was yet a coolness to the air and a kind of winelike vigor that woke in her some little sense of buoyancy. Surprisingly, the night and its terrible scene absorbed less of her imagination than she had thought possible. Crossing the yellow dust of the square, she found a flat-bed wagon and team waiting there, loaded with supplies. Tethered behind was a pair of saddled horses.

Townsite came out of the store.

"I have a cashier's check," she said and held it out to him. "Please settle the account and let the balance stand in your bank."

Townsite grinned openly. "I don't believe," he drawled, "I ever run up against anybody like you. But I got everything fixed."

"What are the saddle horses for?"

"One's yours. Hereabouts you need a horse worse than you need shoes. It's the little strawberry there — very gentle. Other one belongs to the man that's taking you out. Mama, come out here."

A gray, quick-moving little woman appeared from the store. She had, Nan realized, been watching. Townsite said: "This is Miss Avery, Mama."

Mrs. Townsite had snapping, inquisitive eyes, but a kindly mouth and a ready smile. "If you'd just stay over a day," she offered, "I'd like to introduce you to the women of the town."

"Thank you — I'm afraid not."

"Here's your teamster for the trip," drawled Townsite. "Dan Bellew — owner of the Broken Stirrup."

Nan turned quickly, saw Bellew strolling over the dust; and for a moment most of her self-possession deserted her. It was a situation she didn't know how to meet. Half angered, she felt color come to her cheeks. Townsite was speaking: "Dan's ranch ain't far from your cabin, Miss Avery. He's goin' home and agreed to take care of you."

There was no use of pretending, she thought, and met Bellew's glance directly. "I believe you understand how little I like to put you to this trouble."

The challenge was there, as she meant it to be. But once again she was left helpless in front of his manner. He only nodded, the same remote amusement in his eyes — they were a darker hazel than she had first imagined — and went directly to the wagon. Obviously he waited for her, and so she followed, accepting his hand-up. He went around, climbed to the seat, and took the reins.

"You're carryin' a sack of flour for Henry Mitchell," called Townsite.

Bellew kicked off the brake, leaned down to

Townsite. "If anything comes up suddenly," he murmured, "get the news to me." Then the team moved away.

Townsite chuckled at the departing pair. "She's mad enough at him to chew nails, Mama."

Mrs. Townsite said firmly:

"Jackson, she's got a past — you mark my word. I'll bet she's a remittance girl."

Townsite went stoutly to Nan's defense: "I like her."

Mrs. Townsite flashed a humorously understanding glance at her husband. "You'd like anything that was helpless. She won't last out here, Jackson."

"I wouldn't bet on that," said Townsite. "She's a fighter."

The road climbed a gentle grade and presently tipped into a valley; and it was, Nan thought, like putting away from shore. To right and left — perhaps eight miles in either direction — were low enclosing ridges now being slowly blurred by the haze of summer. Northward at a greater distance lay a high and black pile of hills toward which the tawny-grassed flooring ran in long, slow undulations. The road pointed that way straight as a chalk line. A red sun climbed into a sky that was very blue; one gleaming cloud pillar stood alone. Morning's breeze died, and she felt at once the day's sultriness closing in. Cattle lay scattered and apparently motionless all about the flats. Two miles or more onward she looked back to see the whole distance to town marked by a risen banner of dust that clung cloudily to the air.

Dan Bellew had so far said nothing. From the corner of her vision she saw him loosely straight on the seat, his bronzed face soberly composed. Now and then his head described a long arc, as if he regularly searched the horizons, and he appeared to be oblivious of her presence. Presumably he had felt her attitude of resentment and meant to respect it. Yet the situation promised to grow intolerable, even ludicrous; two people could not ride together by the hour and ignore each other. That calm of his was monumental, she thought irritably; yet another reflection, and a fairer one, told her she had set the precedent and so had to make the first overture. Her voice seemed to her to be ridiculously stiff:

"How far is this place?"

"About fourteen miles from Trail."

He had returned the same exact measure of words. She told herself, "He's either trying to discipline me or ignore me," and decided to remain silent all the rest of the way. A long time afterward she was a little surprised to hear him talking impersonally:

"This is plain cattle country, nothing else. Off

to the left rear — where you see a slight break in the ridge — is Simon LeBœuf's ranch. His range comes over as far as this road. Look to the right now and you'll see Gunderson's quarters.'' His long arm pointed, and she discovered the outlines of grouped houses against the foot of that rightward ridge. "LeBœuf and Gunderson control all the lower half of the valley. The upper half, which is narrower, is my range. Broken Stirrup. There's maybe a dozen small outfits here and there, in addition. That's all.''

She had begun to observe that upper narrowing of the flats. Those left and right ridges were gradually closing in. She asked about it, more to avoid embarrassing silence than anything else.

"Yes," said Dan. "They meet up yonder by those dark peaks to form Smoky Pass. Your place is there." A lighter and more indolent manner came to him. "The Indians have a legend about those two ridges. Seems like there once was a maid and a man who quarreled. So the gods turned 'em into hills. That eastern one is Buck ridge; the western one, Squaw ridge. But the maid got sorry, and even stones couldn't keep her away from the man. So there's the result." His arm traced the far-off bending of Squaw ridge. "She went back to the man. Squaw and Buck ridges join at the pass.''

"The man," said Nan coolly, "made no move

to meet the maid?''

"Men are stubborn, I guess.''

"It is easy to see that a man created the myth,'' was Nan's brief retort.

"I was waiting for that,'' drawled Dan. For the first time their glances locked. Nan saw the humor lying quietly in his eyes. It only increased her defensive aggravation. "You seem sure of my reactions, Mr. Bellew.''

"I have a couple previous ones to judge from. As for the man, maybe he thought the maid had him all wrong — and waited till she changed her mind.''

"Quite probably he would think himself the injured one.''

"I suppose so,'' agreed Dan. "But right or wrong, about all the buck could do was wait. If he was right he had an apology coming. If he was wrong he'd naturally suppose the woman was through with him.'' Then he added idly: "Another strictly man's idea, of course.''

"Don't you suppose the woman may have thought the same way?''

"Don't lay that trap for me,'' countered Bellew. "How do I know what a woman thinks?''

"She may have thought this man unjust and blind — and still have gone to him because she couldn't help it.''

"She wouldn't be finished with him?''

"No,'' said Nan, suddenly feeling the conversation out of control. "Not if she loved him. That — that's a weakness. I'm not applauding the woman for it."

"I believe," murmured Bellew, "I would."

"Of course," retorted Nan.

He looked obliquely at her, then turned his attention across the flats to sudden bomblike clouds of dust. The road made a swinging circle toward the eastern ridge and gradually ran a parallel course beside it. The dust cloud rolled nearer, and presently Nan recognized a compact body of horsemen advancing at a set gallop. Dan Bellew was quite silent, and she looked curiously at him, feeling a strange stiffening of his attitude. The direct glance was pinned on the cavalcade; his face had gone quite smooth. Something about him sent a small current of excitement through her. The group arrived within a few hundred yards, broke out of the gallop to a slower pace. Two men spurred abreast the leader — and so the team and wagon came upon them. Bellew said "Who-oa" expressionlessly and halted. "Hello, St. Cloud."

"Hello, Dan."

The name registered instantly with Nan, but for a moment her attention strayed to the two other flanking riders. One — this was Ruel Gasteen, though she didn't know it — she had seen for a moment during the previous night and had re-marked the excessive lower jaw and the tight

53

leathered skin. The other was very short and very broad, with a face quite unrelieved by intelligence or humanity. His wide mouth was indescribably bitter, his eyes intensely glowing; a broad cowlick of hair covered a half of his forehead and hung just above one eye, to give him a sullen, dull-witted appearance. One leg, she saw, was short and deformed. Then her glance passed to the center man and found a quick contrast. This Neel St. Cloud, whose name seemed to be a password of trouble, was a slim, cavalry-figured person as tall as Bellew. He had yellow hair, a sharp, mobile face, a cream-ruddy complexion. And he was, she instantly guessed, rather educated. That air was about him. But the dominating impression he left with her was of a lurking, restless laughter; of a cynical nonchalant cheerfulness at once keying his character. He was obviously sure of himself, almost disdainfully sure, and he made so great a contrast to the more animal types beside him that Nan found herself absorbed. She was, consequently, half startled at the swift answering interest this Neel St. Cloud passed to her. She looked quickly away.

"Trust you had a nice train trip," said St. Cloud to Bellew.

"Been informed, I see," replied Bellew.

"Sure."

"Any objections?"

St. Cloud's ironic smile grew more pronounced. "None, my friend. None at all."

"I don't suppose one man more or less counts much with you," agreed Bellew.

"It is not the checkers that count, Dan. It's the game."

"I judge so."

The antagonism of these two reached out and touched Nan. It was something distinct and embodied. It inflected each of those soft, courteously spoken words. She observed something else about St. Cloud, too. Careless as he was, apparently reckless as he was, his attention remained on Bellew as a sharp, constant thing. There could be, she reflected, no pair so opposed. Bellew was solidity itself, slow and even-tempered, his energies stored away. By contrast, St. Cloud was mercurial, his mobile face reflecting the lightness and darkness of his thoughts. Bellew said abruptly:

"I'd like to see you soon, St. Cloud. For a talk."

"On my way back from town I'll drop over," promised St Cloud and reined his pony around the wagon. In passing he lifted his hat to Nan and smiled directly at her. Then the whole cavalcade went storming by. Bellew put his team in motion.

"He is a rancher?" asked Nan.

"Has a ranch. Beyond the pass, in Smoky Draw."

"Those were his men?"

"Yes."

The reticence of the answers warned her. She thought quietly, "He hates the man, but won't speak." Thereafter silence covered the dusty miles one by one. Heat waves made quivering layers against the earth, and the dry grasses sent up a scorched smell. She could see now the jointure of Squaw and Buck ridges, the little notch of the pass, and the darkly rising peaks beyond. The road took an upward direction, wound along the irregular footing of the slopes. Turning a point of rock, Bellew drew up in front of a small, paintless house. A man walked from behind it — loose of frame and gaunt. He was rather old, she saw, but he had that weathered vigor of an out-of-doors hand worker.

"This," said Bellew cheerfully, "is Henry Mitchell. Henry, you'll have a neighbor. Miss Avery here is going to live in Tanner's place."

She liked Henry Mitchell at once, just from the way he lifted and dropped his beaten hat; his eyes were faded, very honest. All he said was, "Fine, fine." But it was deeply encouraging.

"Sack of flour for you," said Bellew.

Henry Mitchell went to the tailgate, found his flour and dragged it out. Bellew sat idle a moment. "What's news?"

"Lorrie," drawled Mitchell, full of pride, "shot a deer all by himself."

Bellew chuckled. "The kid's a regular Sioux,"

56

he mused, looking around the yard.

"You won't find him," said Mitchell. "He saw you comin'. Ducked out when he observed the lady. He's shy, ma'm. By the way, Dan, I got some advice this mornin'."

Dan looked more closely at Mitchell. "Who from?"

"The doctor," said Mitchell enigmatically. "It was his reckonin' I ought not to travel too much. Specially up in the hills."

They were, Nan knew, speaking in code. Dan's face settled to a thoughtful severity. After a while he said: "Better be careful, then, Henry. You've Lorrie to look after."

"Yeah," observed Henry Mitchell. "Wait a minute," he added and walked behind the house. A little later he returned with a can of water which he placed securely in the wagon. Dan nodded, urging the horses on again. A hundred yards away Nan saw a boyish form rush from one high boulder and disappear behind another. Head and eyes came cautiously around it; a shrill whoop sailed along the windless air.

Bellew grinned. "That's Lorrie," he said and let the team set its own pace up and around a steeper grade. Trees thickened on the ridge's side, and the ground buckled into several parallel coulees. Looking behind, she saw the valley sweep away from her to a misty horizon; and when she again straightened frontward she found the end of the journey. Another house — no different from Mitchell's — sat a few rods off the road, without shelter, without grace. Bellew drove abreast a small porch, kicked on the brake, and got down. Rather stiffly Nan followed suit — uncertain, once more feeling a let-down of spirit.

She had expected little, nor was this any better than her expectations. Crossing the porch, she entered the place and stood aside while Bellew packed her belongings through. There were three rooms — front room, bedroom, kitchen — and these only separated by the scantiest sort of rough-board partitioning which somebody had started to cover with old newspapers. The outer walls were warped, none too windproof; and looking up to an unsealed attic, she saw points of light stabbing through the shingles. A few pieces of improvised furniture remained, an old pair of overalls hung on a nail, the kitchen held a small stove. It was, she thought, nothing better than a primitive shelter — and she unsuccessfully tried to imagine the kind of people who had previously lived in it. Comfort, apparently, was a luxury here. What were the necessities?

Bellew stood before her, his hat off and the black hair aglisten with sweat. "You're moved in," he told her. "That can of water is sitting beside the pump. It's to prime with. Never let yourself get entirely out of water. Your horse is in the barn. Piece of a fenced pasture you can run him in. He won't drift away, and he'll stand on dropped reins. Ever saddle a horse?"

"Yes — I've ridden before."

He loitered, looking down with that old air of judging her. "At night you'll hear a lot of noises. Don't worry. Country's full of packrats. Pay no attention. But as a matter of habit, lock your doors."

"Against what?"

He shrugged his big shoulders. "Against possibilities. There's a new .38 in that mess of supplies. Don't ride anywhere without it. Don't go walking through sage without boots on. If you put your bedding out to air, shake it before you bring it in again. That's for ticks which we have in summer and fall. Should you hear travel on the road after dark, don't display too much curiosity." Paused, he showed a faint puzzlement. Nan, knowing he wondered about her luck in such surroundings, was quick to speak up:

"I can take care of myself."

"One thing more," said Dan. "Don't ride beyond the pass. Not at any time."

"Otherwise," asked Nan, deceptively calm, "I may do as I please?"

"Perhaps I have offered too much advice," said Bellew quietly and went out. Presently going to the door, she saw him driving away with the empty wagon — not down the road but straight west over a roll of land. He was soon out of sight, leaving her with the uncomfortable thought that she had made no effort to thank him. As before, he had relieved her of the need of doing something she didn't wish to do.

shown recently, and has liked him — but not as a lover. For a moment, it noted there was a hint of interest — a faint sense ... of rivalry. But it would give you to reason... she could find no deeper impulse.... He would support her, but if I keep her...

4. St. Cloud's Pronouncement

The last clacking echo of the wagon died out in a coulee, and afterwards the deep silence of the country returned. Nan removed her hat and coat and sat on the edge of a trunk, all her impulses idle and indecisive for the while. Still heat pressed heavily through the house; the boards emitted a baked smell. Looking down at her fingertips, she thought again of the gracelessness of the place, then said quietly: "But I have no reason to ask anything more than plain shelter." The sense of defeat was almost overpowering.

There always had been in her a strain of lucid, self-examining honesty; and even now she was able to explain that feeling of being cast adrift. The Nan Avery who was important to herself and to others, who lived in the midstream of things, who was full of faith, no longer existed. Another Nan Avery sat on the trunk's edge and soberly looked back into ruin. There was nothing left. Yet the warning returned. "I must not go in for self-pity. I haven't the right." And after that the mutations of her drifting thoughts returned her to Dan Bellew. The oddness of it was that a few short weeks ago she would have liked him — but now never could; for in him were mirrored those qualities she no longer trusted — a man's obvious strength, a man's distinct, almost ruthless point of view. Her guard would always be against him; she couldn't soften her instinctive antagonism.

She got up, impatient with herself, forcing her mind back to the present and its necessities, wisely knowing that she had to drop the curtain on what was done. Going out through the kitchen, she surveyed the rear yard, the irregular line of fence, the sheds and the barn. Half interested, she primed the pump. When the water came spouting up she experienced a small feeling of encouragement. It was such a small thing — yet so certain. Water and food, sleeping and waking and the work of one's hands. "I have been living beyond myself," she said and observed that the house had been swept and that there was wood in the box beside the stove.

It was too hot to cook a meal, and so she made a lunch out of cheese and bread and water. She changed into more comfortable clothes and took up the job of unpacking. An ingrained feeling for neatness and order nagged at the supplies piled in the middle of the room, and she worked until her forehead was damp. Then and there she stopped.

"Why should I hurry? There isn't anything here but time."

She felt immeasurably better for having thought of it. Resting on a trunk, she tried to visualize what she could do with the barrenness of the house — how its unrelieved ugliness might be subdued. The bedroom, of course, was first. Refreshed, she swept the room thoroughly, knocked down the cobwebs, created one moderately clean spot in an area of dustiness. She dragged in the iron bedframe, which was part of Townsite's supplies, and put it up. She laid on the springs and the mattress. She arranged the trunks where they would take the place of chests and cupboards; from one of these trunks she got her sheets and quilts and made up the bed, a piece of a popular tune coming unbidden to her mind. It was, "There'll Be a Hot Time in the Old Town Tonight," and it reminded her of Jamie Scarborough.

Out on the road a long column of men went by, headed into the pass. Nan got the sound rather than the sight of them, engrossed as she was with threading a wick into a new lamp. Nor could she help considering Townsite Jackson's thoughtfulness. He had seemed to forget nothing; had, in fact, remembered more items than she would have remembered. And his talk had been very kindly, very shrewd, strongly underscored with sympathy. Nan went out of the bedroom to locate the can of coal oil — labeled by a potato in its spout — and found Neel St. Cloud standing on the porch. Somewhat startled, she straightened to an alert motionlessness.

"Sorry," he said. "Should have given you more warning."

The low afternoon sun struck under his hat and sharpened his smooth, smiling face. He stood there with a sort of negligent ease, yet the slimness of his body and the taper of his shoulder points were such as to suggest a military attitude. For one long moment of doubt she recalled his easy, cynical manner and wondered if he meant to use it on her. It would be natural of him to presume too much. But she was mistaken. He took off his hat, and his yellow head made a slight, courteous bow. He said gently: "If I might step in —"

"If you wish."

He walked through, stood against the wall, surveying the quarters with a swift, estimating glance. "Had no desire to interrupt you," he went on. "Only wished to pay my respects to you as a new neighbor. My place is up beyond the pass — five miles."

"Yes, I've been told that."

His smile broadened. "I supposed you would. I am" — and he paused over the wording of his sentence — "a rather established character. Is there anything I can do to help?"

"Nothing, I think," said Nan. Inwardly she was saying: "How like Jamie in his surface manners."

He made a deprecatory gesture with one arm.

"I don't want to sound grandfatherly, Miss Avery, but if I were you I'd not worry about things around here. To a stranger a great many ways of ours appear odd. Maybe they are. One thing is pretty definite, though. You can always have the help you need by asking for it. Range people are that way."

"I am afraid," said Nan deliberately, "those people will find me rather unsocial."

St. Cloud's eyes were momentarily keen and exploring. It was, she thought, a reversion to his normal man's curiosity concerning her. But he recovered himself quickly. "Solitude? You'll have no trouble getting that. The valley is full of it. What I wanted to say was that I go up and down this road three or four times a week. Should you ever want anything from town, hail me. Please do."

"Thank you. There seems nothing now."

"There will be," St. Cloud said casually. "You'll always be out of matches, or sugar, or nails. The stores, you know, are not just around the corner — as they are in your town."

"How would you know anything about my town?" asked the girl.

"You haven't the earmarks of this country," said St. Cloud.

She listened for the upswing in his voice that would convey the question. But his politeness covered even that; he had not the air of prying for information. He spoke in a matter-of-fact way. She allowed the silence to settle, and St. Cloud — she thought again that his manners were very alert — put on his hat and moved to the door. "I can promise you," he said, "perfect peace and shelter from my quarter, which is anything lying beyond the notch."

"That," replied Nan, "is about all I ask."

"You will, of course, be unable to escape hearing a great deal of gossip. You'll soon enough know all about us. My suggestion is you strain the information through the fine screen of your own good sense."

He was, she understood, asking that discount for himself. "I have my own scale of values," she told him soberly.

He nodded, showing again a touch of speculation. "Some day, when you are caught up, I might persuade you to visit my place? Smoky Draw is almost a town. Other women are there, you understand."

"Possibly," said Nan.

He left it lie as spoken and went to his horse. Watching him to westward in the direction Dan Bellew previously had gone, she suddenly wondered what his inner reaction to that "possibly" had been. Rather regretfully she wished she had not said it. The man was obviously educated, and his kind read too many meanings into plain speech. Dissatisfied with herself, she filled the lamp and sought out the more immediately needed groceries. Sunset was not far away; the valley was a-riot with a plunging, golden light. Going out the back door to fill her brand-new water bucket, she saw Henry Mitchell swinging up the slopes on his horse, followed by the boy Lorrie on a bareback pony. Mitchell arrived in the yard, put a leg over his saddle.

"Thought I'd drop in and see if I could help."

But his eyes passed through the house and around it; and she knew he looked for Neel St. Cloud. It was apparent he had come here out of a sense of responsibility. Remotely she thought she ought to be grateful, yet an uncontrollable irritability grew stronger. She had traveled three thousand miles to escape such an oppressive surveillance; she could stand no more of it. Her eyes went sharply to him.

"Did Dan Bellew tell you to watch this house?"

"Why should he?" countered Mitchell.

"Please understand this: I am quite able to take care of myself. All these offers of help are very kind. But I don't need help."

"Sure, sure," said Henry Mitchell soothingly. He refused to be offended; he was like all other men, discounting her clear desires and clinging to the inevitable male assumption that she was a woman and therefore to be watched, to be shielded. Nan felt anger warming her cheeks.

Nothing, it appeared, could shake a man's urge to be protective. She meant to say something more definite, but old Henry Mitchell spoke before her:

"A lot of little annoyin' things may come up. Your horse might stray. You might have to lift somethin' heavy. Anything at all in that line. Me or Lorrie will be on tap. Just call us. Lorrie, he's nine and as good as a man."

Lorrie had flattened himself on the broad back of his pony and was watching her with intent, lucent eyes. His face was round and darkened by the sun. All he wore was a cotton shirt and a pair of overalls which hung loosely to his too thin frame; and suddenly her anger went away and left her so certain of this boy's needs. Something very wistful and very shy lay mirrored in his wondering glance.

"He don't see so much of women," said Henry Mitchell, slowly. "Kind of interested in you. No, he don't see near enough of women." The man's voice was softened by a slight regret. "Some things a man ain't much good at."

"You're —"

"His granddad."

"Where is his mother?"

Henry Mitchell met the question with a quick blankness of expression. "His daddy is dead."

The girl felt pushed away from something unfortunate. She said softly, "I'm sorry," and walked toward Lorrie. For a moment she thought he meant to bring his horse about and retreat; he straightened, and one hand dug into the pony's mane.

"Lorrie," said Nan, "we're going to be pretty good friends, aren't we?"

"Sure," said Lorrie dubiously.

She wanted to reach up and smooth the tangled black hair, but she knew better. "Sometime," she went on gently, "you might ride over and show me the trails through the timber. I'd like that."

He was watching her very closely, and it occurred to Nan then that his attitude of reserved and suspended judgment was the same thing she had noticed in Dan Bellew. It seemed to be a frame of mind men here were born with — a slowness of decision that had to be eventually sure beyond suspicion. Presently he said in a warmer voice: "All right."

Nan, wondering why she should be so eager about it, smiled and turned. Henry Mitchell's glance was abruptly grateful. "Any time, Miss Avery, you want us two men, just call. Come on, Lorrie, and don't sit on that horse like a squaw."

She watched them descend the slopes, the tall rawboned man and the slender lad side by side. She said to herself, "They are great friends, those two," and a quick recognition of the pathos there came to her. All at once the harsh brightness of the earth vanished, and a still twilight settled across the ridge. Pale blue shadows filtered through the trees; the air began to take on a brief transparency, and she saw the valley sweep away and melt into the southern horizon. A faint breeze rose.

Immobile, watching the tremendous change, she thought: "It will not be as hard to live with myself as I thought."

Neel St. Cloud cut due west from Nan's place, up and down the rolling ravines. Not quite two miles onward he came into a small flat bay of land that butted against the side of Squaw ridge. There — at the junction of valley and high ground — sat Dan Bellew's Broken Stirrup, its face to the open south and its rear darkened by the rising pine slope. Poplars made a pleasant circle about the place; unseen water fell down a gentle drop and sent its music across the dry, motionless air. Passing through the front gateway, St. Cloud's face went smooth and noncommittal, the sharpened cast of expression that comes to a man on unsure soil. Dan Bellew sat in the shade of the porch, but he rose at St. Cloud's approach and stood waiting till the latter had circled and dismounted. St. Cloud took a seat on the steps, reached for his tobacco. In the back angles of the place a blacksmith's hammer suddenly ceased to ring; Bellew sat down again.

St. Cloud, absorbed with the making of his

smoke, said, "Dry summer," indolently.

But Bellew brushed the invitation of preliminary talk aside. Both big fists lay along the arms of his chair, his head tipped soberly toward St. Cloud. "Neel," he said abruptly, "we might as well get this straight. You and I are headed for the same crossing. We stand a chance of collidin'."

"You've just discovered that?" asked St. Cloud, obviously ironic.

"I've known it a long time."

"Of course you have," said St. Cloud. "You're no fool, Dan. If you were, I wouldn't bother with you."

"I had to draw and kill a man last night," mused Bellew. "He wasn't hunting me. He was after Jubilee Hawk. He had no particular reason to bear grudge against Jubilee. He was doing a job because he had his orders. Your orders."

"You sure?" drawled St. Cloud.

"There ain't any other answer."

St. Cloud shrugged his shoulders. "Let it ride like that, then."

"No, I'm afraid not. You're determined to win. But you're not too sure about it. So you figured to make it a little easier by erasin' Jubilee."

"If you think so, I'll not contradict."

"What's there in it for you?" challenged Bellew. "Supposin' you place your men in office. What of it?"

"You don't see it?" queried St. Cloud. He flashed a sardonic smile at Bellew. "You can't guess my hole card? Of course you can't. But it is there. Make no mistake about that."

Bellew said evenly, definitely: "In the first place, you won't win the election."

St. Cloud squared himself about. Into his deliberate stare crept a harder, yellower flame of emotion. "Don't lay any bets on it, Dan. I'll win. Nine days from now my sheriff will carry the star."

"What for?"

St. Cloud got up, threw his cigarette into the dust. "Listen. There's too much law and order in the country. You ought to know I've got no regard for it. You do know it — damned well. Law and order kicked my father out of the valley fifteen years ago. A bunch of pious hypocrites did it. Your old man was one of the bunch that helped drive the St. Clouds back into Smoky Draw."

"That's ancient history," cut in Bellew curtly. "Has nothing to do with the present. The valley drove the St. Clouds out because it couldn't afford to keep 'em."

"It has paid the St. Clouds ever since," said St. Cloud arrogantly.

Bellew nodded. "The rustling has never stopped. You're a clever man, Neel, but you'll be caught some day."

72

St. Cloud's mind was still on the fact of banishment. All at once he was bitter, defiant: "Well, you've got rid of the old man. But I'm still alive. I've lived back there in those damned dreary hills most of my life — an outcast, by God! Your kind has forced me to prowl that country, like some outlawed hungry wolf skirtin' the edges of civilized territory! I've got the right to fight back, Bellew — and that is what I'm doing! I'll win this election, hands down!"

"One way or another," qualified Bellew. "Legitimately or with the gun."

"I make no bones about it."

Bellew struck one fist heavily against the chair. But his voice remained casual: "Two can play at that game, Neel. If you're layin' down the challenge I'll pick it up."

"You've got to," answered St. Cloud abruptly. "I know who I have to lick. It's you — no question of it. You carry the sentiment of this valley around in your watch pocket. I don't know why, but you do. I can cut off the people in Trail whenever I want to. LeBœuf's afraid of his shadow. Gunderson would rather make a compromise than fight me. As for the nesters, they don't count. You're the one that'll get these people organized against me. You see I've got it figured. You're" — and St. Cloud's voice was thin and resenting — "the fair-haired boy."

Bellew remained still a long while. Then he

said, "All right, Neel. I'll have to declare myself in."

"Don't guess wrong on that election," warned St. Cloud. "I'm going to win it. It's been a long ambition of my life. When I do —"

"Go on," prompted Bellew.

St. Cloud's grin was malicious and secretive; and all the reckless, restless nature of the man appeared on his sharp face. "No, I've said enough. But when I win, there will be a further surprise for the valley."

"I'll fight fire with fire," stated Bellew. "Remember that."

"I guess we understand each other," was St. Cloud's even answer. "You're the man I've got to lick. And will lick. So long, Dan."

He turned to his horse and in another moment swept away at a dead gallop toward the hills. It was a signal for the curious ranch crew. The Chinese cook appeared in the front door. Solano, prematurely old and shriveled, walked from a hidden corner with the intent air of having been listening. Link Medders, the foreman, came over from the barn — youthful, but showing the soberness of an early responsibility. He had a gray, smooth face and gave the suggestion of unhurried competence.

"What did that lad want?" he asked Dan.

"Just explainin' himself."

"Not in ten minutes," objected Link Medders.

"It'd take him a month."

One last figure — Mike Shannon — sauntered up with a blacksmith's hammer in his hand. Honest sweat dripped off a currycomb mustache, and his solid Irish cheeks were red from heat. Seldom-speaking, he only listened now.

"He's got something up his sleeve," muttered Bellew. "And it's dynamite."

5. Rendezvous at Nan's

Late in the afternoon, two days following, Nan walked from the cabin to see how her newly hung curtains looked and found Lorrie in the yard, flattened on the back of a pony. A grave patience lined his small face, as if he had been long waiting; nor did he say anything now, but instead held out a package to her. Nan instantly keyed down her sense of pleasure and accepted the gift with a like show of casualness. The boy's shyness was as real as that of an animal — and he had to be met without display. Opening the wrapper, she saw a pan of warm baking-powder biscuits.

She said: "Thank you, Lorrie. These look mighty fine."

Lorrie stared at the distant horizon. "Yeah. Gramp's pretty good at cookin'."

"It was very nice of him to remember me."

Lorrie looked at her with a false indifference. "I sort of thought you wouldn't like it. Gramp said you might. You can cook, can't you?"

"Yes."

"Sure. All women can cook."

"But I don't believe I ever made biscuits."

He looked interested. "That's what Gramp thought. He told me to tell you they only took a minute to make, and that you could have his recipe if you wanted."

"That's fine," said the girl. "Like candy?"

"Sure."

"Someday when you're up this way, we'll make a batch."

"All right," said Lorrie. And afterwards he repeated himself with a stronger inflection: "All right." Then: "You ought to have some chickens for eggs, ma'm."

"Should, shouldn't I?"

"Think I know where I can rustle three-four," muttered Lorrie, full of mystery. "Gramp went to town. Here's a letter for you."

He passed that to her, and when Nan's eyes fell on the bold, familiar writing across the envelope the spell was broken. An instant shadow, she realized, had changed her expression, and Lorrie's keen eyes had seen it. Without another word he turned and galloped down the road. Instantly sorry, she watched him go; and thinking that she must be more careful and more patient, she went into the house and opened the letter. The past had caught up with her, to erase the small feeling of security the last few days had brought. And James Scarborough's note was an exact image of himself, fair yet insistent:

"This comes to you through your lawyer. I don't know where you're hiding, and he won't tell. Nan, I don't deserve this. Lucy got her divorce from me yesterday, and so that miserable chapter is over. I wanted to make it up with you, now you've put your- self beyond reaching. If this is your way of clearing up a bad mess, I can't agree. I've got to make some sort of amend to you. It is not a matter of pride, Nan. It simply is that I will not stand by and let you fight the rest of your battle alone. I've got to come and see you. . . . I think you're somewhere in the West. The reason I do is because I remem- ber telling you one time about the isolation of Montana. I believe that's where you'd run. If you don't write, I'll never stop look- ing.

*"*JAMIE.*"*

She let the note trail between her fingers, trying to force that old recurring misery out of her being. But it was not to be willed away, not to be set aside at bidding. The power of the past was very cruel. Why had she thought to run away from something that followed and probably would continue to follow her through her whole life? There was no surgery, she thought dully, that could separate anyone from the effects of a mis- take. It was like a burn that would not heal. It was like cancer. Jamie's figure was quite clear before her — deprecatory, deceptively slight, full of gentleness and courage. Far better if he had been an outright villain; then her anger could have destroyed him utterly.

She was thinking: "In just three days I did find a little forgetfulness. It is here. But each letter that comes from home will ruin whatever gain I make. I've got to stop it." And in that desperately resolute mood she got out her stationery.

"JAMIE:

"This is the best way. You couldn't help me. If you were here, what would you say or what could you do? I don't want to see you again, and I don't want to hear from you again. If you think anything of me at all — let me alone! *I am writing to the lawyer — telling him to forward no more letters.*

"NAN."

She placed the note in an envelope addressed to Jamie and inserted that in another envelope directed to Thomas B. Devlin, Baltimore. To Devlin she wrote:

"I'm sorry, but I want no more news from the East. Turn back every letter that comes to you."

79

It left her very tired, ridden by the old depression. Going to the porch, she watched the sun flame like fire behind Squaw ridge and gutter out. The pale purple of twilight came again, the soft beauty of another prairie twilight filtered in. Even now the stars showed faintly in the sky; before long the wailing of the coyotes would run down the breeze. All this she had come to expect, to wait for. It wasn't hard to believe she could be a part of this timelessness, this mighty enveloping rhythm of nature. She could submerge herself in it — if left alone.

So thinking, she went about her chores. She watered the pony, led him to the barn, saw that he had grain. She lighted the lamps. She kindled a fire and got her supper. After the dishes were put away she set to work on another pair of curtains. Sometime after nightfall a rider came clattering across the road. A woman's voice said, impatiently: "Whoa, you high-strung little idiot!" Looking through the open doorway, Nan found the dark-cheeked girl of Trail — Helen Garcia — standing there.

"Visitors welcome?" asked Helen. Nan saw the mark of disturbance in the girl's expressive eyes.

Earlier that day Helen Garcia left Trail and rode straight west to the lower tip of Squaw ridge, ten miles distant, and at about seven descended into the Broken Stirrup back yard. Old Mike Shannon was posted like a guard in the shadows. Alert to that, she asked:

"Has it come to this, Mike?"

"If it's Dan you want, he's out, but he'll be back. Gwan in and git some supper afore Chan throws it away."

Helen nodded absent-mindedly, went around to the front. Crossing from porch to living room, she casually lighted a lamp and for a little while roamed restlessly about, tidying up the room with a kind of proprietorship. Afterwards she went out to the kitchen where Chan was clearing up the supper dishes, helped herself to what she could find, and ate with a hungry gusto. Then she heard Dan returning and went immediately back to the front part of the house to meet him, drawling "Hullo, neighbor" in the chestiest tone she could summon.

Dan grinned down at her. "Hullo, Buffalo Bill."

She wore a corduroy split skirt, and an old jersey that hung loosely from her small shoulders. One hand kept flicking a beaded quirt against her trim boots.

"I'm getting mighty tired of eating Broken Stirrup hash and browned potatoes," she complained. "It's all the Chinaman knows."

"Applyin' for the job?"

Helen laughed. "Be careful," she warned. "I

don't need much encouragement."

He rocked gently on his heels, the broad mouth half compressed. In here the shadows put a somber stain across his cheeks. Helen's laughter went away. "Dan, you're running into something. You know it, don't you?"

"What's worrying you?" parried Dan.

"Crossing the prairie last night I ran into a party coming down from the pass. Looked like it was going past LeBœuf's and across the county line. Who else would it be but St. Cloud, Dan?"

"Out on a prowl," reflected Dan.

"What for?"

He shrugged his shoulders. "I don't know."

But Helen remained dissatisfied. "Look here. In the last couple days five strange men get off the train and disappear from Trail. I guess I can smell a sharpshooter as far away as anybody. That's what they are. And they just vanish from Trail."

He said, gently: "I'm glad to know that, Helen. There's not much doubt St. Cloud is recruiting."

"What for?" she repeated.

But he only shook his head. The girl was of a sudden foreboding. "Dan, have you had a definite falling out with St. Cloud?"

He stared. "You're clever, Helen. Nothing gets by you."

"Then you have," she said forlornly. "Dan,

that man won't hesitate a minute to strike you in the back!"

He stopped her with a sudden motion. "What were you doing on the prairie last night?"

Helen went on the defensive. "Looking around."

"You're a good soldier," was Dan's quiet answer. "But I don't want you in this."

"How will you stop me?"

"By just asking."

Helen shook her head. "No, Dan. I won't sit by and watch you get hurt. I'm not built that way."

He said, amused:

"I guess I'll have to hire you."

"You have."

"What's that?"

But she was at once elusive and gay. She tapped his chest with the end of the quirt. "Quit worrying about me. I'm too much like an Indian ever to be caught on the trail Do you expect me to stay in town behind a counter all my life?"

"No," admitted Dan. "You belong on top of a horse, going hell-bent somewhere. You won't ever wither and fade in a ladylike style."

"Unless it be from a broken heart," said Helen tentatively.

"Which reminds me. I heard there was some man in your mind."

The girl's head snapped abruptly upward.

Alarm rushed into her eyes. "Who told you that?"

"Jubilee. Who's the man?"

"He was fooling you," breathed Helen. "I'll break his neck when I see him!"

"That's the girl."

Helen walked restlessly across the floor. She asked: "Seen that Eastern girl lately, Dan?"

"No. I doubt if she likes us very well."

She came back. "She's pretty, Dan."

"All of that."

Helen looked aside. "Well, I've got to be going."

"I don't want you ramming around the dark so much. Remember that."

She was on her horse and away like a whirlwind, passing the stolid Shannon with a quick-dropped "Good-night, Mike!" The words were automatic, for her mind was on the slight change that had come to Dan Bellew's face with the mention of Nan Avery's name. Dimly, distantly she saw her own heart's desire fading; and the cloud of it was across her eyes when she arrived at Nan's and paused there in the doorway.

Nan rose immediately. "You are always welcome. Come in, please."

Helen walked through the doorway and relaxed in the extra chair. Her glance went around the place with frank curiosity. "You know how

84

to fix things up," she observed. "Tanner left it like a pigpen."

"Have you eaten?"

A glinting smile came into Helen Garcia's black eyes. "You're learning our habits. Yes, thanks, I have."

Nan took up the hemming of some curtain material, feeling the direct impact of the other's survey. "She's wondering about me, wondering what I am," thought Nan and then heard Helen Garcia's lazy question:

"Don't you get lonely?"

"I haven't had time yet."

"It is none of my business," reflected Helen. "But I don't see your idea in picking this particular country."

Nan laid down her work. "Perhaps," she said quietly, "it was a case of last resort."

"I'd hate to think so."

"Why?" demanded Nan, surprised.

Helen made an eloquent gesture with her two hands. "It would be so sad. You were meant for nice things. You wear clothes like you were born in them. Really you do. You've lived among educated people, gone to dances and fine parties. Probably never had to shake sand out of your things or scrub the dust off your neck five times a day. You're used to so many things we do without. There's so little here, actually, that you've been accustomed to. I just can't see."

"Don't you like the country?"

"But that's a lot different. I started life in poorer circumstances than you'd ever dream about. Whatever I manage to get is so much more than I had before that I'm plain happy for my luck. Nobody can be very sad over the things they never have had."

"Perhaps," said Nan, quietly, "the things I left behind are not very important."

Helen frowned. "If I was taken away from here, away from my friends and my riding, I'd be lost."

Nan found she had no answer to make. Helen's voice was quick and concerned:

"I'm sorry. I never do have much luck minding my own business."

Nan smiled faintly. "Don't feel too bad about me, my dear. All of us have some fight to make." She slipped deliberately away from the subject. "It's a long way from town. Where will you stay tonight?"

"Oh, I often go on the tramp like this. It's a relief. I'm apt to camp where dark finds me, at Gunderson's or LeBœuf's or at Broken Stirrup. I drift into Broken Stirrup so frequently that Dan keeps a room cleaned out for me.

"Dan Bellew?" asked Nan, curious.

"He's the salt of the earth," said Helen Garcia.

It had the sound of being loyally, defiantly dragged in. Nan made no reply.

"You've got him wrong," stated Helen. "When you're here longer you'll see that."

"Does it matter?" was Nan's casual rejoinder.

"To a great many people it does. What you saw in Trail the other night —"

"Please — I'd rather not think about that."

"You won't be able to avoid it," said Helen. "That wasn't an isolated affair. It meant something. It was the beginning of something. You're not in a very safe place — did you know?"

"Why?"

Helen's dark head inclined to the north. "Those hills —" she began, then straightened, looking through to the back door. Nan felt sudden fear go through her. A man stood there listening. But Helen said calmly: "Come on in, Pete. I've been waiting here half an hour."

He came forward with a show of reluctance, uneasily watching Nan. He was, Nan thought, not very strong and not very old. His chest was thin, his face pinched. He did then a curious thing — he backed into a corner and stood erect against it.

"This is my brother, Pete Garcia," said Helen. "Pete, don't skulk!"

"There'll be a bunch comin' down the road in a little while," said Pete. "Well, I'm here. What was it you wanted to see me about?"

"You've got to back out of this," said Helen.

Pete's face went hard and stubborn. "I didn't

come here to be preached at, sis. Quit it."

"Pete — you've got to come out of those hills and stay out."

"If that's all you got to say, I'm gone," retorted the man.

Astonished, Nan suddenly caught on. These two had arranged for a rendezvous in her house without her knowledge or consent. She felt, in fact, temporarily dispossessed. Both were for the moment oblivious of her presence. Helen had risen, the lithe young body rigid. Nan broke in, suppressing a too obvious resentment.

"I don't see why you find it necessary to stage this quarrel in front of me. I'll go out and leave you alone."

Helen raised an arresting hand. "Don't," she said. "There's nothing you shouldn't hear."

"You sure?" asked Pete Garcia, embarrassed.

"Everybody in the country understands you've turned crooked," said his sister bitterly. "Miss Avery might as well know."

"I've heard enough," growled Pete Garcia. "Risked my neck coming here in the first place. I can't be visiting folks any more, Helen. I'd be suspected. I'd be considered a tale bearer."

"You've developed a set of morals all of a sudden," said Helen.

"It's my skin I'm takin' care of."

"You've got to get out of this mess, Pete. There's going to be a fight. You'll be on St.

Cloud's side, against all the people you know. Pete, you can't do that! Haven't you thought about it?''

"Made my choice," said the man, uncomfortably.

"You didn't make any choice," said Helen, flaming up. "You took the easiest way! Why, you darn fool, you'll be hurting the only man that ever troubled to help you! You'll be riding against Dan Bellew! Don't you see?"

"They've all treated me like a bum in this valley," muttered Pete. "Why should I worry about 'em? St. Cloud's all right."

"That's all you've got to say?" demanded Helen.

The man looked at his sister, and for a moment his eyes showed a hunted, harried expression. Then stubbornness settled at his lip corners. Helen cried out desperately:

"All right. If you're too ungrateful to consider Dan, then consider me! What are you doing to me, Pete? Don't you see? Here I am — sister of a crook — sister of a St. Cloud rider! How can I face Dan Bellew? What will he think of me?"

"He won't change," was Pete's dogged reply. "Everybody knows you ain't like me. I got nothing against Dan. I wouldn't lift a finger against him. But as for the others, they can go to hell! That's final."

"I won't let you do it!" said Helen. Roused like

that, Nan thought critically, she was nearly beautiful. And somehow very admirable. "Go on, Pete."

The man looked anxiously at Nan. "I'd rather not have you say anything about this," he said. Without waiting for an answer, he left as he had come, soundlessly through the back doorway. Helen turned, tired and dejected.

"You think a great deal of Dan Bellew, don't you?" It was something Nan hadn't meant to speak of.

Helen said a slow, disinterested, "Yes."

"Why did you ask your brother to meet you here?"

"It was the easiest place."

Nan asked coolly: "And perhaps you wanted me to hear something of Mr. St. Cloud's character?"

"You've heard it. It is only what everyone knows."

But Nan was critical.

"I can do my own judging in my own good time," she told Helen. "I suppose I should thank you for trying to enlighten me. But I won't."

Helen went as far as the porch and paused. "You don't deserve what will come to you," she murmured.

"What will that be?"

Helen shrugged her shoulder and passed on. A little later Nan heard the girl's horse pound recklessly down the grade toward Trail.

Pete went back to his horse which had been posted in the timber and rode a circle through the higher hills. He hit the road somewhere beyond the pass and about twenty minutes later came against a series of stray shadows motionless in the night. At once a voice, brisk and dry, challenged him — the voice of St. Cloud whom he feared. St. Cloud said:

"Garcia?"

"I rode across the narrow end of the valley," grunted Pete. "And saw nothing that looked like trouble."

"No evidence of other riders out?"

"No."

St. Cloud was silent for a long moment. Then his curt order struck into the waiting quiet: "All right, boys. Come ahead." That line of shadows rippled across the lighter grayness of the road. Pete fell in behind and so followed the party through the notch and into the flat of the valley. Once, looking to his right, he saw the Broken Stirrup lights cutting yellow holes through the black.

6. Riders by Night

Mechanical as the chore was, Nan could not keep her mind to the sewing. This long day had come to an unsettling climax with the visit of Helen and Pete Garcia, and that scene remained vividly in her mind. It was of course none of her business, yet she could not escape the feeling of being involved; something of the oppressiveness that had weighed on her spirits the night of the Trail shooting returned now to disturb her profoundly. The truth, she thought soberly, seemed to be that nobody could remain neutral in this country. People's affairs here were peculiarly interwoven. One could not stand alone, even so desiring. The quarrel of the Garcias, for instance, had its beginnings and its endings in the lives of many others.

She rose, walked to the porch. The stars were very dim in a velvet sky. A soft wind ran freely from the west, the barking of Henry Mitchell's hound arrived in softly diminished currents of sound to accent the loneliness of this still night. Helen Garcia obviously had been fighting for Dan Bellew, fighting for his safety and for his good opinion — and thus here was another situation that entangled him. Thinking about it, Nan was remotely surprised at recollecting how many stray circumstances had revolved around the man. Around him and around Neel St. Cloud. These two seemed magnetic poles on which the current of the land slowly and surely fixed itself.

The loneliness was absolute. She never had felt it so keenly before. Her own troubles lay darkling in her mind; and beyond those was some new, strange emotion she could not define. Bellew's strongly outlined face was very distinct before her, and she could not help wondering what his attitude was toward this Helen so obviously, so wistfully in love with him. Not quite realizing why, Nan made an abrupt decision. Putting on hat and jacket, she went out to saddle the pony. Afterwards she rode westward in the direction of Broken Stirrup.

She had the letter to the lawyer in her pocket for mailing, and that was an excuse. But below the excuse was a prompting so unlike her that she would not logically examine it. More or less aloud, she said: "Why should I ride to him? I must not do it again." Over a roll of land she saw Bellew's ranch lights, warm and heartening; and for a moment she paused, on the edge of turning back. What checked the impulse was a gruff query:

"Who's that?"

"Nan Avery," she answered, half startled.

The man advanced, stood beside her; a match made a sudden crimson nest in his cupped hands. Her question was no less sharp than his own: "And who are you?"

The light died. "Just Mike Shannon," said the man. "Go right ahead."

She went on, perplexed at the little mystery his silently stationed body made there. Passing down an alley of trees, she came against the house's long porch and there dismounted. An open doorway beckoned.

"I wondered," Bellew's voice said, "if you'd ever ride my way."

He was in a black corner of the porch. He had been quietly sitting there, but he rose now and walked forward. Her own voice was coolly collected.

"Why should you waste your time wondering about me, Mr. Bellew?"

He was faintly smiling. "Afraid it's one of those things I'm not going to be able to avoid doing. Step inside."

Going in, she had another of her curiosities satisfied. It was a big room, typically a man's living quarters. A few worn pieces of furniture were scattered about. One comfortable rocker faced a fireplace above which hung a photographed picture of cattle. A rack of rifles inconsistently kept company with a bookcase near by. Bellew pushed the rocker around for her, moved over where he could watch her.

"I had a letter I wanted mailed," she said. "Will you be going to town this week?"

"Mike goes in tomorrow."

"The one I met out yonder?"

"Give you a start?" asked Bellew, showing concern.

"No-o." She lifted the letter from her pocket and placed it on the near-by table, wondering why she had come. The letter became a flimsier and flimsier pretext. Slightly irritated she let the silence remain at his disposal.

He said: "Getting along all right?"

"Yes."

"Not too much to yourself?"

The calm, shrewd insight put her instantly on the defensive. "Is that something else you've wondered about?"

"Yes," admitted Bellew.

"Don't," Nan told him curtly.

"I'm not trying to be inquisitive," said Bellew patiently. "Rather not have you think it."

"No, you're trying to be kind, and I can get along without kindness."

He shrugged. "Don't believe I understand. You're two steps ahead of me. And we're scrapping again."

Of course he didn't understand. But she understood him. His was a man's mind, always seeking to reduce uncertainty to tangible shape. They were a thousand miles apart. Once, too, she had demanded an orderliness in her reasoning as well as in her life. But there was nothing much left now, no logic, only a despair born of her hurts. She would not again trust, not again share. The small sense of relief at being here vanished utterly, and she felt once more that rising antagonism she could not stave off. A quick, clear thought came to warn her that it would probably always be so between them. Another man she might ignore, but Bellew's insistent strength threatened that inner isolation she meant forever to defend.

He said very gravely: "And what could you be thinking about to look so lost?"

She got up.

"I'll run along."

"Did you come straight from your place?"

"Yes."

"Meet anybody outside of Mike? Or hear anything?"

"No."

"Anybody ride through your neighborhood today?"

She watched him. "Helen Garcia dropped in for a moment." Instinctively she avoided any mention of Pete. "But you probably knew about that."

"How would I?"

"She was here, wasn't she?"

Bellew spoke in the manner of making his explanation unmistakably clear: "She's often here. I think a great deal of her. So does every other person in the valley." He followed her to the porch, calling: "Solano."

A fatigued, disinterested voice answered; Solano's small bent figure came into view. It was, she recognized, the man who had met Bellew at the train.

"Take a little trip toward the south," said Bellew and walked around the house. She was in the saddle when he came back with his horse. "I'll ride along with you," he explained.

"That isn't necessary."

But for once he caught her thought. "You'll be under no obligation to me," he said a little dryly. "I make this scout every night."

Silence fell like a wall between them for a half-mile or better. Nan thought of Lorrie. "Tell me," she asked, "where is Lorrie's mother?"

She thought his answer was a long time in coming. And it was reserved: "Same as dead."

It piqued the girl. "You people believe in keeping your secrets."

"As you desire to keep yours," said Dan. They were then descending into a coulee. Dan's horse wheeled. Dan reached swiftly over and caught Nan's reins, drawing her to a halt. Nan stiffened, and Bellew murmured sharply, "Keep still."

The report of fast traveling was on them at

once, swelling up to a rapid rushing of hoofs along the bottom of the coulee. Riders went by, making ragged silhouettes no more than a hundred feet ahead, and a man's metallic voice struck up the slope. "Turn a little left — keep closed up." After that the party swept away southward.

Bellew's arm dropped. They went on down the incline into a risen dust and up the yonder side.

"Who were they?"

"Just a bunch of riders in the dark."

But she realized it to be only a half-truth. "He knows," she thought, "but the code is not to tell." There was no more talk until they rounded in front of her house. Nan saw his face by the lamplight; it had become more angular.

"A week from today," he said, "there's an election in town. Usually always a dance at the same time, over Townsite's store. Would you go with me?"

"You and I," Nan answered, "only succeed in being unpleasant to each other. Why should we go on with it? Thank you — but no."

He nodded, and wheeled away.

Their meetings, it appeared, would always end with this abruptness. Stabling the pony, she walked through the back doorway.

At once she noticed change. On the front-room table was a long silk shawl.

Beside it lay a note:

"Sorry I missed you. I had hoped for a pleasant chat. You've no idea how much of a change that is for a lonely man. Please do not misunderstand this gift. The evenings up here can be very cold — and the shawl has been idle in my trunks for ten years. It belonged to my mother. If the idea of a gift is not to your liking, consider it a loan. Looking forward to another day, I am most humbly,

"NEEL ST. CLOUD."

Lifting the shawl — it was richly, gorgeously Spanish — she experienced a quick touch of fear. "I've got to get this back to him," she said and laid the shawl aside with plain distaste.

Solano left Broken Stirrup at a slow lope, the small, rachitic body loosely bent in the saddle. Two miles due south he crossed a casual arroyo and there halted long enough to dismount and study the ground by furtive matchlight. What he saw drew out only a murmured grunt; but thereafter he made a right-angled turn and proceeded at a faster gait. It brought him presently to a solitary cottonwood and here again he repeated his surreptitious survey. This time he aimed westward as rapidly as the pony would carry him.

A quarter-hour later the looming bulk of Squaw ridge dropped its footslopes dead to the fore. Solano wheeled into timber and went up a sightless trail.

Neither yet nor for another good twenty minutes was there any obvious purpose in the circuitous wandering. But Solano knew his destination, and when he stopped again he had made a four-mile detour into the ridge and had come out on the valley floor at a point where a rock monolith sat slightly removed from the main course of the high ground. Here he loitered, smoking one cigarette after another, until the muffled pacing of a pony drifted up. Solano dropped his smoke, backed against the monolith.

The rider sent out a subdued call:

"Hello, there."

"Yeah," droned Solano.

"It's the second time in the hour I've circled this rock," said the other severely. "Where have you been?"

"Couldn't get away," replied Solano. "Finally Bellew sent me out to have a look."

"What for? He suspect I might be riding tonight?"

"Dunno. He never said. Just told me to have a look."

"You've stuck pretty close to him the last few days?"

"In earshot most of the time."

"Learn anything?"

"Him and Hawk and Townsite had a long

palaver at Trail three days ago. I got most of that — but it was nothing you don't know, St. Cloud. Dan's been around the ranch mostly since. Tonight that Avery girl came to see him."

St. Cloud said interestedly: "So? I'm glad to know that. What else?"

"Nothing."

St. Cloud seemed dissatisfied.

"You've got to brighten up your eyes, Solano. He won't sit idle. He'll hit back. I've got to know how — before he does any hitting. That is your job."

"Yeah," said Solano. "But listen. For God's sake don't let anybody discover this arrangement between us. If Broken Stirrup catches on, I'm dead."

"You're safe."

"Keep it to yourself. Don't tell Clubfoot or Gasteen — and don't tell Garcia."

"Think Garcia would squawk on you?"

"He's got a sister, ain't he? She's fond of Bellew, ain't she?"

"I wonder," said St. Cloud and turned back into the farther prairie. Solano waited a few moments, then aimed straight for Broken Stirrup.

Perhaps ten minutes later a long-shadowed body dropped down from the rough summit of the monolith and stood where Solano had been.

"Thought so," said this one in a kind of surprising breath. "All these recent tracks around

101

here meant something. Knew damn well they did. Six nights of waitin' ain't gone for nothin'. Sorry business to run into treachery — and if I go tell Dan now he'll run Solano clean over the Rockies." The tall form stood still. "No, I better keep it to myself a little while longer. Give Solano rope and he'll hang himself. Tell Dan later. That's the ticket."

Having decided it, the man found his horse, and cantered east.

Fifty minutes later Henry Mitchell arrived home.

7. The Scales Tip

Lorrie halted at the intersection of the two high trails and bent downward from the back of his pony. Watching him sympathetically — in the elapsed week she had gotten behind his barrier of shyness — Nan thought the youthful face could on occasion be very shrewd, very mature. Yet it was somehow saddening to see him so grave, to see him rushing so rapidly through boyhood. Lorrie looked up, a sparkle in his eyes. "Somebody's been along here this morning."

"How would you know?"

He made an explanatory gesture with his hands. "If these tracks had been here overnight the dampness would of smoothed 'em a little."

"Lorrie, where did you learn all this?"

He looked obliquely at her, as if afraid of skepticism. "Gramp — he used to be scout with the cavalry. He tracked renegade parties." And a little while later he added with a false impartiality, "He's pretty good."

From this high point Nan looked across descending pine spires to a valley rolling away beneath the nooning brightness. Her own house stood visible two miles westward. In all other directions the timber shut off the horizons. Lorrie's meandering explorations had led them this far and here appeared to have an ending. Pointing north, Nan said: "What lies over there, Lorrie?"

"Just a lot of canyons and trees."

"Shall we ride that way?"

He was at once reluctant and troubled. "It's an overgrown trail."

"Some other time, then," she suggested.

"That's Smoky Draw country," he said hesitantly.

"What about it, Lorrie?"

He had odd reticences; Henry Mitchell, she thought, had taught him that little-speaking habit. Presently Lorrie added a casual afterthought: "If I was you I don't believe I'd ever ride beyond this point. That ain't a good place yonder."

"We'd better turn toward home."

Single file, they passed down the trail and within a mile arrived at the lower and more open part of the ridge. Two riders went hastily southward on the valley road, ripping up the yellow dust; and from this little elevation Nan saw Bellew's cattle widely scattered across the upper end of the flats. Mitchell's house and her own were gray squares against a chrome-and-tawny soil. The summer's heat remained a constant thing, the sky was brilliantly and flawlessly blue. She had the feeling that beneath the still brightness of the day the earth slowly swelled.

"Where do you go to school, Lorrie?"

"There ain't any outside of Trail. I went there one year, a long time ago."

It required a light touch. This lad answered better to suggestion than to direct advice. "That's too bad. Other boys will get ahead of you." They came across the rear of her place and found Henry Mitchell waiting on the shady side of the barn. She could see he had been slightly worried. Wondering why, she explained: "Lorrie showed me the hills this morning."

"Nobody knows the country any better than him," said Mitchell and moved away, pretending an interest elsewhere.

"If you'll stay awhile," said Nan, "I'll get something to eat."

"That's nice, but we've got to go home."

She had seen Mitchell only once during the week. Looking at him now, it came to her that he showed increasingly his age. The long lined face was gaunter than she recalled; as he walked to his horse she observed the distinct stoop of his ordinarily Indian-straight body. In the saddle, he looked down, speaking for her ears alone: "You notice the boy's wearin' his shoes? It's somethin' I never could make him do. That's your influence, Miss Avery. He thinks a great deal of you."

"I want him to."

"I'm mighty glad," said Henry Mitchell gently. "I want him to amount to somethin'. He can be — he's got the makin's of a fine, upstanding man. Same as his father would of been if he'd lived."

"He's always welcome here, Mr. Mitchell. I like to have him around."

"He'll come. As I said, he likes you. You know how to handle him. One thing about the boy — he'll go through fire to keep the good opinion of those he's fond of. If you get his trust you've got it till the end of the world." Mitchell looked across the yard: "It's taken a load off my mind. I won't be here forever — things happen sudden in this country. I'd always figured Bellew would take him if I went. He thinks Bellew is absolutely right. But there's some things a woman does best — and raisin' kids is one of them."

"You shouldn't be worrying about yourself."

Mitchell's shrug was somehow fatalistic. "I'd like to be around when Lorrie's twenty-one, just to see how much he resembles his dad. But that's askin' too much. My life has been full of chances. I've been mighty lucky — but there's always a last time to everything."

He wheeled abruptly away. Riding beside Lorrie, he said affectionately: "You sit like a squaw — straighten up." Lorrie grinned; and then they went down the slope together, two straight figures against the harsh light.

Presently she went in and got a cold lunch. Afterwards there was nothing to do, and so she took a chair to the shady side of the house and sat there, purposeless and reflective. The work of establishing herself had brought with it a distinct happiness, but that was done, and the leisure she dreaded so much lay ahead. Looking down at her supple hands, she realized her trouble. "I was never made to be a spectator. Never. I've got to be doing things. Not to be useful would destroy me."

Bellew, she suddenly reflected, had known this about her; and suddenly she wondered why, in the seven intervening days, she had neither seen him nor heard of him. Utterly impatient with herself, she got up.

"Why should he come? Haven't I refused all his offers? Nan Avery, you fool, find something to believe in, and stick to it!"

The echoes of a team ran up the road irregularly. Going about the house, Nan watched two fine blacks whip a light buckboard across the rutted yard and halt. Mrs. Townsite Jackson said, "Hello there, lady," and dropped to the ground. She explored the place with a glance that was bright as a magpie's.

"Well," she said, "you've had ten days of this — and how does it suit you?"

"No complaints," answered Nan. "I suppose you know this house pretty well."

"I've lived in many like it," said Mrs. Townsite and sat momentarily on the edge of the porch. "You can't trail around with a man such as Jackson for forty years and not find yourself in some odd places. He's dragged me to every corner of creation. I've heard coyotes howl and Indians whooping it up. I've seen murder and grief — and things you'd scarcely believe." She drew in a sharp breath. "It's been sort of interesting."

"I like your husband."

"He's the best man I know," said Mrs. Townsite soberly.

"Come inside."

Mrs. Townsite rose and went through the door. Her black eyes absorbed the details instantly, approvingly. "This shack never looked like this before. You know how to fix things up, sister."

"The trouble is," said Nan, "it's all done. What is there left?"

"I know. You're like me — always running out of work. Not the kind to fold your hands in silence."

"Well, what else is there for me to do?"

Mrs. Townsite went off on an apparent tangent. "How old are you, anyhow?"

"Twenty-three."

"That's your trouble."

Nan showed her curiosity. Mrs. Townsite went blandly on: "I'm not exactly a believer in the unqualified blessedness of matrimony — I've seen too much misery and scandal. But there isn't any other institution that will take you away from yourself any quicker."

"That," was Nan's quiet reply, "isn't the answer."

"It will do," retorted Mrs. Townsite, "till women find a better one. You should have married five years ago."

"At eighteen? I couldn't possibly have known any real thoughts toward any man."

"No, and you won't at twenty-eight or forty-eight or sixty-eight. That's the chance you take. What of it? You don't seriously expect to be either right or happy more than half the time, do you?"

"Why not?"

The older woman shook her head, sadly shrewd. "Young people all have the idea life owes us something. It doesn't owe us anything. What we get we pay for and work for — and never are very sure then of getting it. Happiness comes when we find we've made or won something we didn't have too much right to expect. I don't like all this fa-la about happiness, anyway. Nobody goes anywhere by sitting on the fence wishing. It's like Jackson says, nothing tastes good unless you've sweat for it."

"Pride?"

"Certainly."

"I'm not sure," said Nan, slowly, "that it is enough."

"Why not? If we start from nothing, we ought to be proud of whatever we earn. But, lands, why carry on like this? I came out thinking you might like to drive into Trail and put up with us tonight. It's election day. Townsite always gives a dance over the store."

Nan had not realized then how anxious she was to get away from the ridge for a few hours. The quickness of her reply surprised her. "Yes — wait till I lock up."

"Don't change that pretty dress," warned Mrs. Townsite. "But bring along breeches and boots — you may have to come back on horse."

Nan went out, watered the horse and stabled him. She bolted the rear door, rolled her riding outfit into a bundle, caught up a hat and coat, and followed Mrs. Townsite to the rig. Mrs. Townsite sent the rig rapidly down the slope. At Mitchell's house the girl waved at Lorrie; then the road swung around a toe of the ridge and straightened into the length of the valley. Far to the southwest she saw the dust wake of a fast-traveling party. Mrs. Townsite spoke:

"Sister, your business is your business. I think you're in trouble and decided to run. Bless you, I hope you lick it. But speaking out of considerable experience with the two-legged creatures hereabouts, let me warn you. Don't dilly-dally with our men. You can't treat them like your laddies back East. It would seem like flirting. If they think you've made a contract, they'll see you go through with it. . . . Ain't it a pretty day?"

"What have you heard about me?" challenged Nan, annoyed.

"St. Cloud's been to your place."

Nan's answer was faintly ironic. "The man you have all made into the devil's image?"

"So we have," said Mrs. Townsite imperturbably. "We may be right about that, or we may be wrong. We'll soon enough know."

"How?" asked Nan.

Mrs. Townsite shook her head. She had ceased to smile.

In those seven days Bellew made searches that revealed nothing. Each night Solano reported no sight of the St. Cloud riders. Mike Shannon camped on the lip of Smoky Draw pass and only once witnessed the passage of men — an inbound party of four. Apparently St. Cloud was idle. Link Medders, scouting the very edges of St. Cloud's ranch, found the place crowded with riders.

"He's been gathering every friend he could find for the election."

"Why should he gather them up there?" argued Dan. "He doesn't need to ride herd on his voters. They've got their orders. That isn't the answer, Link."

"Then he's hiring new hands from outside."

"Yes, but they couldn't vote. What's he hiring 'em for?"

Two mornings before the election, Helen Garcia swept off the prairie on the dead run and provocatively rounded Dan in his yard. She said, in her chestiest tone, "Hullo, pardner," and looked down with a gay, flushed face. "Where you going, so important?"

"Top of the pool."

"Right with you, mister."

She vaulted boyishly to the ground and fell in step, impatiently whipping off her hat. The Broken Stirrup back yard went two hundred feet forward to the rubbled edges of the ridge which curved semicircularly around the ranch. Out of a small gorge of this ridge ran a thin stream of water; beside the miniature gorge a rugged trail rose at a forty-five-degree angle. Helen scrambled across the rocks and said, "Who-a, Dan, I'm no goat. Gimme your paw."

Dan drawled: "Papa carry baby?"

"Baby scratch," retorted Helen and took hold of Dan's coat. Thus towed, she came hilariously behind him. It was a stiff climb, but brief. Four hundred yards onward the ridge leveled temporarily, and the curving fissure made a wide abyss before them. Eighty feet below lay the still, unsunned surface of dammed water. The drop was sheer. At the bottom, below a falls created by the pool's overflow, Mike Shannon worked with a pick.

"Still fooling around with this water?" inquired Helen. "What's the idea?"

"Some home-made engineering," explained Dan. "We're building a diversion tunnel and ditch. Afterwards I'm putting in a real dam. Irrigation, my lamb, is the thing."

"Don't call me that," Helen said impatiently. "Can't you get it through your head I'm a grown woman?"

Dan grinned. "Even if you are, what's wrong with the name?"

She looked into the chasm, sent a rock spinning through space. "It's — it's kind of complicating, mister. But never mind. I ran into something last night."

"I told you to quit riding after dark," said Bellew unfavorably.

"I happened to be a couple miles over east of Trail, riding by the tracks. You know where the trestle crosses that draw? Well, there was a bunch of men camped in it. I got down and crawled along the trestle and counted ten of them. Saw them by their fire and didn't recognize a one. I'd guess they rode up from the south. That draw is part of the old cattle trail, you know."

He accepted the information silently, thoughtfully, and walked down the slope, Helen tagging behind. In the yard she said:

"I'm going to get hold of Pete and pump him. He knows what St. Cloud is up to."

"No. If St. Cloud ever thinks Pete is carrying tales, he'll slaughter the boy."

Helen's dark eyes were suddenly not far from tears. "Pete's put his hand against you, and still you try to protect him. Dan, you're awful damn kind!" She stepped into the saddle. "Listen to me. Don't come to the election without your men. And don't get drawn into a fight." She was away before he could answer, her little figure soon dimmed by the distance.

That evening Dan sent a call down the valley, and the next night, which was the Friday eve of election day, the five men he had summoned met in his house. Two, Jubilee Hawk and Henry Mitchell, were valuable for the personal examples they set. The third, old Townsite Jackson, commanded a following because of his unique position as first citizen. But it was to Tom Gunderson and to Simon LeBœuf that Dan looked for voting power. He told them so.

"Lumped together, you fellows have about forty-five hands. It is absolutely essential you get every last one of your men into Trail tomorrow for voting. It will be very, very close."

Gunderson, a spare and active man to whom everything was definitely white or definitely black, said: "He won't win, Dan. If he does we'll run him out."

"He might not run," grunted Simon LeBœuf, a great and awkward figure, as unkempt as the worst of his riders. "I'd be willing to bet he'll run a blazer of some kind on us. That's the St. Cloud habit."

"Yes," agreed Dan. "That's what we've got to watch for."

Townsite said: "If he does win, boys, this country will run red. I'm telling you."

"He warned Mitchell to quit riding around Smoky Draw," mused Dan. "He's got something up there he doesn't want us to see."

"Maybe," suggested Mitchell, "he means to swamp the town tomorrow with his men. Forcibly prevent people from votin'."

They sat deeply silent awhile. Jubilee finally spoke. "The first jug-head to try that at the polls will get pounded."

"Careful," warned Dan. "It may be what St. Cloud wants you to do."

"I'll do it, nevertheless."

"We've got to keep away from an open fight," said Dan, looking at both Gunderson and LeBœuf. "When you get your men voted, pull them out of town. Here's another thing: Put your riders on the trail tonight to remind the homesteaders about coming in. I guess that's all."

The meeting broke up. But LeBœuf, mounted and ready to go, had a last sober word: "You don't carry help enough on this place, Dan. If St. Cloud means to get anybody, it'll be you. That's been plain to the whole valley for some time. I'll be in Trail by tomorrow late afternoon." Then the group went cantering away.

The next day Dan carried on with the work around the pool until about two, then left Chan in charge of the ranch and headed for town with the others. Three miles into the prairie, he remembered having left one thing undone. "I clean forgot about those two Mormon families up in the middle of Squaw ridge. Solano, you strike off there now. We'll meet you in town." So, with Medders and Mike Shannon, he reached Trail around four.

It was worse than he expected. The town was jammed. Men he had not seen for months cruised the walks; groups of them collected on the four corners of the square. Almost solid lines pressed restlessly in and out of the Golden Bull, and he was quick to note that the drinking had been heavy. The crowd spirit was electric; after eight o'clock, he reflected, when the counting began, Trail would be in effect a powder magazine at the mercy of any careless incendiary.

His first chore was to stable his horse; then he led Medders and Shannon straight to the courthouse to vote, finding Jubilee and half a dozen others guarding the place; St. Cloud, it was evident, also had his watchers on the ground. When he finished voting he plowed his way back to the street and waited for Medders and Shannon.

"You'd better rustle home," he told them. "Chan's all alone."

But Link and Mike Shannon had obviously been talking it over. Link's answer was definite: "Not now, Dan. This town ain't safe for you. You're crazy if you think so. We'll just trot behind."

Dan shrugged and turned into the milling tide, at once confronting Nan, Mrs. Townsite, and Helen. All three were hooked arm in arm. Nan seemed freer and gayer than he had ever observed. The crowd spirit, he thought to himself, had taken her away from herself. Mrs. Townsite, too, appeared pleased with the hectic atmosphere; but Helen was unsmiling.

"Bellew," said Mrs. Townsite, "do you smell powder?"

"You like to be right in the middle of a crush, don't you?" drawled Bellew.

"Can't change my habits," sighed Mrs. Townsite. "I love to see things move."

Helen said, soberly: "Will you be at the dance, Dan?"

He nodded, going past them, wondering at that last oblique glance Nan Avery had thrown at him. There was a sudden jam in the middle of the street as Gunderson's riders filed off the prairie. A man straightened from the wall of the Golden Bull and cheered the sight of them; and another man reached over and clapped his hand across that one's face — the act of a thoughtful head. Dan elbowed his way into Townsite's store. Townsite came over for a hurried word.

"Figure this out. Part of St. Cloud's crew came in early, voted and went out. The rest of that gang ain't showed yet. Neither's St. Cloud himself. Where's LeBœuf?"

"He'll be along."

"Come to the house for dinner. We've got the Avery girl."

Dan shook his head and left, mind centered on St. Cloud. There was nothing he could do, Dan reflected irritably, but wait; turning up the hotel steps, he found a chair and sat down. At five-thirty Gunderson found him there.

"Where's LeBœuf?"

"Late as usual. You better get your crew out of this place. It's dynamite."

Gunderson said, "Not till LeBœuf shows up," and instantly was absorbed in the restless mass. Sometime beyond six Dan went in to eat a tasteless meal; passing out later, he saw Neel St. Cloud enter at the head of his column. Profoundly worried about LeBœuf, Dan looked at his watch. It was then seven, and the guitars and fiddles were tuning up in Townsite's dance hall. Link Medders came beside him; he sharply challenged his foreman.

"Have you located Solano?"

"Not here yet."

"LeBœuf's got just an hour," muttered Dan. "That's cutting it too fine."

Nan stood in a corner of the hall with a party that included Helen, Mrs. Townsite, and some other women to whom she had been recently introduced. Rows of bracket lamps flooded yellow light down on the weaving couples; the rhythm of the music went on and on, suiting the temper of these boisterous people who seemed never to get tired. It turned insufferably hot, the confusion increased. Townsite stood in the middle of the floor, frankly sweating, and called the turns of a square dance; one man ducked in and around the crowd, scattering wax. Babies wailed along one wall where a double set of benches had been arranged for them; there was an endless levee in front of the punch bowls. She had, she thought, never seen anything so uproarious, so hilarious. Yet she could not escape certain contrary signs. Detached as she was, the sense of suspended judgment grew very strong in her; and she noticed men, one moment openly amused, turn toward the stairs with an instant soberness. Townsite strolled over, his chore completed, and stood a moment with his wife. Their talk was brief and worried.

"Any news?"

"LeBœuf didn't get here."

"Lands!"

Dan Bellew came in during the intermission, pausing to search the walls; and she observed, with an acute interest, that his appearance was enough to dampen the strong tone in the hall. Townsite cut quickly over, and the two of them stood momentarily near her. The sense of generous humor which she knew Dan to possess was altogether gone; and his eyes, once touching her, passed by without recognition. Helen stepped from the wall, caught his sleeve, and said something that he answered with the smallest of smiles; then the music began, and the two revolved away. She was a little surprised that he danced rather well; somehow it hadn't fitted into her picture of him. A moment later they were in the center of the room. Helen had her face lifted toward the man. Both of them were extraordinarily grave.

"Doesn't he know," thought Nan, unaccountably irritable, "that the girl loves him?"

Something happened. The music stopped on a rising tone — stopped raggedly. A man walked hurriedly into the hall, a young, red-headed man. He saw Bellew, went over with a hand oddly lifted outward. And as softly as he spoke, his words carried clearly through the hush.

He said: "St. Cloud's got it, Dan."

She didn't know why it should be so, but a

sharp sensation of fear went knifing through her. Mrs. Townsite's "Oh, Lord!" was heartfelt. Nan, strangely stirred, watched Bellew. Whatever his faults, she quietly thought, he had the one supreme stark quality of strength. It flowed out from him at this moment as a tangible thing to draw and to comfort the dispirited, uncertain crowd. It gave him an unquestioned leadership — every last soul in the hall was now watching him. She wondered if it were not a visual trick, until she discovered that she too had pinned her faith on him.

8. Terror

Posted there in the center of a hall gone dead still, Dan Bellew felt Helen's two hands rigidly gripping his arm; and looking briefly down, he saw she was close to tears. But it was Jubilee Hawk that demanded his whole attention at the moment, for Jubilee's temper strained against the hard muscles of his face, and a gusty emotion ripped wickedly across the gray-green eyes. When the red-head spoke again, it was with a singsong flatness:

"I'd hate to think LeBœuf sold us out."

Dan said impassively: "What's done is done."

"Nothing's done. Something tough has started. It may be you, it may be me, or it may be St. Cloud — but somebody's apt not to get out of this town tonight."

"Don't lose your head now. We'll take our licking and we'll like it — this time."

"Easy to say," muttered Jubilee.

Townsite and Gunderson quickly crossed the hall. Old Henry Mitchell walked up the stairs and joined the circle. For a moment nobody said

122

anything. The roof had fallen in, and they were still struggling out of the wreckage. Helen murmured a word Dan didn't catch and slipped away. Dan put his two fists in his pockets, stared at the others. "We'll take our licking and like it — this time. Now we're going to get out of Trail before trouble starts. Some stray fool might start shooting. No election is worth a widow. Gunderson, you round up your men —"

"It ain't so simple," said Gunderson. He jerked his head upward. "Listen to that."

All the hall windows were open, and the deepening voice of the crowd came in. There was a resounding smash out there, like the collision of vehicles; a half-frenzied phrase javelined through the turmoil. It woke angry answers, dangerously immediate answers. On the far edge of Trail a gun began exploding.

"Somebody ought to kill that fool," muttered Dan.

"Somebody prob'ly will," retorted Jubilee. "Well, what are we going to do?"

Henry Mitchell looked to the landing of the stairway and said, very quietly, "Now we'll have some news." Solano limped slowly across the floor, his thin body gone slack. He returned the united scrutiny with a flitting briefness, placed his lackluster eyes on Bellew. "He couldn't come," he said. "He ran into trouble."

"Why?"

"I went to tell the Mormons. A mile south of them I saw a lot of LeBœuf's cattle milling off west of the ridge. Looked like a steal to me, so I ran for LeBœuf's and told him. He went out on the run with the whole crew. I waited till six. Heard some firing. Then I came on here."

His dismal voice trailed into silence; he looked dispiritedly around the room. Dan made a motion of acquiescence at the group. "There's St. Cloud's trump. He dragged LeBœuf away deliberately."

Henry Mitchell stared at Solano. "How was it you come so properly onto this rustlin' business? You couldn't see anything from the Mormon places."

"I went to the skyline trail from there."

"Why?"

Solano's eyes met Mitchell's and slid aside. "Always a habit of mine to scout. That's what Dan pays me for."

Dan interfered, frowning at Mitchell. "Solano's my rider. I'd trust him to the limit. Don't get the other idea in your head, Henry. This was St. Cloud's trick. He timed it just right."

The sounding of the gun on the edge of town stirred Jubilee. He repeated his question: "What are we going to do now?"

"St. Cloud's won the county," decided Dan. "Let him run it. We'll find Gasteen, Jubilee, so you can hand over your star."

"Hand it?" grunted Jubilee. "I'll throw it in his face."

"Careful. We'll start nothing tonight. Not in this crowd. You're coming home with me. Gunderson, you've got to snake your men out of Trail."

Townsite made an empty gesture. "There is not one of us," he said simply, "who can count on tomorrow. It is going to be just hell. I'm not a scary animal, as you boys well know. But I make this guess, and I make it because I know what happens to a country when it becomes an outlaw strip: One or more of us will be dead before the month is out."

Dan's answer was very soft: "We can fight back, Townsite."

"I propose to. When you want me, you know where to send for me."

"More news," drawled Henry Mitchell.

It was St. Cloud. He came across the floor with a careless stride, the yellow head thrown back and a high flush of high pleasure on his mobile face. The sharp grin included them all and dismissed them all, save Bellew. On Bellew his attention centered fully.

"I told you," he said, amused, "I'd win this election."

Bellew's cheeks were shadowed and set. "By a trick."

St. Cloud showed a quick mockery. "Part of

125

the game. I don't deny it."

"I told you before that two can play at trickery."

"Within the law, I hope," said St. Cloud. "Don't put yourself outside the law, Dan. There's a new sheriff."

Bellew let his answer drag into the profound stillness; and the tenor of it was definite and final and unchangeable: "I want this understood: I am going to smash you."

St. Cloud's cheeks went slimmer, sharper. The lurking malice faded before a swift blaze of anger. He said nothing more but made a slight, stiff bow and walked on to that end of the hall where Nan Avery stood. Looking there for an instant, Bellew saw the man smiling again, turned to the perfect cavalier; then Bellew wheeled and went down the stairs to the street, the others trooping thoughtfully behind him.

Solano lagged behind, more obviously limping. As the others walked into the street, Henry Mitchell abruptly pivoted, barred Solano's way. In the semidarkness of the stairway he bulked hugely over the little Broken Stirrup hand. "Solano," he said, "I let you have too much rope."

Solano stiffened, placed one hand against the wall. "What's the matter with you, Henry?"

Mitchell's big fist clenched. "You godblasted runt, you sold your saddle! I ought to've settled the balance the other night at Rooster Rock when you met St. Cloud. But I let you have too much rope. I don't understand a yellow-bellied lizard like you, and hope I never may. You're through on Broken Stirrup, Solano. You know that, don't you?"

Solano stood motionless, the wind springing violently in and out of his chest. That hand supporting him on the wall began slowly to slip downward. His eyes went luminous with fear.

"You know it, don't you?" roared Henry Mitchell.

"If you say so," said the little man, sullenly.

"Shannon or Medders would tear you apart. Dan's too easy. All he'll do is send you over the hill. But he wouldn't believe what I told him, and anyhow I wasn't born to squeal. You're going to tell him yourself tonight and fade out of here fast. Understand?"

"All right," muttered Solano. "I'll do it."

"You bet you will. I'm riding to Broken Stirrup in the morning. If I find you there I'll drag you over Squaw ridge at the end of a rope."

The edges of a suddenly compressed crowd spilled into the stair doorway. A long yelling rose and died, and some sort of an uneasy quiet took hold of those on the street. Henry Mitchell was instantly restless, worried for his party out yonder. Closely eyeing Solano, he saw another surreptitious drop of the little man's arm. "All right — if you want it here," he muttered.

"No!" yelled Solano.

"Then get out ahead of me!"

Solano sidled around him, beat a hurried passage through the packed ranks. More and more alarmed, Henry Mitchell elbowed his way across the walk and out into the street. Down by the Golden Bull was a pool of light, and right there seemed to be the trouble. Somebody talked in rapid, arrogant phrases — Gasteen, he thought, as he butted the impeding onlookers aside. Breaking into the cleared, bright area, he at once knew the worst of the night waited here for a too sharp word or a too sudden gesture. Gasteen's raw hillbilly frame towered up in the yellow radiance, placed against a solid row of St. Cloud hands. He had the sheriff's star newly pinned to his vest, and his long lantern jaw thrust itself obstinately toward Bellew, confronting him. Jubilee and Gunderson were near by, and the two Broken Stirrup men; and over to one side, suggestively massed, were all the Gunderson hands and the additional Bellew sympathizers. The line of cleavage was definitely drawn. Old Henry Mitchell had seen too much violence in his lifetime not to feel the slow, cumulative advance of it now. Coolly deliberate, he took his stand near Bellew.

"You are not tellin' me what to do," challenged Ruel Gasteen. "Your days of authority are clean over. You'll pull no more wires."

Bellew said: "You've got your star, Gasteen. But I want this understood: Stay off Broken Stirrup ground. I never fed or sheltered a St. Cloud rider, and I'm not beginning now."

Gasteen's gleaming eyes were red-shot, full of fury. "I told you the night you killed Tom Addis I'd not forget it. I ain't. I want your gun, Bellew."

"You're making an arrest?" grunted Bellew.

"I said I would."

Bellew's answer was smooth, frigid. "Your mistake. You are not making this arrest, Gasteen."

"Don't try to slide out of it," warned Gasteen. "I'm not bluffing. You know it. I do what I say I'll do. Pass over the gun and come on to the lock-up."

Bellew's black head tipped forward; all his features were dark and bitter-drawn. "We might as well get it decided now. You're making the issue, not me. My answer is I'm not a football for the Smoky Draw crowd to kick around. Your pants belong to St. Cloud. He bought you a long time ago, and he's set you up in this job to be a monkey on a stick. There never will be a time when I surrender to you."

"I'm not afraid of your reputation," said Gasteen implacably. "I'm willing to make the try. And I'm askin' for that gun. It is the last time I ask."

"No," said Bellew. The sound swelled into the utter silence.

Nan saw all this from a second-story front window of the hall. The scene was directly below her, so near that she felt drawn into it. Those two tall men faced each other, and their talk, deliberate and barren as it issued from them, was freighted with an incredible bitterness, a burning hostility. The words lashed like whips, struck like blows — each one leaving an indelible mark on her memory, each one pushing nearer to that climax even she could foresee. The tension of the crowd increased; it reached up and caught her in its insufferable grip, to produce a feeling of half suffocation. When Bellew's "No" struck out, she involuntarily stiffened, expecting a consequent explosion. In that moment all the faces revealed by the saloon lights registered one uniform emotion — a strained, blurred savagery. Gasteen's ungainly body poised slightly forward at an angle; he had gone motionless. As for Bellew, she had not seen him stir all through the parley. His will seemed literally to beat against the new sheriff.

It could not last — it did not last. But the change was unexpected. She heard a dry voice calling forward: "Just a minute there." And then there was a swaying of bodies as the yellow-headed St. Cloud made his way to the circle. It

130

was as if he poured a quick stream of water on fire. One hand waved Gasteen back.

"That's enough," he told the new sheriff. "You ought to know better than to start a fight in this crowd."

"I'm not afraid of him," muttered Gasteen. "I want him to know that."

"You've made your demonstration," rapped out St. Cloud. "Now drift."

Bellew said emotionlessly: "So the tail of the dog wagged too soon?"

"The metaphor is unfortunate, Bellew," answered St. Cloud, "but we'll take that up later."

There was another long moment of deadlock. Then Bellew's black head nodded, and he turned away, and the crowd, released from the tension, began a slow milling. Nan swung from the window, tired and restless. For the first time she observed that Mrs. Townsite and Helen had been all this time watching through the same window. Helen's face was white.

"I think I'll go on home tonight," Nan told Mrs. Townsite.

Mrs. Townsite's mind was elsewhere. "You can get a horse," she said absent-mindedly, "at the stable."

Nan went down the stairs and back to the living quarters of the Jacksons, behind the store. She changed into her riding clothes and returned to the stairway hall, instantly bumping into Bellew,

131

who was apparently coming back to the dance. The sultry anger flickered on his face. He spoke rather sharply: "The street's no place for you until this crowd scatters."

"I'm going home. Where is the stable?"

"Ready now?"

"Yes."

He nodded to her, opened a way for her across the square. A little short of the stable, deep in the confusion of the collecting Gunderson party, they met Mike Shannon with three ponies in tow. "Miss Avery will use yours," Dan told Shannon. "You rustle another."

"Really, I'd rather hire my horse and ride home alone."

"Unfortunately, that's not possible."

She shrugged her shoulders, not willing to make a point of it, and accepted his hand-up. He stepped to his own saddle, escorted her to the head of the restless Gunderson column; and a little while later she was sweeping out of Trail. Henry Mitchell rode directly behind her, Medders and Shannon were abreast. A little to the fore, Bellew and Gunderson talked in a brief let-down fashion. Among the others was a heavy silence; all the desert lay dark and vague, and the stars were very frosty. Short of the halfway point the Gunderson party faded off to the right at a full gallop; at Mitchell's house the old man dropped out of the line with a sober "So long, everybody." Medders and Shannon wheeled into a coulee westward — and so Nan arrived at her own front yard, feeling Dan Bellew's simmering temper like an actual heat. What she had been thinking all along the road came out of her candidly:

"I'm glad for one thing — I'm glad the quarrel ended short of bloodshed."

"A postponement," said Bellew indifferently.

"I don't understand you very well," Nan reflected. "In the hall you ordered your men to avoid a fight. I liked you for it. On the street, among all those people, you seemed willing to have one. Why did you change?"

"Because the situation had changed," Bellew said briefly.

But the little devils of logic sat in judgment again, criticizing him, condemning him. "Save for St. Cloud's intervention there would have been a fight, probably a terrible fight."

"Yes."

"You were willing to assume the responsibility of men being killed. You were not willing for others to do so. Tell me — why?"

He sat silent a moment, and she felt rather than saw his friendless glance. "The difference," he said, "lies in the men involved. The challenge was there. I had to meet it."

"But what harm could there be in an arrest — if you are sure of your ground?"

"It wasn't," explained Bellew, "an arrest. It was a challenge."

"Oh. Other men may act humble, to avoid the spilling of blood. But humbleness is not for you. It amounts to that, then?"

They were coldly and civilly quarreling again. They were hurting each other. She saw the rim of his hat rise, his shoulders straighten. "I don't suppose I could make it clear to you," he stated. "Probably not worth trying."

"Probably not. It seems quite queer, though, that the man you all consider a conscienceless outlaw should be the one to quiet an extremely dangerous situation. He, apparently, thought more deeply of the possible widows than you did."

"Let it stand like that," said he laconically.

But she was suddenly, hotly angered. "No, I can't let it stand like that! I am disappointed in you! I thought I knew you better — and I thought I liked you better! It doesn't seem very broad of you to rebel against a sheriff and risk a horrible scene just because you dislike him and are too proud to admit his authority. You set yourself up to be law-abiding. Your acts make a hypocrite of you."

He said nothing for so long a while that she slipped from her saddle and handed over the reins of the horse. Bellew accepted them; then spoke for himself:

"You don't get the angle of sagebrush politics. The transfer of that sheriff's star means something more than you think it does. If you want the thing plainly stated, it makes Gasteen's kind lawful people. It makes an outlaw of me. Tonight I had to do one of two things: either submit or announce the fact I was willing to be an outlaw."

"You speak of Gasteen, but you mean St. Cloud. Why not say so?"

"I don't like to talk about people in front of their friends," said Bellew and abruptly swung off with the led horse.

"I'm not necessarily —"

But it was no use talking at so much blank night. He had planted his shot and gone, leaving her directly hit. Badly stung, she clenched her fist and walked half blindly into the house, at once knowing she could not let the rebuke stand. It was utterly unfair, utterly untrue. "No man," she told herself bitterly, "has the right to presume I've admitted St. Cloud to friendship! Dan Bellew shall not presume it!" In the morning, she decided, she would ride directly to Broken Stirrup and fight it out.

In spite of the evening's turmoil she fell almost instantly asleep. Thus the sound of the single shot which later broke flatly across the area came to her like the disturbing fragment of a dream. It did not wake her. What did wake her, somewhat after

135

that, was a pounding on the house door and Lorrie's half-choked call. "Miss Nan — Miss Nan!"

She sprang out of bed instantly, an odd premonition striking through her, and hurriedly put on a robe. When she unbolted and opened the door, the boy threw himself in, and his fists beat against her body with an unconscious rage. His small frame was racked by emotion, ripped by violent muscular spasms. The breath strangled in his throat, and his cheeks were hot as fire. But it wasn't fear, she knew. It was shock, it was outrage, it was grief.

"They got Gramp!" he cried wildly. "They got him!"

"Lorrie!"

"They got him!"

"Oh — my dear, dear boy! Who?"

But he had stopped speaking, and she felt the stiffening of his body even as he clung to her for comfort. He would never, she realized, answer that question; Henry Mitchell had taught him to be a man. Tightly holding him, sharing the cruel pain of his tragedy, she thought: "He is my boy to care for now."

9. The Weaving Net

Friday following the election, in the middle of another blaze-hot afternoon, Nan walked around the house and found St. Cloud waiting by the porch. He had come very quietly and was still in the saddle. At sight of her he lifted his hat, smiling.

"I thought," he said, "it was a proper time to take up your promise."

"What promise?"

His cheerfulness was disarming, a little apologetic. "Maybe I'm presuming too much. It's only half an hour's ride over to Smoky Draw — and I'm proud enough of my place to want you to see it."

A sense of uneasy surprise passed through her, and she thought instantly of Mrs. Townsite's warning. It was as she had suspected. St. Cloud had read too much into her words, which had been without encouragement.

"I think my exact answer to your invitation," she said, determined to put him in his place, "was that I might possibly come. Does that sound like a promise, Mr. St. Cloud?"

"To a lonely man — yes."

"I'm afraid you take too much for granted."

He further surprised her with the shrewdness of his understanding. "You're drawing a line for me to see. You want it quite plain between us — isn't that so?"

"Exactly."

"I like you the better for it," was his frank answer. "I won't trespass, and I won't give the valley any grounds for gossip."

Nan was a little curt with her reply: "I am not worrying about the thoughts of other people. What I do is none of their business. I am quite old enough to make my own decisions. The point is, I don't want you at any time to twist my words into something more than they mean."

He watched attentively, deep interest framed in his eyes. "I see. Then what was the meaning of that 'possibly'?"

"That was common politeness," said Nan. "It is clear to me now I should have been blunter. Politeness out here seems to be a sign of weakness."

Unexpectedly his smile returned. "You know, you're a very positive woman. You've stopped me in my tracks. I admit the error humbly. Now suppose we start all over, and suppose I make the invitation again?"

He was, she realized, very clever. For while he accepted her rebuff, he also accepted her stated independence of the valley's gossip. It was in effect a challenge of her sincerity. She had made the mistake again of asserting her freedom of thought too forcefully and now could not afford to cheapen her declaration with a refusal. But, even as she understood it, her silent resolve to go with him was influenced by another consideration equally independent. She was very curious about Neel St. Cloud. Not quite trusting him, she had no sound basis for such distrust. It was another point of pride that she wanted better evidence than the hostile opinion of the valley people. Deep in her mind she recognized, too, the influence of her resentment toward Dan Bellew.

"It's only a little way up and a little way back," prompted St. Cloud.

"All right. Wait until I write a note for Lorrie."

His brows went up. "You're keeping the boy?"

"Yes. Why?"

"Splendid thing for you to do," he said. "I'll saddle your pony meanwhile."

She wrote the note and left it on the kitchen table, telling Lorrie where she was going and when she would be back. Catching up a hat, she went out and waited for St. Cloud to bring her pony around. Afterwards they rode briskly into the throat of the pass.

The note to Lorrie was unnecessary. Crouched behind a tilted slab rock near the road, the boy saw them go, his bright black eyes full of fury.

There was a padded echo as the small dynamite charge blew a cloud of gravel and fine dust across the Broken Stirrup yard. Dan and Jubilee and the rest of the crew came slowly out of shelter, returning to the sloping edge of the ridge. The fumes settled gently away from a newly created mouth of the diversion tunnel; Mike Shannon lifted his shovel and started clearing aside the blasted rubble.

"That's all," said Dan. "Day after tomorrow we'll go up the canyon and blow out the plug in this tunnel. The pool ought to drain overnight. Then we've got a good month ahead of us building up the dam. I'm going to Trail and see if they've set those stock cars out on the siding."

"Therefore," said Jubilee, "so am I."

The two swung out of Broken Stirrup at a casual gait. Dan Bellew aimed a little east of the true course of Trail, but after an indecisive half-mile he straightened back, Jubilee's slanting lids compressed a little.

"Not going over to the girl's place?"

"No."

"That boy ought to be living on Broken Stirrup, Dan."

"He needs gentling. It was a fine thing for her to take him, Jubilee."

140

"Yeah, but if Mrs. Wills ever gets her hands on Lorrie —"

"If she does I'll step in. Meanwhile, the less said about it the better. Neither Lorrie nor the girl knows about Mrs. Wills."

Jubilee scowled against the slashing sunlight. "Nothing ever comes out right in this confounded world."

They detoured through a scattered bunch of Broken Stirrup stock, they went cantering on down the valley with a long ribbon of dust behind them. Gunderson's distant window panes, struck by the sun, sent brilliant lances of light across the flats. All the adjacent folds of Buck ridge were alternately tawny and black. It was a dry world, a motionless world waiting for the reviving coolness of night. Bellew stared straight to the fore, features thoughtfully engrossed; Jubilee was never still, but kept his glance turning from one quarter to another, as if seeking some fact he could not find yet knew to be present in this cloudless day. About three o'clock the road dipped into the gentle draw and entered Trail.

They split here, Jubilee hauling up before the Golden Bull and Dan going on to the railroad station. His stay there was brief and concerned itself only with the livestock cars standing down the siding; afterwards he went to Townsite's store.

"I don't seem to see Gasteen."

"He ain't been in Trail twice since last Saturday," grunted Townsite. "Where you suppose a good St. Cloud hand would make his headquarters? Up in Smoky Draw, naturally."

Dan sat on a nail keg and curled himself a smoke, brooding over the chore. "Too quiet these days. You'd think this country was dead. I wonder if St. Cloud's trying to put me asleep."

"Your next move is plain to me," stated Townsite. "I think you're being damn careless runnin' that ranch with four men. Fourteen would be more like it."

"What makes you say that?" asked Bellew.

"This filtering in of hard mugs never seems to stop. They drop off the trains and they pop up from every sagebush."

"Sure. It's a safe county now for a crook. News like that spreads fast." Bellew pushed his square shoulders upright. The hazel surface of his eyes showed a concentrating attention. "Now I wonder if such was St. Cloud's purpose in winning this election? Easy way to get himself a following, ain't it?"

"A couple boxes labeled 'Machinery' was delivered to Major Cleary other day," muttered Townsite. "But if I don't know the shape of a case of rifles I'm a fool. Rifles. For St. Cloud, of course. It may interest you to know St. Cloud's been writing letters to a couple of towns down the trail. First to Logan Gap. Second one to Anna Creek. He got replies both times. See? Whoever he is writing to is on the way north. Letters indicate it."

"Too bad," drawled Dan, "a postmaster can't open letters."

"This postmaster would," said Townsite soberly, "if it'd do any good. Only St. Cloud wouldn't be careless enough to say anything plain to the curious eye. Who's moving north — and what for?"

"We'll know pretty soon."

"Why don't you get more men on Broken Stirrup?"

"I'd just as soon have him think I was daydreaming," mused Bellew. "As it stands, I'm no safer with an army than with what I've got. I'll do my recruiting when I know what I'm up against."

Townsite's gesture was one of disagreement. He walked to the closed-in corner that represented Trail's post office, found a letter and brought it back. "Read this."

Dan smoothed the paper, studied the writing on it through the trailing smoke of his cigarette:

"Postmaster, Trail City, Montana:
"In the course of settling legal affairs this office is looking for a Nan Avery, formerly of

143

Baltimore, now thought to be in the West. Do
you know of her whereabouts? If so, please
write and oblige.

"JAMES T. SCARBOROUGH."

Townsite said suddenly: "Sounds like a form
which he's probably sent all over the country.
I've figured a long time she was runnin' away
from something. Ain't my place to guess what,
but it must be important or this man wouldn't be
queryin' postmasters."

"What are you going to do?"

"Not allowed to give out information like
that," said Townsite. But he added afterwards:
"What should I do? What would you do?"

Bellew got up, walked aimlessly around the
room, cheeks drawn solid. "Her life is her own,
Townsite. It is none of our business what she does
with it."

"Ain't it?"

Dan flung up his head, touched by the older
man's tone of slight doubt. Townsite went on:
"I'm not blind, my boy. You've made her business your business already to the extent of pro-
tecting her. You like her. You like her a lot. If I
didn't think so, I'd never have mentioned this
letter. But if you want, I'll throw it in the waste-
basket."

"People seem to know my affairs better than I
do," was Dan's dissatisfied answer.

144

Townsite's words were gently kind: "Everybody watches you. We all prospect on your next move. It ain't inquisitiveness — it's interest. You can take that as a compliment."

Bellew said thoughtfully: "If she's hiding, we shouldn't interfere. I think she's trying to get rid of something on her back trail. Trying to forget it. Everything she does or says is more or less colored by what is behind her. I feel that. She's been hurt. This is her way out of it."

"So the letter dies here?"

"Wait a minute. If running away would do her any good, I'd say let the letter go unanswered. But she'll never be happy as she is. You can't ever successfully run away from what's in your head. You can't bury something that's alive. That's the way it is with her. I know of only one way to handle it."

"Which way?"

"Face it and have it out."

"Supposing it's something serious they want her for?"

"She couldn't do anything really wrong," Dan said swiftly. "You know that."

"You won't get any thanks for this."

Dan shrugged that aside. "How will you get around the regulations?"

Townsite grinned. "I'll just write and say I'm not allowed to give out such information, but that if he writes a letter to this office I'll see it's forwarded. He'd be dumb not to catch the answer."

"She ought to have a showdown with herself," Dan mused.

"That's your way," pointed out Townsite. "It may not be hers. Men and women don't think alike. Some women enjoy their sorrows."

"Not Nan Avery. She's had the habit of being square with the world. She isn't now — which is what worries her."

"There'll be a man in it."

"Yes."

Townsite stared. "That makes no difference to you, Dan?"

Dan's face was at once blank. "Why should it? Don't ask me a question like that."

Townsite reached out and laid a palm on Dan's shoulder. "I didn't know it was that bad with you, son."

Jubilee, feeling much better, idled out of the Golden Bull and along the shady side of the street. He had once been marshal, once sheriff, and the habit of squaring himself with his surroundings was hard to break. Abreast the door of his former headquarters he slowed down, looked in, and saw nothing. He cut across the yellow dust, ambled through an alley, emerged to a side street well screened by the interlaced tops of ancient locusts. At this point his fruitless wandering betrayed itself; over on a porch Helen Garcia swung gently in a hammock.

Jubilee went that way and sat down with the outer evidence of great weariness.

"The day," said he, "is a trial to the spirit."

Helen sat up. "Dan in town?"

"What of it?" grumbled Jubilee. "I'm here, ain't I?"

"That's some help," admitted Helen.

"Now I suppose you got to dash right over and see him," said Jubilee.

But she relaxed in the hammock, looking very small, and let one white arm trail to the floor. Her black eyes narrowed as the rest of her slim face turned more and more sober. "You've been around the ranch all week. Has Dan visited Nan Avery?"

"What for? To get his neck bit? Naw."

"They've quarreled?" asked Helen in a faint voice.

"It ought to be happy news for you."

"You don't know much, Jubilee. People never quarrel unless they hurt each other. They don't hurt each other unless they care."

"Him and her?" Jubilee overdid it. "Not a chance."

"So you know it as well as I do," said Helen softly. "Everybody knows it, I guess, except they themselves."

Jubilee pinched a smoke together, lit it, took a

drag. He shoved back his hatbrim irritably, and a loose coil of raw red hair dropped across his forehead. The light points in his gray-green eyes sharpened. His voice could hurt, as it did now. "It is about time," he said roughly, "you put away your slate and your hoop, Helen. you're too old for toys. While you're about it, put away some of your kid dreams. There's a lot of pains with growin' up. Better get 'em over with now."

"Dan?"

Jubilee dropped the cigarette and forgot to be curt. "I wouldn't knock Dan for a million dollars. And I wouldn't hurt you for ten times that. But it's no go. This girl don't change it, one way or another. Point is, you'll do for Dan's small sister — that's all. I know him better than any other man in the world. It's time you caught on."

She was very still, her face oddly intent and shaded. "Why are you telling me, Jubilee?"

He stared down the street, angular cheeks gone homely. "I don't want to see you building yourself up for a worse fall. If it could be otherwise, I guess I'd be mighty pleased. You're all the girl anybody to want. You're swell, Helen. But —"

"Why are you telling me?" she repeated.

"I'm here," he said gruffly.

"Mean that, don't you?" she said quite gently. "Thanks, Jubilee. But I don't change easily. Maybe I'll grow out of it, maybe I won't. I've known all you've told me for some time. I guess

I can step aside and not cry in public."

"I'm here," insisted Jubilee.

"You wouldn't like being second best."

He got up, turned away. "Far as you're concerned, I'd be seventh best and like it."

Her slow answer followed him: "You deserve something better than that, Jubilee."

He went along the street, turned a corner stiffly, and crossed the square to Dan, who waited at Townsite's. Both rode solemnly out of Trail. A long time later, past Gunderson's, Dan explained why they didn't take the slightly shorter route across the valley. "Got a couple letters for Miss Avery."

"Find anything new?"

"No-o. Same things repeated."

Jubilee tipped his head to the brass-and-blue sky and grunted. "It won't last. Can't. I'd give a leg to catch the inside of St. Cloud's mind for ten minutes."

"Where'd you go?"

"Over to see Helen."

Dan suddenly grinned. "I'd like to see *that* happen, Jubilee."

"Oh, hush," was Jubilee's aggravated answer. They passed the vacant Mitchell place, both glancing silently at the rectangle of fresh dirt on the higher ridge; they turned the last loop of the road and crossed Nan Avery's front yard. Lorrie sat huddled on the porch. When he saw them he sprang up and ran over to seize Bellew's bridle. The youthful eyes were brooding, unhappy; his mouth was very straight.

"I'm going home with you for good, Dan," he said.

"Hold on here, youngster."

Lorrie's fist clenched, his voice broke shrilly: "She rode up Smoky Draw with St. Cloud! I'm goin' home with you, Dan! I won't stay here another minute!"

Dan, Jubilee thought, showed worry. He spoke to Lorrie with an accented patience. "Don't get her wrong, son. She doesn't know about St. Cloud. She's only being neighborly."

But Lorrie was stubborn, beyond persuasion. "I can't help it. She's had truck with him, and I won't stay. I liked her — I liked her a lot, Dan. But if you don't let me go with you I'll run away."

Bellew thought about it over a heavy spell of silence. "You sure? You're going to make her feel mighty bad. She's trying to make a nice home for you."

Lorrie shook his head, the outrage simmering in him, maturing his young cheeks. It hardened him against all argument. Seeing that, Dan suddenly got down and walked toward the house. "All right. Get your things, and I'll write her a note."

10. Smoky Draw

Two miles north of the pass St. Cloud and the girl entered a heavy pine belt and at once got beyond the scorching beat of the late sun. The road ran like a tunnel through the false twilight, bending gently to the left; and then abruptly fell out of the timber and into a shallow gulch that seemed a natural corridor leading onward into the peaked hills. A dozen gray, paintless buildings lay along the gulch. Turning before the nearest and largest house of these, St. Cloud dismounted.

"My particular kingdom," he told her smilingly. "The name of which is anathema to all the good Christian people of the valley."

Nan instantly resented that faint suggestion of being classed outside the valley group. He was, she thought, trying to make up her mind for her as he had done before. Yet for the moment she said nothing, but crossed the porch and walked into the house. She was at once surprised. The room, quite large, had a full furnishing of fine oak pieces — all good and all old — suggesting a past period of life at once more polite and more formal. In one corner stood a piano, obviously unused; above it hung a mirror framed ornately with golden cupids. The fireplace was a huge thing faced incongruously with marble, and near by, on a kind of pulpit stand, lay a great metal-bound family Bible. An inner door led into the recesses of the house. A stairway climbed stiffly to the second story. Save for certain discrepancies this might have been the living room of a fashionable Baltimore home; the mark of taste was evidenced here, but of a taste covered with dust and neglect and the rather heavily flamboyant additions of another hand.

She accepted the chair St. Cloud offered her, realizing that his keen glance awaited her reactions. He had a certain eagerness that somehow demanded an answer.

"How," she asked, "does all this come away up here?"

It was, of course, the expected question. He stood in front of the fireplace, the soldier-straight body stirred by a characteristic, ever-present restlessness. "Ancestral belongings," he drawled. "Descended to an unworthy son. All this stuff came around the Horn to Portland in 1860. My father had it freighted to the valley. He could have gotten along without it, but my mother was a proud lady and wanted all the relics of the past around her. That," he added, shifting to irony, "was before evil days came upon us."

"You once lived in the valley?"

His reply was interrupted by the opening of an inner door. A woman's husky and strident voice came from behind Nan: "You'll want supper at the same time tonight?"

Nan, quite curious, turned in her chair.

"Mrs. Wills," said St. Cloud, "this is Miss Avery. Mrs. Wills is my housekeeper. Her husband works for me."

Nan acknowledged the introduction silently. Mrs. Wills's eyes were unhappy and too old, and her disposition was written clearly on a face that once had been buxomly handsome but now was scored by acid lines of violent emotion. Her mouth, Nan thought, gave her away. It was thin and compressed. She was, perhaps, thirty-five. Thirty-five and controlled by a sulky, tragic temper. Her hair, a frowsy yellow, showed gray threads. St. Cloud's answer was clearly one of dismissal:

"Dinner at the same time, if you please."

Mrs. Wills's direct stare was offensively knowing. But she soon turned to avoid Nan's cool inspection and closed the door definitely behind her.

"My father," went on St. Cloud, ignoring the interruption, "was one of the first settlers in the valley. He grazed all the land where LeBœuf's place is now. I was born there. Yet here you find me in this year of grace, 1899, camping in the wilderness."

Nan sat immobile in the chair, studying the gloved tips of her idle hands. Her perceptions, always sharp and useful, were building up St. Cloud's character for her. The allowances she had made for him previously were less truthful now that he stood in his own house. Behind the surface courtesy, below the surface pleasantry was another person that kept eluding her understanding. He was complex, he was contradictory; and these things were baffling in a man. Baffling and untrustworthy. When she mentally placed him beside Dan Bellew he suffered by the comparison, for Bellew's lucid and straight-spoken character made St. Cloud seem less honest, less substantial. Nothing, excepting that reckless, ironic face, was clear-cut. He was, she thought critically, the shadow to Bellew's substance. More acutely regretting her trip, she could not reason away the sense of being involved in something that was gray and surreptitious and unclean.

St. Cloud had kept silent. Lifting her face, she caught the intentness of his look. It was as if he tried to follow her reasoning. Suddenly he said:

"Do you believe what you have heard about me?"

"Don't you think that's more personal than necessary?" she countered.

"I want your good opinion. I want that more than you believe."

She shrugged it aside. "It would do you little

154

good, even if you had it. I warned you before not to read meanings into what I say."

He took a quick breath, turned across the room and back. "You came here because you were curious. Probably because you wanted your own picture of me. All right. That's fair."

"I'm not asking for your confession," Nan told him dryly. "I don't particularly care for explanations."

"My father had the best of everything out there in the valley," he went on, "until other cattlemen came in. There was friction. Never mind what it was all about. Cattlemen, especially the big ones, are graspers. They're used to power, and they always want more power. They made a target out of my father. They drove him beyond the valley. Up here. Here's where he died. I'm the only one left. I've inherited this accursed barren spot in the hills. It isn't my birthright. My rightful place is down yonder. But here I am, like the archangel, barred from heaven. In the opinion of those people I'm worse — I'm a wolf skulking the edges of the settlement."

She watched him, refusing to speak the answer he plainly begged for. A darker, more suppressed mood rode him. "That's the background. It may explain to you how bitter I am. Maybe it'll also explain why I feel perfectly justified in taking whatever steps I can to fight back. I'm fighting back, you know. And I do not hesitate to use the same means they have used on me and my family."

"Wait a minute," interrupted Nan. "You are telling me you'll take what you can get, however you can get it?"

"As they did. Don't forget that fact."

The relentlessly logical mind over which she had no power drove her insistently on: "You would force Dan Bellew off his place if you could? You'd drive him out?"

The pleasantry had quite departed from his mobile features. Lips and nose were thinner; the light eyes flickered mordantly. "You're quick, you're very sharp-minded," he applauded. "The thing is between Bellew and me. We both know that. I guess everybody else knows it."

"Why?" demanded Nan. "Why should it be Dan Bellew rather than anyone else?"

"The man," said St. Cloud half angrily, "is a god to those people. Why should he be? Don't ask me. I only know he is. He's got a damnable control over them all. They'd ride to ruin for him. Yes, they would!"

Nan found herself saying very quietly: "Loyalty is not given to a man unless he deserves it."

His answer was abrupt, contradictory: "Make no mistake about him. I had hoped you'd see him as he is, not as people think him. Dan Bellew wants power, too. Just as much as any other man. He wants to give orders, not take them. He was born with a heavy hand, and he will not surrender."

She cut in: "You've not answered me directly. You mean deliberately to fight him?"

His grin was rather saturnine. "So you must have things in black and white? Listen to me. I am no spectator. I've got to be up and doing. I wasn't meant for compromise or safety or sweet reasonableness. If people hurt me, I will not turn the other cheek. Never! I could not live as a poor man or a quiet one. I have ambition — the same as Bellew has. I am a fatalist. The ending doesn't matter, for it is sure to come anyhow. The years between now and then are all that matter. Either I make a large winning or I come to a quick finish. The highroad for me or the bottom of the canyon."

"All those words, boiled down," she said, "mean 'Yes.' That's your answer?"

"I can say it no clearer," retorted St. Cloud; and at that moment she thought she saw him exactly and completely. His words betrayed him, and his body betrayed him, drawn rigid as it was, the head tilted back and the face colored as if from drinking. For herself, she meant to be final beyond the chance of another mistake, she meant to close the door against him definitely.

"It is clear enough. You are setting up to be another Robin Hood. Did you ever stop to think that, all the fiction and romance set aside, he was just a common thief?"

"Here — here!" he broke in roughly. "Don't be so ready with your judgment. I gave you credit for a better understanding. This isn't the East, you know."

"I didn't know there was any boundary line to ordinary honesty."

His lips made a thinly angered line. Obviously on the margin of blunter talk he turned toward the doorway. The girl's eyes traveled over there as well, to see the chunky, off-balance body of Clubfoot Johnson sidled against the opening. He had, she knew, been there for quite an interval; the air of absorbed attention lay on that swarthy face which seemed so conscienceless and so cruel. The coarse black hair tumbled across his forehead to increase his air of cunning. He was grinning openly.

"Well?" challenged St. Cloud.

"Just a word," muttered the other man and made a furtive gesture. St. Cloud mechanically excused himself and went out. Rising, she heard the two go along the porch, heard them rapidly talking. The inner door opened, and Mrs. Wills came hurriedly through. Queerly disturbed, Nan wondered at the cold hatred she saw mirrored on that prematurely haggard countenance; and more clearly she felt the presence of an unbridled temper. It had done this much to Mrs. Wills; in another few years the woman would be a common slattern.

"How's Lorrie?" asked Mrs. Wills.

Nan was puzzled, but she answered calmly enough: "Very well."

"Like his new home?"

"I hope so. Why are you asking?"

Mrs. Wills put her hands on her hips, openly sullen. "Why shouldn't I? He's my son."

"Oh, not really —" said Nan, dumbfounded.

The other woman was instantly ablaze. "Oh, yes, really!" she sneered. "Don't you suppose I can have a son? Well, he's mine. Don't forget it, either. One of these days I'm coming after him. I —"

But St. Cloud was returning from the far end of the porch, and Mrs. Wills bit off the phrase and half ran through the inner door. St. Cloud came quickly in, at once throwing a glance that way. Afterwards he studied Nan with a more composed manner, plainly seeking a friendlier ground.

"After all," he said, "we still don't know each other very well. Let's not quarrel about it."

Nan's answer was ruthless: "Don't you know when you have been rebuffed?"

St. Cloud grinned. "I'm a gambler, always hoping for better luck next time."

She went directly past him, out to her horse. In the saddle she looked around to catch the same intent and weighing expression. "I shall see you

159

again," he said. "I'm sorry I can't ride back with you."

She put the pony to a quick trot and soon passed into the trees, glad to have the gulch behind her. The sun had dropped below the western rim, and the pervading cobalt blue of another long prairie twilight washed the land. In the thickness of the timber was a premature darkness. Beyond this wooded belt Nan turned to the left and, instead of following through the pass, cut into higher ground. Aimless as the act was, it only mirrored the confusion and the heavy fears dredged up by the revelation of Mrs. Wills.

It was hard to believe that this woman, so nearly self-destroyed, could be Lorrie's mother. Yet that was only the initial shock. What plagued Nan as the pony took her upward into the cupped irregularities of Buck ridge, what roused her to furious defensiveness, was the threat of returning the boy to Mrs. Wills. It was unthinkable, it was cruel. Normally fair-minded, she could not now admit Mrs. Wills's rights. The whole case was summed up and dismissed in one scornful thought: "If she was his mother, why did she leave him like that?" No, she would not surrender Lorrie. Not ever.

"I've got to watch him," she told herself. "I've got to keep him in my sight."

But there was a shadowing uncertainty, a lingering doubt of her position. Supposing Mrs.

Wills did come for a boy legally her own? To what extent dared she resist the woman? If she did resist, it meant only one thing — the use of a force she hated. She recoiled from the possibility, but it would not let her alone, and presently she found herself wondering what Dan Bellew's answer would be. Exactly at that point she saw the man in a new, far more revealing light. In Trail on election night he had met a like issue and had replied. What was right one day could not be wrong the next; what was right was to be fought for. So he had answered — Nan realized — without change and without compromise. And in that moment she applauded Dan Bellew for the very rigidity of purpose that had until now seemed nothing but arrogance. The next moment her preoccupied eyes lifted and found two men stationed in a gully below. The rest of it was purely involuntary. Wrenching the pony back, she retreated quietly to a protected spot and there halted.

They were two hundred yards away, and the evening had deepened to the prairie's lovely dusk. But she recognized them. One was the new sheriff, the other was Solano of Broken Stirrup. Little as she understood the laws of the range, she did know this to be wrong. No Bellew man could have any possible business with that St. Cloud outfit Bellew so urgently opposed — and so what she saw below was treachery. Increasingly feeling the danger of her position, she watched Ruel Gasteen swing an arm southward. Solano bent in the saddle and spoke a few brief words. Afterwards he rode directly into the farther pines. Gasteen went up the gully and also disappeared, apparently bound for Smoky Draw.

Nan waited a good ten minutes before venturing forward. Beyond another heavy stringer of the hills she saw her own house standing darkly by the road and swung toward it. Sliding down the slope, she suddenly realized she had some duty here. What it was, she couldn't for the moment determine, so complicated and interwoven were the articles of faith and action of this strange, mysterious land. Beneath its serenity was the smoldering of conflicts and ancient hostilities. Was that why all its people spoke so sparely and so invariably watched the horizons with half-hidden eyes?

She didn't see Lorrie, but thought nothing of it. Probably he waited out on some high point for the flash of the house light to beckon him in. Entering, feeling somehow guilty for her lateness, she lighted the lamp and at once saw two letters from the East and an open note on the table. The note, from Bellew, was very brief:

"MISS AVERY:
"The letters were in Trail, so I brought them.

Lorrie has decided to live with me. This is his decision, not mine. I believe you'll understand why he is doing it.

"DAN BELLEW."

11. A Warning Disregarded

The cruel and unforgiving briefness of that note left her momentarily stunned. She felt a physical hurt, a kind of sick emptiness; she had the odd illusion of Bellew looking across the shadows at her without sympathy. Things, she thought dimly, happened like this out here — bitterly swift and unexplained. Turning toward Lorrie's bed, she found his personal effects gone, and immediately a silent cry went protesting to her deepest being. "Dan Bellew hasn't the right to do this to me! What have I done to deserve it?"

But below this helpless unstrung feeling her temper slowly took shape. She had always been a fighter, and if her courage in the past few weeks had remained still and ineffectual it was because she had deliberately recoiled from a world suddenly turned unkind. Her strong pride had been beaten, but not her spirit. She had, she abruptly realized, been wrong in one thing. She had been wrong in believing she could build up a barrier that would protect her from further hurt and intrusion. The truth was, she could not ever escape the chances of living. This added catastrophe demonstrated the flimsy quality of her isolation.

At once she was bitter and defiant, unable longer to remain still. And her instinct to strike back usurped that cool second-reasoning which always had so strongly colored her personality, had so accented her charming individuality. Half furious, she ran out to the horse and went galloping off toward Broken Stirrup. Beyond the third coulee she caught Bellew's house lights. Near the yard she heard Mike Shannon's challenge strike out of the dense shadows, but she rode speechless past him, dropped to the house porch, and walked swiftly in. Bellew's black head was bent over a ledger on the table. He looked up at her, and even with an angered phrase taking substance in her head she had time to see he had somehow withdrawn his faith. The man's solid face was deliberately noncommittal, as it had been that election night in Trail when he turned to Neel St. Cloud.

Nan spoke impetuously, bitterly: "Am I being punished?"

"No," said Bellew. He didn't rise; his two big palms closed together on the table's top.

"I don't believe Lorrie would do this on his own account."

"Then you don't know Lorrie."

"It's — it's unfair!"

Mike Shannon strolled up the porch and looked in. Dan waved him back. "I asked Lorrie to think

165

it over," he said. "He refused. I told him that whatever you did was entirely right because you thought it right. But that's no line of talk to make any impression on a nine-year-old boy. He came with me. I don't want you to think I drew him away. I've always thought he needed your help. I do now."

"Then send him back to me."

Dan slowly shook his head. "He wouldn't come."

"What have I done that is wrong?" challenged Nan.

"You went to Smoky Draw."

"Is that wrong?"

"Lorrie thought so."

"Do you think so?" pressed Nan.

"We're looking at it Lorrie's way, not mine," Dan reminded her. For a little while she had nothing to say. The flush of her cheeks deepened, temper turned her fine, direct eyes stormier and stormier. She was profoundly aroused, deeply stirred. He could see that clearly. He could see, too, some other strange shift in this really beautiful girl. That air of aloof and critical disinterest was quite gone. Her guard was down, and she was at a fighting pitch. She was, he thought, swept clean away from that indifference against which he had so frequently and painfully collided. She made a picture of grace and vitality there against the lamplight — the level eyes blazing at him, small fists unconsciously closed. Her shoulders were rigidly square. Fundamentally there was nothing placid or helpless about Nan Avery, and the discovery queerly touched him.

"I want him back," said the girl, after the studied pause.

"You'd want me to drag him back by the fur of his neck?"

"No — not that way," said Nan swiftly. Then her anger became a white-hot flame. "This pleases you, doesn't it?"

"Of course not," interposed Dan. "Get rid of the idea."

"Oh, yes, it does! Toward your enemies you are very hard. You see no good in them — and no good in those that speak with them. You sit there and you think I am getting exactly what I deserve!"

"Do you see some good in my enemies?" countered Bellew, quiet again. "In St. Cloud, for example?"

It was her turn to put him back on the main subject. "We're not talking of St. Cloud now."

He nodded his agreement. "But you've got me wrong. I'm not trying to rub it in."

Nan drew a deep breath, fell from anger to an anxious pleading. "Listen to me. I want Lorrie back. If I've got to beg, then I'll beg."

"Like him, don't you?"

"I love Lorrie," stated Nan.

"You'd go a long ways to keep him," mused Bellew. "You'd swallow your pride. You're doing that now."

"Yes."

"I like you the better for it," said Dan quietly. "If an apology will do you any good, you've got mine. I'd figured you a little selfish. I was wrong." He paused, scowling at the desk. "But I don't see any way out of this."

"Why?" insisted Nan. "Why should he be so bitter toward me all at once? I don't understand it." Facing him, the words came reluctantly out. She was revealing more than she wished him to see. "I know he feels certain things deeply. I know he is shy. I have been very careful not to force myself on him. Really I have. I'd do almost anything to gain his confidence. I thought I had it, and I can't feel he would turn against me so swiftly."

"You went with St. Cloud," pointed out Bellew. It was to him a complete answer. But to Nan it remained aggravatingly obscure. It brought her head against the strange, unfathomable hatreds of the land.

"What does that mean to him?" she asked.

"Maybe I'm to blame for not speaking sooner. Lorrie's dad was a mighty fine man. Lorrie's mother was a girl of the valley, but a kind of a high jumper. When Lorrie was about two years old another man got interested in her. There had to be a quarrel between the men, and there was.

This interfering party shot Lorrie's dad dead and ran for the hills. Lorrie's mother followed and married him. They're up in Smoky Draw now. Henry Mitchell took the boy. Henry Mitchell never mentioned the woman to Lorrie, but it was the main point of his life to let the boy know how rotten that Smoky Draw crowd was. That's the whole story."

"Why didn't you tell me?" cried Nan, feeling the futility of her hopes.

Dan shrugged his heavy shoulders. "Maybe I'm to blame. But we keep our scandal to ourselves out here. The habit of saying nothing is pretty strong."

"I met Mrs. Wills."

Dan showed a fresh interest. "What did she say to you?"

"That she might come after Lorrie."

"Not in my time," grunted Bellew. "But if she feels that way about it, Lorrie's better off on Broken Stirrup."

A side door came open, and Bellew raised a warning hand toward Nan. Lorrie, heavy-eyed from disturbed sleep, stood on the edge of the big room and stared across at the pair. Bellew spoke very casually:

"Miss Avery feels pretty bad about your going away, Lorrie."

The boy said nothing. He looked directly at Nan, then soon away.

"Wouldn't you like to come back?" Nan asked him gently.

Lorrie shook his head, speechlessly stubborn. Nan's lips moved, but she only said, "Goodnight, son," and stood still until Lorrie had gone back, shutting the door behind him. Bellew rose, turned about the room.

"I guess that is all," said Nan, no inflection in her voice.

Bellew stopped in front of her. "You had your own perfectly proper reasons for going with St. Cloud. I don't question them. But you can't expect a boy to understand the fine-drawn distinctions of your thoughts. With Lorrie it is either black or white." A darker tone subtly took possession of his words. "For that matter, I guess all of us in the valley look at it either black or white. I don't say it is very enlightening. But I do say we can't afford to be either charitable or generous."

"I shan't bother you again," said Nan, turning away.

"It might be a good idea," pointed out Bellew, "if you'd come over frequently. Might change Lorrie's attitude."

She shook her head, speaking with the same uncolored listlessness:

"No use, I'm afraid. He's your boy now."

He walked with her to the porch. On the steps she hesitated, thinking of the scene between Solano and Gasteen. Rather indefinitely she thought she ought to tell Bellew about that; but at this particular moment the affair seemed of little importance to her, and such inclination as she had was changed by a recollection of Bellew's phrase: "The habit of saying nothing is pretty strong." She had made many mistakes from not knowing the ways of these people. She would not transgress again.

That silently decided, she got into the saddle and turned homeward, overpowered by a sense of black defeat.

When she reached her yard, she suddenly felt the presence of somebody on the edges of it, and she wondered — with a final remnant of anger — if St. Cloud was paying another visit. Putting up the pony, she went to the house. The distinct odor of cigarette smoke lay in the front room; on the point of locking the front door, she was quite startled to see it open before her. Pete Garcia slid in, closed the door quickly, and backed away from the immediate light. Knowing him to be Helen's brother, she wasn't afraid, but the surreptitious air of the man and his roving, uneasy manner caused her to challenge him sharply:

"What is it you want?"

Garcia got a sealed envelope out of his pocket and offered it to her.

"Been waiting here about as long as I dare. I want you to take this letter to Bellew."

171

"You're able to ride, aren't you?"

"Me? Think a minute, ma'am. What would happen to me if I set foot on Broken Stirrup? Take it. He's got to get that right away."

"Not from me," said Nan impatiently. "I'm not your messenger or his. You'll have to get your sister —"

"I ain't got time to ride to Trail," insisted Garcia. "Didn't I say he's got to get this right away?"

Nan put her hands behind her, refusing the letter. "I won't be involved in your affairs."

Garcia showed his irritation. His thin frame went very still, and he seemed to listen for stray rumors beyond the house. The brilliancy of his eyes increased. "I don't see how you can be so foolish. Figure it out. If it wasn't blamed serious I wouldn't risk my neck coming here, would I? I'm on St. Cloud's payroll, ain't I? Well, why would I be dickering with Bellew if it wasn't powerful important? Think it over. You see?"

"Get out of here and take your letter with you," ordered Nan.

Garcia sighed, shook his head. He came forward with a characteristic abruptness, laid the letter on the table, and swung to the door. "See that he gets it right away. I'm not fooling you — not me. If it don't reach him tonight, there sure will be hell to pay. You're Dan's neighbor, ain't you? Well, then, do what you're supposed to do."

Having delivered that parting injunction, the man sidled from the room and went across the porch at a dead run. Nan remained in her tracks, hearing Garcia's pony beat up into the ridge. Turning deliberately from the table then, she walked into the kitchen to find something that would serve for a cold meal.

She had gone to Bellew's once this night; no power could take her back to that scene of humiliation. At this hour nothing was very important.

What Solano said to Ruel Gasteen at their meeting in the ravine was:

"Dan's drivin' beef to Trail tomorrow sundown. He'll be going along the Buck ridge trail."

"St. Cloud will want to know that."

"I'm telling you, ain't I?" countered Solano and rode immediately into the pines.

12. Disaster

At five o'clock the next afternoon Dan rode
across the flats to a point in Buck ridge behind
the Mitchell place, there joining the rest of the
crew. Eighty head of three-year-old steers lay in
an easy pocket, waiting out the hot day. Dan said,
"Time to go," and thereafter the beef was turned
into the twisting trail that led to town. Solano cut
through the brush and took the point of the herd.
Medders and Shannon rode the flanks; Dan kept
Jubilee with him in the dusty rear. Evening's cool
came with sunset, which was Dan's favored time
for driving, and he established a slow pace to
preserve tallow. The cattle went steadily, darkness drifted down, the rustling, scuffing echoes
of the stock played against a surrounding quiet.
A breeze blew out of the west. Jubilee's match
burst crimsonly against the thickening shadows.

"Fifty-seven days without a drop of rain.
We're due for a swell bust of weather. I feel it."

Link Medders's sharp "Hi-hi-hi!" slid through
the pall; the march momentarily got hung up
ahead. Dan's pony, needing no advice, surged
into the brush, threw a steer back into the ranks.

Then the forward motion was resumed. Link Medders cursed melodiously. Jubilee spoke again: "Had a talk with Lorrie yet?"

"About Mitchell?"

"Ahuh."

"I asked him if he saw the man who fired the shot. He was in bed and didn't. But he heard only one rider. Mitchell was standing in the doorway with the light behind him. I don't see how Henry, old a hand as he was, would do such a trick. Killer apparently was waiting for that, probably been posted for some time. After the shooting, Lorrie said he heard the man run into the timber."

"No question in my mind," mused Jubilee. "Don't forget Mitchell was warned to quit riding around Smoky Draw."

"A guess is all we'll ever have."

"A guess is enough."

"For our purposes, yes."

A long riding silence fell. The cattle wet their feet at Lost Miner creek, filed into the mile-long run of Redoubt gulch. Night's blackness thickened here, the wind strengthened and turned colder. Beyond this defile lay a flatly open area across which the narrow column made an undulating progress. Part of a moon shed frosty light on the ragged surfaces of butte and pine. They were high up, and in the distance Gunderson's ranch lights cut glimmering points through the low-lying fog on the prairie. Dan struck a match against his watch.

"We're making good time. Trail by eleven."

Jubilee Hawk emerged from long reverie. "We've had about all the breathin' spell we're going to get. St. Cloud is a restless man, my son."

"Yes."

"I wish I knew."

"We are dealing with a fertile brain, a dangerous brain. Medders, ride on up to Solano and tell him to slack off. We're strung out too far."

"Listen," said Jubilee, "haven't you got any idea?"

"I'm not trying to forecast what St. Cloud will do. If I put up my guard in one place he'd hit me in another. I see nothing very clear — except an eventual fight." Paused, Bellew listened into the night with his chin risen. His added words were very thoughtful: "It will be bloody — and a lot of dying goes with it. That's all I see."

"It's you he's trying to get."

"I don't feel it, somehow. Usually I smell trouble coming. This time I don't."

"Nevertheless, it's you," insisted Jubilee.

Something was wrong with the column. It had lost its forward momentum, and the rear beasts were straying out into the flats. Of a sudden the line disintegrated, and all the men fell to a swift circling. Link Medders called angrily to Dan: "I told Solano to slow down, not stop! What the hell's the matter with him?"

176

Some definite pressure up to the fore recoiled against the cattle strangely. Cutting against the strays, Dan shouted to the little man somewhere ahead on point: "Solano!"

Solano's voice was faint, remote: "Yeah?"

"What are you doing?"

There was no answer. Dan stopped his pony, scanned the shadowed earth. Down left, the margin of timber stood blackly against him. To the right the ridge was broken by small stringers of land showing jagged crests in the moonlight. Seeing that, he launched a quick order to Medders:

"Take Solano's place. The man's asleep. We're a quarter mile off the trail."

The cattle kept drifting to the rear, gently pressing into the riders. Jubilee shot abreast Dan. "Something funny here. What's makin' 'em shy away?" He swung on then, set his horse against the increasing mass of the steers. Shannon angled out of the obscurity and said, "This is odd, Dan." But Bellew, not yet moving, only half heard. A vague form detached itself from the nearest stringer of land a hundred yards to the right.

"Solano — come over here."

That figure never answered. Instead it drifted silently forward a short distance and halted; at the same time a whole series of formless shadows rose to the rear of the man and came abreast. A sibilant word sheered the dark, and all Bellew's nerves went tight and cold. Almost conversationally, he called to Jubilee and to Shannon: "I think this is it, boys."

"What?" grunted Jubilee. He wheeled, reached Bellew's side; he swore tautly. "By God —"

"Who's there?" challenged Bellew.

"Watch it!" roared Jubilee and laid the full force of his pony against Dan's. Both men went shifting back into the mass of moving steers. That sibilant word again passed like a knife through the dim light. "Down!" shouted Jubilee. Medders's voice came out of the distance in aroused puzzlement: "What's the trouble back there? I don't see Solano. Solano!" And then the utter silence of those breasting figures over by the stringer of land was blasted apart. A guttering row of muzzle lights flashed vividly; the concerted gun detonations made an avalanche of sound that swelled across the open, struck the far trees, and rebounded in pulsing fragments. Jubilee's Apache yell lashed shrilly back. A steer beside Dan grunted and fell instantly dead; the rest, hit by an immediate panic, stampeded into the timber, the crushing force of their retreat adding a wild note to the flat wail of a continuing fire.

It was, Dan coolly thought, St. Cloud's trump play. That whole group sat yonder in the saddles and fired as though at target practice. The whole thing was thus dispassionately planned. All this occurred to him in fractional intervals of time. He had drawn, he had wheeled behind Jubilee and Shannon, who stood shoulder to shoulder. He yelled "One of you get behind that dead steer," and plunged into a circling lope. The breath of following lead touched him, the crying of a barrel-toned voice in St. Cloud's outfit rose and fell, rose and fell. He saw the mass of a high rock dead ahead, he cut about it and dropped there. He had that long line flanked. Seizing his rifle from the saddle boot, he began smashing at them with an enfilading fire.

His shots struck. A horse sagged, the rear end of that line wavered, a man capsized and emitted one fading cry. But the heavy voice lashed out insistently: "Rush him — rush him!" And afterwards part of the outfit broke from formation and drove at the rock. They were squared against the faint moonlight, their shapes grew bolder before him. Bellew thought, "You fools, you're dyin'," and laid his barrel on the steadying rock. He fired twice, saw the targeted figures tragically melt; those saddle-empty horses pitched across the advancing group, got it into a snarling tangle; his bolt crashed another shell into its seat, and the veering muzzle stiffened on a spreading torso that for one moment stood advanced and alone in the confusion. The man was as good as dead then; but as the rifle fired, the pitching horse reared up on its hind legs and took the bullet in the chest. It dropped, and the rider went sidewise to the earth. Dan Bellew relentlessly sought him with the gun, lost him in the quick churning of dust. The man appeared on his feet again and raced away with an up-and-down gait that identified him at once. It was Clubfoot Johnson. The attacking wave had spent its strength; those left alive retreated — and Clubfoot Johnson seized a passing rider's leg and was pulled into the sheltering dark.

The long line of St. Cloud hands had unmistakably broken apart. A piece of it advanced on that dead steer behind which either Jubilee or Shannon lay — and fell back; elsewhere in this mad night a quick and furious fire lifted roiling layers of sound into a sky gone oddly dark. Medders, near the trees, was singing out his epithets with a blistering casualness. Then Dan caught one more view of Clubfoot Johnson reaching for a horse. It was what he wanted to see. Leaving the shelter of the rock, he trotted forward.

The affair was over in three or less violent minutes, its swiftness of beginning matched by an equally swift ending. The Broken Stirrup hands were intangible shapes blended with the dark, and St. Cloud's party had lost its initial advantage of surprise. There was a long, arresting cry. The guns beat up the flat echoes once more, and following that last volley the ambushers whirled and weaved across the open area. Jubilee Hawk spent his last shots at thin shapes. The firing quit altogether, uneasy quiet came trembling back. For a long, motionless interval the Broken Stirrup men waited, hearing St. Cloud's men crushing the earth beneath them in departure and at last passing eastward beyond earshot.

Jubilee said: "Everybody all right?"

Solano's muted voice arrived from a distance: "Medders, what was you hollerin' about before all this started?"

Medders spoke rapidly: "Mike — Dan!"

"That ought to teach St. Cloud a lesson," said Mike Shannon. "How about it, Dan?"

Into the waiting silence no answer came. Medders and Shannon walked slowly to the center of the area, paused there. Solano's body made a still streak under the moonlight. Jubilee Hawk rapidly hoisted himself to his knees.

"Hey, Dan!"

After another straining period Jubilee jumped to his feet. The four men came together. Medders muttered uneasily, "He was behind that rock a minute ago," and made for that position on the run. His voice presently drifted back. "Not here."

"Mister Bellew," snapped Jubilee, tension shrilling his voice, "don't be coy."

"Maybe he lit out after 'em," suggested Shannon.

"No," called Medders. "His horse is here."

"Good God!" rapped out Jubilee. "Don't just stand there!"

Medders ran toward the looming stringers of land, torso bent at the ground. Jubilee looked at Solano, who hadn't yet moved. "Don't stand there, damn you!"

"Stop cussin' me," said Solano, openly sullen. "My leg hurts. They shot my horse from under me."

"I wish," snapped Jubilee, "they'd busted your fool neck."

"Why light on me?" complained Solano.

"You led us off the trail — you got the beef all balled up. At a time like this."

Medders was a hundred yards off. He dropped to all fours suddenly, and he called out: "Come here."

Jubilee swore. He leaped ahead, Shannon on his heels. He said: "Him?"

"Yeah," grunted Medders.

There was a long, motionless shape on the earth in front of Medders. Jubilee bent down. Medders let a heavy sigh out of him. "His heart's workin'."

Jubilee reached for a match and struck it. The yellow glow slid across Bellew's face and turned oddly crimson. Bellew's eyes were half opened, and he breathed like a man sleeping; but a mask of blood stained the whole left cheek from temple to neck. Jubilee's hard, glittering eyes bent nearer and nearer. The match went out.

"If it was a clean hole he'd be bleedin' worse. Looks like it creased him."

"Light another match."

Jubilee obeyed. Medders's fingers gently crept across Bellew's head. "I don't see anything else. Dan — come on, boy, sing out."

The three of them hung over Bellew; and the last flicker of the match showed the hungry anxiety of their brooding faces. In the following darkness Mike Shannon took the lead. "It's a mile nearer the ranch than it is to town — and better travelin'. You boys get him home. I'll run for Trail and have Doc Nelson on the job by the time you reach the house."

"That's right."

Jubilee ran back for his horse, brought it up. Solano came limping over and stood a yard away while Jubilee swung to the saddle and the others lifted Bellew up to him. Then he said, curiously: "What about the beef?"

"To hell with the beef!" snapped Jubilee. "Shannon, get goin'!"

Shannon was already on his way, pounding across the clearing into the broken terrain southward. Jubilee swung into the trail, Medders behind him. Solano was left to himself.

"If he passes out on us," stated Jubilee in a barren voice, "I'll ride to Smoky Draw, Link. So help me, I'll kill that —"

"Jubilee," said Medders, "it seems mighty queer to me how St. Cloud knew we'd be in this spot at this time."

Doc Nelson reached Broken Stirrup a few minutes beyond ten o'clock. Shannon was with him, and also Helen Garcia and Townsite Jackson. Medders met them on the porch and silently pointed to the lower bedroom. "Still breathin', but knocked clean dumb."

Helen let out a sharp sigh, following Doc Nelson into the room. But in another moment she returned, paler than before, Jubilee holding her arm. Nelson put his head through the door. "Boil up a kettle of water and bring me a couple more lamps."

"Is it bad?" demanded Helen.

"How do I know?" grunted Doc Nelson. Jubilee motioned Chan to the kitchen, himself going for the lamps. The others made a silent, grim group in the living room. Helen turned from one end of the room to the other, unable to halt, her eyes constantly reverting to the bedroom doorway. Townsite rolled a dry cigar between his teeth.

"How did this happen?"

"They were waitin' for us — that's all,"

growled Jubilee. "If Dan —"

"Don't say that!" cried Helen.

Uneasy quiet returned for a little while. Solano slid quietly into the room and paused, slightly removed from the group. Jubilee's glance snapped over to the little man with an odd alertness. "Solano," he demanded, "how did you happen to get off the trail? You could ride that country with your eyes shut."

"Half asleep, I guess," muttered Solano. "Up most of last night scoutin'. I let the pony pick the way."

Jubilee's mouth tightened. "Why would your horse leave a well-beaten trail?"

"How in thunder do I know?"

"What difference would a half-mile make?" asked Townsite, deeply interested.

"St. Cloud's boys were waitin' for us, wasn't they?" pointed out Jubilee.

"Listen," broke in Solano, "I don't want to hear any more nonsense like that. I'm the oldest rider on this ranch. I worked for Bellew's father. I helped drive the first Broken Stirrup cattle onto this range. Don't stand there and look at me as if I was a chicken thief!"

"We got off the trail — and right there St. Cloud's bunch met us," said Jubilee in a level, insistent manner.

"Probably he had us scouted from the moment we put the beef in motion," said Solano. He stood with his feet apart, his flimsy body apparently ridden by fatigue; and the secretive, dust-colored eyes met and avoided the long, thoughtful inspection of the others. A feeling of straining, speechless suspicion came into the room. Even Helen Garcia halted her aimless wandering and watched the little man. Townsite thought to light his cigar, narrowly staring into the match flame; and it was his next remark that broke the spell: "I have told Dan it was a mistake to run so shorthanded. He should have twenty men on this place. He won't see it."

"Different from now on," said Jubilee flatly. "There will be a dozen of his best friends on Broken Stirrup by tomorrow night."

"That's the talk."

Medders broke in: "I don't think St. Cloud was in that party. But I did recognize Clubfoot. Dan shot his horse down. It was probably when Dan went after Clubfoot that he got hit."

"Of course St. Cloud wouldn't be along," muttered Townsite.

But Jubilee interposed a warning: "Don't discount his courage. He'd been there if he figured it necessary."

"And now what do we do?" grunted Medders. "Take it and like it?"

"That depends," answered Townsite and motioned toward the bedroom; and once more a nervous, gloomy quiet oppressed them all. Doc

Nelson came out, bringing swift attention down on himself. Helen Garcia stopped in front of him.

"How is it?"

"Bullet shaved three inches of skin off the side of his head, and a small amount of bone. I think it's probably a case of concussion. Won't know how bad it is for another couple hours. Where's that water?"

Helen went quickly after it. She took the steaming kettle into the room and returned to the group with round, frightened eyes. Townsite gently patted her shoulder. "That boy," he drawled, "is too tough to kill."

Helen said: "He looks so helpless!" Then she wheeled away. "I'm going out. Be back very soon." She went to the porch, to her horse; she climbed into the saddle and sat there a moment, watching the strong light flooding out of Dan's room. Old Mike Shannon strolled to the porch, saying, "Don't ram too far from this yard." But Helen went off at a strong lope, not quite sure of her destination till she topped a coulee two miles to the east and picked up Nan Avery's house beam. Then she knew, and rode straight for that beacon. She didn't bother to knock, but opened the door and walked in. Nan Avery's head rose from an unfinished letter on the table before her. Some flash of apprehension shone momentarily in her level eyes and then was absorbed by a quick concern; for Helen Garcia's cheeks were tragically drawn, the vivid features overwhelmed by the darkness of despair. It was so plain, so contagious that Nan rose with a swift question:

"What is it?"

The smaller girl's shoulders dropped. She was not far from crying. Her breath rose and fell rapidly. "Dan was shot down tonight by St. Cloud's man."

"Helen!"

"Doc Nelson is taking care of him at Broken Stirrup."

"Is it bad?" breathed Nan.

"Don't know yet."

"But — how could anybody do that!" cried Nan.

"I told you once before," was Helen's dull answer, "you didn't know this country."

Nan didn't hear. It was as if some strong support had been withdrawn from her. She stood mutely there, physically sick. She was thinking of Bellew with a kind of hungry interest, and the solid, easy-muscled shape of the man came quite clear before her. It was impossible to believe that anything could happen to him, so lively and rugged were her pictures of him. He was, she told herself faintly, too strong to be caught by the ordinary accidents of life; he was a riding man.

"I've got to go over there, Helen."

"I knew that."

It was so wistfully said that Nan was roused to a more outward interest. "Helen — why?"

Helen Garcia leaned wearily against the wall, watching emotion play through the tall, fair Nan Avery. If she had any lingering doubts as to her own share in Dan Bellew's life they were dispelled now. This Avery woman who could be proud and aloof and untouchable was after all only human — with the same feelings and the same desires. It was very clear and very saddening. Like went to like. Dan Bellew, who admired pride and courage and self-possession, would be finding it in Nan Avery. That was the way it was; these two were made for each other.

"Do you want to know?"

"Yes."

"You are in love with him."

"That —" began Nan — and swiftly closed her pale mouth.

"That is so," said Helen. "I knew it days ago. People don't go out of their way to hurt each other, as you two have done, unless they feel something else."

"You — you shrewd child."

"What good does it do me?" brooded Helen. "Well, we've got to get back there."

But Nan suddenly straightened and went paler than before. "This is all my fault! Look here."

Pete Garcia's letter still lay on the table. She took it up, passed it to Helen. Seeing that handwriting, Helen said abruptly: "How did you get it?"

"Your brother brought it."

Helen ripped the envelope nervously. The note was very brief, and unsigned:

"St. Cloud is going to surprise you on the drive."

"You never opened it?"

"He asked me to take it to Dan last night."

"And you didn't?" Helen's dark face blazed. "You ought to be slapped!"

"I had been to Broken Stirrup once that day. I humbled myself. I couldn't go again."

"So you let your pride interfere!"

"I didn't know it was that serious," said Nan slowly. "I really didn't know."

"Haven't you been warned about Smoky Draw? How long are you going to trust that yellow-headed killer up there? Oh, but you're a fool!"

"Dan will have to know," Nan murmured.

"You bet he will."

"Tell him."

"Me?" said Helen. "What would Dan think of me for carrying tales? Tell him yourself."

"You think that much of him, Helen?"

Helen Garcia swung toward the door, concealing her face with an impatient, weary manner.

"Let's get out of here."

Nan lighted a lantern and ran to the barn. She was soon back in the saddle, and the two went side by side across the coulees to Broken Stirrup. A little distance from the porch they came against Mike Shannon's stationed figure. Mike said roughly: "You oughtn't be rammin' around like this, neither of you. Dan's all right."

Nan felt a cool, streaming relief pass through her. Helen Garcia murmured some indistinguishable phrase and jumped boyishly to the porch. When they walked into the big room, Doc Nelson was pulling down his shirt sleeves, jaded and ruffle-haired.

"He came out of it," he said. "Never know just what concussion will do for a man. Sometimes it just blows out the light, sometimes it doesn't. It's up to you to see he stays on his back three-four days. I want that cut to heal. Go on in if you want."

Nan turned on her heels, paused at the open door. She felt embarrassed for a moment at what she saw — which was Lorrie standing at the head of the bed and trying not to cry. Dan lay flat on his back, white bandages making a complete helmet around his head. He grinned, faintly drawling:

"Do I have to get shot to draw you over here, Miss Avery?"

"This is my fault. I had a letter of warning

brought to me. I didn't deliver it."

"Honesty is a swell thing to have."

"No, I'm not trying to be angelic. I didn't realize what was in the note. And at the time I didn't care. I'd just come from here. I couldn't come back."

"Think no more of it. If the cards fall that way, there's nothing you can do about it. The business was in the book before you or I was born."

Helen Garcia stood in the door's opening, watching that scene with a shadowed intensity. She had a quick, glad phrase framed in her throat, and there it died; Dan never saw her. Dan's eyes were absorbed in Nan Avery, and the strengthening light in them told Helen the complete story. As quietly and as softly as possible, Helen retreated, faced the silently grouped men.

"I'll go home with you, Doc," she said and went to the porch.

Jubilee walked after her, rounded her in the semidarkness. "I'll take you home."

Helen lifted her pointed, passive face; the glow of her eyes dimmed. "You belong here, Jubilee. But thanks. Jubilee, you're nice. And you were right."

"Don't let it hurt too much," growled Jubilee.

"I guess I can stand it," murmured Helen. But there was despair in her, and it came violently out: "Jubilee, it's so damned hard to grow up!"

Jubilee put a hand under her chin. "Some people cry when they lose. You ain't that type. Get it, Buffalo Bill?"

"Jubilee — I didn't ever know you were so kind."

The man cleared his throat, and his cigarette tip made a glowing arc in the shadows. Whatever he meant to say was checked by the approach of Doc Nelson. In another moment Nelson and the girl were riding off toward Trail.

Said Nan: "It was Pete Garcia who brought me the note."

Dan tried to shake his head. "The boy will only get himself in trouble. I've got to see Helen and have her tell him —"

"She was here a moment ago," said Nan and turned to the living room. Jubilee was just then coming in, and she asked him.

"Went home," muttered Jubilee, and his frowning glance locked significantly into the girl's. Nan slowly nodded and turned back. "She came with Dr. Nelson," she told Dan. "And then rode to tell me."

"A fine kid."

Nan interposed a sharp correction. "She's more than that. She's a wonderful woman."

Dan's tone was gentle. "That's right. I keep forgetting she's grown up."

"Are you really going to let me off this easy?"

Lorrie slid off the bed and eased himself from the room with a show of self-consciousness. That made Dan grin. "That boy has got the sensitiveness of a woman. He feels he's one too many right now. Look here, let's quit scrappin'."

"All right, Dan."

He put up a hand, and she came forward to take it. The pressure of that big black fist was sudden and genuine. He had turned very sober. "I told you once it wasn't possible for me to keep from figuring about you. Remember that. Take it for whatever you please."

"Would you mind if I stayed in the house tonight?"

"Feel comfortable if you would," Dan said. He was, she saw, keeping his eyes open with effort; and disengaging his hand, she quietly turned down the lamps and went out, closing the door behind her. The men in the living room stopped talking with a telltale suddenness, and for some reason their turning attention embarrassed her. Somehow her calmness had gone, and almost defensively she walked to the porch and on into the lone roadway between the poplars, quite responsive to the soft pleasantness of this night and the silver beauty of that thin moon suspended in the south. She had no power over the lifting, gay mood so abruptly possessing her; and absorbed by it as she was, she almost collided with Mike Shannon, who stood there by a tree silently smoking.

"Ma'm," said old Mike, "you like him, don't you?"

"Yes."

"Sure — sure."

"This was my fault, Mike. I could have stopped it."

"Now I'd not be blamin' yourself. He's alive, ain't he? Well, then."

Nan turned quickly toward him. "I have got to tell you something. Perhaps I'm wrong — it is so hard to know what the right thing is, and I have made so many mistakes. But all of you should know this: Coming back from Smoky Draw last evening, I happened to see that new sheriff, Gasteen, talking to Solano."

Mike Shannon's pipe slanted upward between his teeth. There was a long pause. Then he said gently: "You're sure of it?"

"I couldn't be mistaken."

Shannon seemed to study the sky; she saw the stolidly honest face settle. Yet his next phrase was oddly irrelevant: "It's late, ma'm. Maybe you'd better stay over for the night."

"I thought to."

"Come with me." He led her back to the living room. "At the head of the stairs," he explained, "is your room."

Nan went halfway up, turned.

"Good-night, gentlemen."

They were, she thought, fine-mannered people. Their hats came off, and they all answered her with grave courtesy. And so she passed up and into the room.

Mike Shannon said in a slow voice:

"Where's Solano?"

"Out somewhere," answered Jubilee.

Shannon looked from one to the other — to Townsite and Medders and Jubilee. "The girl," he went on in the same gentle manner, "said she saw Solano last evenin' talkin' with Ruel Gasteen."

Jubilee's angular face broke into a hard, wicked shining. "That squares with tonight's funny stuff."

"I might as well tell you," drawled Townsite, "I've suspected it for some time. Henry Mitchell hinted it to me a couple days before he died."

Jubilee started for the door, to be stopped by Shannon. "No," said the Irishman, "this man's been ridin' with me for years. I'm bound —"

Solano came into the room with his catlike tread. Shannon took out his pipe, tapped it against the side of the fireplace. "Well, somebody's got to ride the circle before bedtime. It'll be Solano and me. Come on, boy."

Solano hesitated. "I'm tired as a dog —" But Mike went up to him and walked out with him, shoulder to shoulder. None of the other three said anything for a long, long while. There was the report of hoofs on the packed drive, a rhythmically dying scud in the looser soil beyond. Medders's face went more and more taciturn, and Jubilee Hawk stared straight against a wall.

It was Townsite who broke the lengthening pause:

"Nobody knows Shannon till they see his loyalty roused."

"Mike?" grunted Medders. "Mike would cut off his arm if Bellew wanted it."

Jubilee said: "We've got the answer now to how Solano happened to see LeBœuf's cattle bein' rustled. It was arranged by St. Cloud he should go pull LeBœuf away from the votin'."

"What would the little runt want to be that way for?" demanded Medders. "Why, damn him —"

Two curt reports cut the outer stillness, killed Medders's talk. Those three stiffened, and their faces turned to the door's black opening — all changed to expressionlessness. Jubilee muttered:

"Night's full of sounds. It's maybe a coyote dyin'."

"Get this straight," said Medders, "we're all telling Dan the same story — Solano was killed by parties unknown."

"There's another who is not to know," warned Townsite. "That girl told us. It'd break her heart if she thought —"

One pony came beating back, neither hurried nor delayed. Townsite turned and walked the length of the room, his head dropped.

"This," he muttered, "is what a range war is like." Mike Shannon came in. He said gently:

"I rode a ways with him. I told him to stop, and I called him for what he was. He had his chance, and he took it when he saw what was up. Had to give him a clean break, didn't I? It was my shot you heard last."

13. This Turbulent Land

Gabe Trono was a Mormon squatter with a wife, four yellow-headed children, and a pack of hunting dogs in which he took considerable pride. He had a cabin at the foot of Squaw ridge six miles below Broken Stirrup, and he had twenty heads of stock grazing alternately on LeBœuf and Bellew soil with no complaint from either rancher. Gabe didn't own an inch of ground, and the beef was only the natural increase from three cows long ago left to their own devices. Things just happened to Gabe Trono; he was a great believer in letting well enough alone. During the busy seasons he rode for the big outfits, and that little labor fed the household through the year. Otherwise Gabe could be found doing any irrelevant thing — washing the Monday clothes, following the hounds, or leading his flock on a camping trip that never had destination or limit. The fact was, Gabe led a placidly satisfactory life, neither eaten thin by ambition nor stirred to pretensions of wealth. He got along, and his family was happy.

On this unimportant person the collecting

storm next burst, at once wiping out his substance.

It was three nights after Bellew's ambush on the ridge. Gabe had wound up his eventless day. The small chores were done, the lamps trimmed and lighted, his cob pipe drawing well. Mrs. Trono had left the doors open to dissipate the odors of boiled cabbage, and Gabe rocked himself in the cross draft of pungent evening air. The children were in bed. "Tomorrow," said Trono, listening to the far yammer of a coyote with a sense of deep ease, "I got to get at the well." And then the coyote's wail was overborne by the steady fall of hoofs rising from the northeast and coming rapidly on.

Mrs. Trono stopped in her tracks. She said, a little anxiously: "They're passin' toward LeBoeuf's again, Gabe. I wish they wouldn't come so close."

"We never done them no harm," reflected Gabe. Yet he lowered his pipe and ceased to rock, and he was keening the night like one of his own hounds. The trembling impact of that party telegraphed itself stronger through the earth; of a sudden the dogs began to bay.

"Close the door," said Trono's wife.

"What for? It's a free country."

"I know, but I'm afraid."

The night party broke out of the enclosing dark, wheeled in Trono's yard. He saw the curveting horses, the closing ranks. One man moved deliberately into the steady beam of house-light. "Trono, step out here a minute."

"Don't go," whispered the woman.

"Now, now," cautioned Trono. But a slow and worried frown settled across his face. That yonder man was clear in the light, lopsided body and sullenly cruel countenance and all. Trono rose, cast one doubtful glance at his gun standing against the wall, and walked through the doorway. Wise in the ways of his country, he saw that the group — twenty strong — was bent on business. There was no friendliness in the men. Still, he kept his voice casual:

"Hello, Clubfoot."

Clubfoot Johnson moved in the saddle. Mouth and eyes and hatbrim made narrow, hard lines against the scorched-black cheeks. "Trono," he said, "get your family out of that shack inside of two minutes."

"Lord sakes," muttered Trono. "Why?"

"Get 'em out!" barked Clubfoot.

Trono's anxious glance passed along the silent line of riders and was then drawn off to the southwest, off toward LeBœuf's. What he saw yonder astonished him beyond measure. A great column of red flame piled up into the sky. "Hey," he said, "what's burnin' over there?"

"Another nester's shack."

"That's Nick Wales's. Say, boys, we ought

to ride and help."

"We just come from there," grunted Clubfoot ironically. "Now get out of that shanty and do it sudden."

Comprehension came to Gabe Trono with a catastrophic suddenness. "No," he said strongly, "you ain't doin' that trick to me, Clubfoot!"

"Ain't I?"

Trono's wife ran through the doorway. "Listen here, you crooked-legged thief, why don't you let us alone? Don't you dare touch this place! You hear? Trono is an honest man, and he never raised a hand against St. Cloud in his life! You're not going to burn our house!"

Clubfoot laughed. "Missis, you want your husband alive, don't you?"

Trono's wife let out a gasp and said nothing more. She ran back into the house. Clubfoot spoke over his shoulder: "Bill, go in there and pile up anything that will make a quick fire. Sim, put a match to the straw in the barn."

"Now, Clubfoot," pleaded Trono, "what's this all about?"

"We're burnin' you and Wales to the ground. That's a warning to all nesters in this valley. If it ain't enough of a warning, then we'll be back. Get to hell clear of the country, Trono. Don't let daylight find you around here."

Trono's wife came out, herding the children in front of her. One of the St. Cloud men passed in, brushing the woman roughly aside. All this Trono saw with a heavy eye. The kids were scared, and that hurt him worst of all. But he knew these men; and he understood on what dangerous ground he stood. There was nothing to do. "Let me get my belongin's out first, Clubfoot."

"You ain't got enough to worry about," jeered Clubfoot. "Let 'er go, Bill."

A long lance of fire stabbed through the barn door, a roar rising as the hay ignited. Trono moved stupidly toward his children. He caught up the youngest and beckoned the rest to follow him farther into the desert. The lamp in the house smashed to the floor, the St. Cloud rider walked from the place with a quick crimson glow behind him.

"Put up the sign," said Clubfoot imperturbably.

Trono's wife lashed at him despairingly: "Oh, you'll get your reward one of these days! You're the cruelest thing that breathes! Go tell that to St. Cloud! Tell him I'll be glad when Dan Bellew kills him! I'll be glad!"

"You're through in this country," said Clubfoot. "Don't forget it. And let me tell you somethin': Don't go to Bellew's or LeBœuf's. If you do, Trono, your life won't be worth much."

"Is there no pity in you?" cried Trono's wife.

"I never had any use for a nester, missis. Far

as I'm concerned, you ain't even people. Come on, boys."

The barn shook with the swelling heat, and in the house the licking tentacles ran hungrily up the walls. St. Cloud's men went beating away. Trono felt the heat on his face, and he retreated again and put down the youngest one. His wife was crying bitterly; Trono put a hand awkwardly to her shoulder.

"We've started before, and we can start again."

"Trono, I loved that house, and now we've got nothing — not even clothes!"

"Never mind. They let the horses out of the barn. I'll get 'em for you and the kids to ride. Wait right here."

"Where will we go?"

"Bellew's."

"You were warned not to do that."

But this easy-going man's temper was rising. "I ain't that certain to scare," he said gutturally. "By God, they'll pay me back!"

Clubfoot's men had driven down a stake with a cardboard on it. Trono went over there, guarding his face against the heat, to read the sign:

NOTICE TO ALL NESTERS: LEAVE THE VALLEY
BY DAYLIGHT OF THE
FOURTEENTH OF THIS MONTH.
NO EXCEPTIONS AND NO EXCUSES.

"He'll pay for every inch of it," gritted Trono, turning about the solid flame that had been the barn. His two horses were drifting off, and he spent a good twenty minutes getting them. Afterwards he hoisted his family aboard and started off to the north, to Bellew's. His wife had ceased crying, but the youngest was whimpering. Trono walked on with that little wail in his ears, hurt and shamed and outraged by it. He never looked back.

Clubfoot led his band diagonally across the flats to Henry Mitchell's place and left it a high plume of crimson against the night's dark. He went on to Nan Avery's house and called roughly. "Come out of there, you!" This evening's destruction woke all the illicit, brutal pleasure of which his sullen mind was capable. He was pleased with himself, proud of his luck. Yet his trail was written vividly across the prairie sky, and from time to time he looked with some degree of uneasiness off to the quarter where Broken Stirrup lay. Having no answer from the house, he went in, found it empty. He kicked over the furniture, made an inflammable pile against a wall. One of Nan's dresses hung from a clothes hanger, and he came out with this, maliciously grinning.

"Neel might like this trinket."

Fire began to glow behind the shanty windows, but Clubfoot made no immediate move to go. He sat in his saddle, watching the blaze catch hold, eyes reflecting some of that fire's hot heat. "She's got herself to blame for this. Neel would of took her. But she give him the mitten. She's a fool. Any woman that turns St. Cloud down is a fool."

"Why you suppose she did?" said one of the crew.

"Dunno," said Clubfoot, puzzled. It was past his understanding. There was little room in his warped mind for such oddities of conduct, no light and no shade; nothing but a faith in the man who owned him that was like the fealty of a serf. "She'll regret it in another week," he muttered. "Let's go, boys."

When he reached Smoky Draw he slid from the saddle and tramped into the big house with Nan's dress hanging over a thick arm. He tossed it to a table, the evilness of his blackened visage deepened by a humorless smile. St. Cloud stared from that dress to Clubfoot and angrily hurled his question at Clubfoot:

"What did you do?"

"Just burnt the place. Girl wasn't there. Found the dress. Sort of a trinket for you, Neel."

St. Cloud said with a sort of breathless quiet: "If you ever touch that woman, Clubfoot, I'll slice the heart out of you. Understand me?"

"Why, chief, I did nothin'," countered Clubfoot plaintively.

"Had I wanted that dress I would have asked for it."

"Yeah," mumbled Clubfoot.

"You did what I told you to do?"

"Yeah," said Clubfoot, once more grinning.

That grin, which more widely spread the grimy evil of Clubfoot's character across his face, exploded Neel St. Cloud's rage. His words were brutal and contemptuous and insolent beyond measure: "I ought to smash you with a whip! Maybe I've got to spend the rest of my life among dumb animals like you, but by God, you'll at least mind me! Get out of here!"

Clubfoot departed as one whipped; nor was there any power in him sufficient to raise his head to the yellow blaze in St. Cloud's eyes. Clubfoot knew that mood and feared it. This misshapen man was that primitive; answering only to the emotions of loyalty and fear.

There was another meeting of the stalwarts at Dan Bellew's house. Gunderson said, as he had said before: "If we've got to smash him, let's do it now. He doesn't scare me."

"Take your time," put in LeBœuf dryly. He sat in a chair, his wide bulk crowding it; and a settled worry camped on his face. "There's no big rush about doin' something we'll have to do sooner or later. I want to know what St. Cloud's intentions are."

"Ain't they plain by now?" queried Townsite. "He tacked those warnings all over the valley."

"Why?" persisted LeBœuf, whose mind kept worrying at the problem.

Dan Bellew lay propped half upright in his bed. He mended the burst seams of a cigar, he lit it; he smiled faintly at Nan, poised in the doorway. Then the small show of humor faded, and he turned to LeBœuf. "Testing out his luck."

"It's holding good," said LeBœuf grimly. "The Mormons moved out this morning. They passed me as I was on my way here. Leavin' the country."

"What?" grunted Jubilee. "They won't scrap?"

LeBœuf had a more discriminating view: "Why should they scrap over something which don't concern them very much? It ain't their land — it is ours."

"They live on it," pointed out Link Medders.

"Plenty more land to live on," stated LeBœuf. "When a man's got a wife and a herd of kids to consider, he ain't so eager to buck up against bullets." He turned his heavy head toward Gabe Trono, who stood in the background. "Never gave you no reasons, uh?"

"Clubfoot said St. Cloud was running all nesters out. That was the story."

"It ain't the answer by a long jump and run," meditated LeBœuf. "And he never gave you a chance to get your belongin's?''

"No. He burnt us out complete.''

"There's the size and substance of St. Cloud for you," LeBœuf drawled.

"Was there any previous doubt?" asked Townsite gently.

Bellew shifted in the bed. "Trono, the sensible thing for you to do is obey St. Cloud's order. No use for you to throw in with us. Next time any St. Cloud man caught you he'd kill you. I've got a quarter-section south of town you can move on.''

Trono's sun-baked cheeks settled to a greater stolidness. "I can't do that, Dan. He burned me out. Everybody knows I'm a peaceable fellow. Never raised my hand against nobody. But I can't swallow this. No, sir, I can't.''

"Somebody's going to get hurt," said Dan quietly.

"That's all right.''

A considering silence fell over them all. Faint currents of air entered the room and disturbed the heavy tobacco smoke. Nan withdrew, her light steps tapping across the barren floor. At the sound Dan's eyes lifted and followed the girl's sure slender body as far as the kitchen. He didn't realize it, but that slight shift of interest was observed and understood by every other man in the room. They were watching him.

"Well," said Gunderson, "the man's powerfully recruited. We'd better brace him now before he gets any more help.''

"The truth is," reflected Dan, "he's scarin' the nesters away to cut that much support from under us."

"Look here," proposed Gunderson, impatient to arrive at something definite. "Why don't we go up to Smoky Draw tomorrow night and burn it out?"

"Too obvious," said. Dan. "St. Cloud would expect us to do some such thing. Anyhow, I'm in this deal, and I can't ride for a few days."

"In that connection," said LeBœuf, "when are you going to increase your crew? You're more exposed than any of us."

"Well," broke in Gunderson, "is it to be some more waiting and watching?"

"Just that," said Dan. "The worst thing we could do would be to try and outguess St. Cloud. Let him make all his false starts and fake moves. When he tires of feinting and comes for the showdown — then we act. Not before. We'll have to strengthen our patrols. My men will scout as far as the Pinnacle. You boys send your patrols to that point. In case of trouble, get a rider on the road."

Gunderson was dissatisfied and said so. But LeBœuf, the older and steadier man, nodded his head in agreement. He rose, which was the end of the parley. Presently they all filed out of the bedroom; but after they had gone, Dan called Jubilee back.

"Go to Trail and get as many good men as you can find. I leave it to your judgment, but I would like Peach Murtagh and Joe Gatch if you can locate them. Do it quietly, and warn them to say nothing. Don't bring them with you. Each man is to drift here after dark."

"The same as done," said Jubilee, turning out. He narrowly avoided colliding with Nan, at that moment entering with a tray, and afterwards he flashed a brief, amused glance at Bellew and disappeared.

Nan put the tray across Dan's lap, punched an extra pillow at his back, and sat on the edge of the bed, watching him. It was a little difficult for him to eat, and this unaccustomed handicap of movement always roused a slight sense of rebellion. Seeing that rise now, a glow of amusement touched her eyes.

"Humbleness, Dan, is always the hardest virtue to acquire."

"Are you laughing at me?"

"No. Preaching at you. You can't help yourself. You hate to be confined like this. It just outrages your sense of self-sufficiency."

"Wisdom in that. All I can do is lie here and think. I don't like it. I'm not a thinking man."

"So there have been no compensations?"

"You're here."

211

Nan colored a little. "I wasn't fishing for compliments."

"It wasn't a compliment. It was a statement of fact. Why have you gone to all this trouble of waiting on me?"

"Making amends."

Dan scowled. "If it is just the payment of a debt, consider it paid. Is that all?"

"Now, now," said the girl. "Let's wait —"

Lorrie ambled into the room, a little embarrassed at finding the two adults so engrossed with each other. He said, after a moment's awkward silence, "Be all right, Dan, if I ride up into the ridge? Link said I better ask."

"Sorry, old man. All Broken Stirrup hands are confined to quarters today. We might have company — and I'd need you."

"Sure," said Lorrie, gravely. "Hadn't thought of that. Gettin' better?"

"Be in the leather right soon now."

Lorrie's eyes glowed against the absorbed darkness of his face. He said, "That's mighty fine," and put both hands in his pockets and started out. He had looked only once directly at Nan, and then with an air of uncertainty. Nan glanced at Bellew, making an odd gesture; then she spoke to the boy:

"I'm sorry, Lorrie, I went over to Smoky Draw. I didn't know about that place."

Lorrie stared through the doorway. "Sure you

didn't," he answered. "That's all right, ain't it?" Then he added, "Sure," indefinitely and went out. Nan sat very still on the bed, a shadow across her eyes.

"That," mused Dan, "was a wonderful thing for you to do."

"It was an apology."

"He didn't have one coming."

"But I can't let things stand this way, Dan! I don't want him to feel so foreign toward me!"

"Nevertheless," Dan said firmly, "you have offered the peace pipe. Don't do it again. It is up to him now."

"If there was anything I could do —"

"Don't. He's got to learn to be a gentleman sooner or later. Got to figure out this give-and-take business all by himself. If he doesn't, he's not the boy I think he is. In any event, you don't want his affection if it has to be coaxed."

Nan got up, smiling again.

"You're very fair, Mister Bellew."

"Now don't run off and leave me picking at the covers all afternoon."

"Have you nothing to think out?"

"That's done. I know all the answers."

"To everything?"

"To everything," said Dan and met her eyes directly. "If I'm wrong about one of those answers, Nan, I'm wiped out."

Nan turned her back to him, glancing into the

living room. "I should hate to see you hurt. Do you know how much I'd hate that? I know what it is to have the ground simply drop away —"

Hoofbeats skipped nimbly across the dry, still air. There was a swift flurry at Broken Stirrup's door, and a girl's husky voice said: "Stop that, you dumb beast." Dan chuckled at the sound of those quick and sure steps in the living room. And when Helen Garcia paused in the doorway, her alert and boyish figure swaying slightly from inner restlessness, he drawled:

"Buff'lo Bill, howdy."

"Who's this strange man wearing a nightcap in Dan Bellew's bed?" said Helen.

"Where've you been?" Dan grumbled. "I've missed you."

"You're a poor liar," stated the girl. Her glance met Nan's and remained engaged for a long sober moment, then whipped back to Dan with a kind of subdued brightness. Nan said nothing, but slipped quietly from the room.

"Feeling all right?" asked Helen. She stood in her tracks, slim hands crossed before her.

"Terrible."

"You won't die," decided Helen. "Just feeling ornery. Don't like to lie on your back and watch flies crawl across the ceilin', do you? Good for you, just the same."

"Where's your sympathy?" complained Dan.

Helen's voice sank from the flippant note.

"You don't need mine," she said gently. "Well, I've got news. I spied a column of St. Cloud's men marching down that same gully under the railroad bridge last night. Followed 'em, too. They faded southeast. Something over there draws 'em powerful strong."

"So?" muttered Dan, full of interest. Then: "When are you going to quit that?"

"Told you once I was one of your crew, didn't I?"

"Now look here, honey —"

Helen turned swiftly on her pointed boot heels. "Cut that out, mister —"

"I'd like to give you a wallopin' —"

"That's the boy," applauded Helen and turned to him, the glimmer of humor showing through. "Be good — and don't fuss. See you sometime. So long."

"What's the rush?" asked Dan.

But Helen had gone from the bedroom. She went rapidly to the porch. Nan stood there, looking away at the fogged heat of the afternoon. "Nice of you to leave the room," said the younger girl. "Always thought you were a good sport. But it wasn't necessary."

"Helen, do you feel badly toward me?"

"Why?"

But Nan didn't answer the question. It was unnecessary. Its meaning lay between them plainly. Helen's sharp, mobile face was for once

215

quietly composed. "No," she said, "of course not. That's the way things happen. I'll get over it."

"I wish I thought so."

"Believe it," said Helen swiftly. "That's what I'm doing." She touched Nan with a brief pressure of her fingers, strode down to the horse, and presently was streaking across the flats in the direction of Squaw ridge. That strict expression on her dark cheeks never gave way; but in her eyes was a cloudy, wistful hunger. "He was the first man ever to show me a kindness. He's been so darned white — like a father. That's the trouble — like a father. He can't change from feeling like that. So — I guess I've got to do the changing."

It was then only one o'clock. She reached the high ground of Buck ridge near two-thirty and went cantering across that clearing which had been the scene of Dan Bellew's ambush. Afterwards the trees absorbed her mysteriously; nor did she appear from them again until the long and oppressive day had gone dark Taking station beside the main trail to town, she sat idle as the night deepened and the stars broke more brilliantly through the velvet sweep of sky. The moon, filling from quarter to half, hung low in the south as if suspended by a giant cord; and all the remote voices of the hidden creatures began speaking from thicket and cairn. Surrounded by

216

this mute beauty, this pervasive melancholy, Helen Garcia scarcely moved through the ensuing half-hour.

"I would have been good for him," she thought sadly. "But so will Nan be. I wonder if he knows he loves her. Well, it makes no difference. I've got to see this thing through."

Points of sound broke the silence northward and died out. A moment later the fast fall of a pony's hoofs strengthened and neared. Helen straightened and drew a swift breath. She moved a few yards back on the trail, crossed to a more open area, and reined around. Afterwards those quick impacts were muffled in some deep arroyo. Helen said audibly: "I've got to stop him before he gets deeper in this mess." Then rider and horse came streaking down the trail.

Helen slid her horse fore and aft into the trail and sharply challenged.

"Draw up there, Pete."

The rider's form weaved far back. He said, in a brittle, nervous voice, "Dammit!" The pony beneath him felt the obstruction ahead and grunted from the quick tensing of his muscles.

"Want to talk with you, Pete."

Pete turned, rode beside her. He was breathing hard, and his torso kept swaying from side to side. "Don't ever do that again, Helen! I almost drew on you!"

"You're nervous as a cat. Blame the miserable

sort of a life you lead."

"No preachin'! How did you know that I'd be along this way?"

"You ride it every night. What for, Pete?"

"Don't try to pump me."

"What's down in the south that interests St. Cloud so much?"

The man said anxiously, "What do you know about that?"

"I know."

"Kid," pleaded the man, "keep out of this. You don't understand what sort of an outfit you're snoopin' at."

"Oh, yes, I do. Listen, St. Cloud's going to break out again, isn't he?"

"You figure it."

"Soon?"

"I can't tell you. Stop trying to pump me!"

"What's down in the south that he's looking for all the time?"

There was a long pause. Then Garcia said reluctantly: "Bad medicine. Now don't ask me any more."

"You've got to get out before any more damage is done!"

She expected anger, yet this slack brother of hers for once showed a streak of reason. "I wish I could, kid," he said. "I'm tellin' you straight — I made a bad mistake joining that bunch. It ain't like I thought it was. It's worse. Those fellows don't give a damn for anything. They're pretty tough. You get it? They'd even put a bullet in you if they thought —"

"Then get out of it."

Garcia's answer was foreboding: "Too late. If I tried I'd die. I'd never ride far enough to get clear of St. Cloud. He's cold as ice. Yesterday he half killed a man with his bare fists for talkin' too strong. No, I've got to play this through."

"You know what will happen to you?"

"I don't see any end," muttered Garcia. "Whichever way things go, I don't see how I'll come out on top. The valley's against me. St. Cloud doesn't trust me much. I'm walkin' a rope, and one day it's goin' to bust."

"You poor kid."

"Yeah," grunted Pete, "ain't I? I've learned my lesson, and it won't do me any good. I'm finished. But you keep out of it. Don't try to see me any more. Good-bye."

"Wait a minute, Pete."

But he was flailing down the trail and soon beyond sight and hearing. Helen sat immobile in the saddle awhile, thoughts burning into the substance of this affair. "It will be soon," she reflected, "and it will come from the south. I've got to get Pete out of it. I've got to."

She turned the pony toward town; the fugitive voices of the night creatures began softly speaking again after her departure.

14. St. Cloud Hits Twice

Jubilee reached Trail around three o'clock of that afternoon and ran unexpectedly into a visiting St. Cloud party. Sidling into Townsite Jackson's rack, he got down with a trigger-quick feeling of personal danger. Four men loitered on the store porch and ceased to speak as he approached; looking elsewhere along the street, Jubilee recognized the sign of some sort of an arrangement. Quite a group stood by the sheriff's office farther down. A pair of hands strolled heavy-footed along the front of Major Cleary's hotel. A bunch came along from the railroad station and entered the saloon. This apparent purposelessness impinged sharply on Jubilee's roused senses, and so did the lack of other townspeople. Those had withdrawn, leaving the streets to the St. Cloud outfit. Jubilee walked around his pony and stepped to the porch with a lazy lift of his muscles. The four in front of him were motionless — a politic immobility as admonitory as the clanging of a brass gong. One of these men was posted athwart Townsite's door. Jubilee halted, casually speaking.

"If you ain't rentin' that spot, Sim, move aside."

Sim was built like a pole; his head came down, and one half of a mirthless mouth pinched in a cigarette while the other half let out the slipping syllables.

"How's it feel to be plain folks again, Hawk?"

The man, Jubilee saw, was full of liquor. That made it worse. Jubilee knew the makings of a bad jam lay right here, and his natural shrewdness warned him to take care. There was no accounting for the acts of a drunk. He said mildly: "Pretty good, Sim."

"You was a lousy sheriff," said Sim.

"I've heard it said before."

"Our meat-chawin' man is shore full of humbleness today," sneered Sim.

"Move aside, Sim."

"Move me aside!"

"I can do that, too," said Jubilee, thoughtfully.

One of the others broke in abruptly. "Get out of the way, Sim."

Sim showed surprise. The avid mouth widened and then closed entirely. He drew himself along the wall, gesturing with an exaggerated courtesy. Jubilee passed into the semidarkness of the store, hearing a quick, muted talk spring up behind him. Townsite, rising from behind a counter, said curtly: "What you doin' here today?"

"What's all this about?"

Townsite shrugged a shoulder. "I don't know what brought 'em. But they're mean over something. Now you go back to your horse and fade."

"To hell with that!"

"They'd like to rip-rap you out on that street. Use a little judgment."

But the tom-toms were beating up Jubilee's reckless spirits. "I'm hoistin' no white flag to those monkeys. Townsite, I've got recruitin' orders."

"About time."

"Seen Murtagh or Gatch lately?"

"Gatch is in the saloon, where he oughtn't to be. Murtagh's out of town."

"I'll see Gatch."

"Don't go to that saloon, you fool."

Jubilee made a flat, pushing gesture with one hand and walked into the bright sunlight. The St. Cloud men were gone from the porch. He saw the Sim fellow at that precise moment shouldering into the saloon. Jubilee thought: "It's a demonstration that they own Trail. I'm going to have a sweet time —"

He wheeled over the square, intercepting a man just then leaving the Star stable. "Hello, Cortwright."

Cortwright whipped himself about. Alertness went out of his eyes, and surprise came in. "What you doin' here, Jubilee?"

"Want a job?"

Cortwright said shrewdly, "Broken Stirrup?"

"That's it."

"I'm your cooky. Say, if you want those five lads down at Willow Springs —"

"Good boy. Get 'em. Now don't go out of here like you was on business. Bring these fellows across the valley after dark. Say nothing — say less than that."

"Billy Burt is campin' out on Long Creek."

"Pick him up. Or anybody else you see that's ridden with Dan."

A brace of St. Cloud partisans swung around a corner and walked slowly past. Jubilee said rather loudly, "If you see any of that beef driftin' on Buck ridge pick it up and Dan will pay you." He went along the walk, proceeded up Railroad Avenue, and breasted the saloon door. He gave one covert side glance that revealed more of St. Cloud's party drifting down toward Major Cleary's hotel; and then he passed in. The left half of his vision embraced Joe Gatch standing alone at the long bar; the right half stretched to include the quarrelsome Sim and six others grouped around a rear table. He knew none of the six; they were strangers to the land, imported on St. Cloud's order.

He walked toward Gatch, who stood with both arms idle on the counter and a half-filled glass between them. Joe Gatch's face was bemused, taciturn. But the glance he flashed on Jubilee had that same element of relief and surprise the latter had witnessed in Cortwright the moment before. Gatch's eyes went the other way, touched the withdrawn barkeep. He said quietly: "You're a fool for bein' here, Jubilee."

Jubilee held up a finger to the barkeep, got his glass and poured himself a jot. The barkeep retired again, as if wishing no talk with these two. There was a murmuring among the St. Cloud hands. Jubilee said in the same monotone: "Where's Peach Murtagh?"

"I can find him."

"Do that. Bring him to Broken Stirrup tonight. Quietly, my boy."

"If I ever get out of here," muttered Gatch.

"So," said Jubilee with a stronger emphasis, "if you see any of that stray beef, tell Dan about it."

Sim broke out of his position at the table and walked rapidly across the room, bent his body against the door and disappeared; his passing seemed to be a signal, for the other six faded through the rear way — and the saloon was thus left to Jubilee and Gatch and the barkeep. Gatch drew a deep breath, pushed his whisky distastefully away. "I was here and they moved in on me. I thought I was a goner, till you showed up. Watch your step. You're big game for those mugs. Gasteen's in town."

"Broken Stirrup — tonight," said Jubilee and

walked to the street. This aimless milling around was familiar to him, being the time-worn prelude to trouble. Restless anticipation lay in the air, the sense of a purpose not quite definite. Sim, he saw, had crossed the square and stood now near his, Hawk's, horse. The rest of the crowd made a kind of loose skirmish line from Townsite's to Cleary's hotel. He thought once of crossing the street and skirting that line, but the suggestion died of its own futility. "This is no way to play poker," he told himself bitterly. A hard, collected anger cleared his mind entirely of doubt; his part in this was as plain as breathing. He understood that with a sudden spectator's understanding. And then he went directly on to the square.

Out on the near desert the afternoon's train lifted an undulating "whoo, whoo whoo" across the crisp stillness. All those moving men had lifted a fine screen of dust across the square. Certain things hit him with remarkable clearness — the shadows along the east walls, Townsite standing in the store opening, Cleary's fat body spilling over a hotel porch chair. These were incidentals, coming unbidden into a scene that narrowed down at each pace to so many men blocking his path and so many apertures between them. He thought: "I'll take that nearest opening. If it closes on me, I'll waste no time arguin' —"

He expected it to close, but it didn't. His shoulder brushed another shoulder, and he felt the attentive faces wheel around and watch him turn the rack and step up to Townsite's porch. "What's the matter with their scheme?" he puzzled. "Something's wrong —"

The lank Sim broke that locked stillness with a ripped-out oath. Sim moved along the rack in angered hurry. He ran up the steps. "Gasteen wants you in the lock-up, see? If he ain't here to do it, I'll do it! Come on, now!"

"Hold that," challenged Jubilee.

"Come on!"

"You're a worse fool drunk than sober," grunted Jubilee, caution frayed thin.

It was flame applied to powder. Sim's gangling arm swept semicircularly downward, knees and torso springing with the intensity of his effort. Townsite's chesty roar of warning to the others on that street rolled over Jubilee with a tidal massiveness, "Stand still, all you brush poppers!" Jubilee took a catlike step aside, watching Sim's shoulders rise. He never saw Sim's gun — only the upper half of the man reacting to this deadly play. Down Railroad Avenue came the clanging bell of the transcontinental and the quick release of live steam; Jubilee, finding Sim's face a rigid mummy's mask, let his hammer fall at the high point of the traveling gun's arc. That beating, barking echo exploded the tense calm of the street; Sim staggered half around from the striking force of the .44 slug. His own bullet ripped an aimless track across Townsite's wall, and he fell off the porch awkwardly, landing in the powdered dust.

Jubilee stretched his long legs backward, whipped himself inside of Townsite's doorway, wondering why those other St. Cloud men had not opened. He saw why a moment later when the metal blue snout of Townsite's rifle dipped and disappeared. Townsite sidled away from the doorway. "You didn't materially damage him, Jubilee."

"I can't drop a drunk," growled Jubilee. "Now what've we got —"

"Trouble!"

The yonder calm was grimly overbearing. Sim's half-wail rode the stillness. "Somebody come give me a hand. For God's sake —" The deep blast of the engine's whistle rattled Townsite's loose windowpanes; the train moved out, steam snorting from its cylinders. Poised inside the doorway, Jubilee saw a small file of men coming down Railroad Avenue headed by Ruel Gasteen. Gasteen rolled forward, his clodhopper's gait swaying the ungainly body from side to side. He cut across the square, halted; Jubilee made out the flash of the man's eyes, the formidable stubbornness that afterwards arrived. Gasteen tilted his head to Townsite's store.

"Hawk, come out of there."

"I'm satisfied."

"You don't get away with it!"

"Come an' take me," taunted Jubilee. "This is a good place to make a scrap."

"I'll camp on you till you're starved out! Hear me?"

"Ever hear of anybody starvin' in a grocery store? Mister, I pick my places."

A cool assured voice said, "Pardon, gentlemen," and a small, slight-figured man cut deliberately through the St. Cloud ranks and walked across the square. The act was so indifferent to the situation that Jubilee marveled, and then placed the fellow as a pilgrim; no man knowing the country would so place himself between fire.

"What have we got here?" grumbled Townsite.

"You name it."

The fellow turned into the store and halted. He put down a small grip, and he surveyed the pair with a mild, shrewd glance. Momentarily diverted, Jubilee observed that this stranger had a face that might be misleading; it was a kind of neutral face, very mannerly, soft and yet definite enough, schooled to a certain blandness of expression. His clothes were Eastern, tailored to him.

"For heaven's sakes," protested Townsite, "get out of that doorway."

The stranger smiled. Some flicker of greater light appeared in his eyes; and his glance, turning

228

behind to the street and back to those two obviously beleaguered, was somehow casual and comprehending. Afterwards he lifted his grip and walked away from the opening.

"Well, gentlemen, if you have another gun —"

Townsite only grunted. Jubilee said, "Don't ever sit in a strange game, mister."

"The only fun I've ever got out of a rather dull life," said the man, gently, "is doing just that. I think you can trust me with a Colt. I carried one in Cuba for two years. There's four ounces of Spanish lead in one of my flanks right now."

"Hawk," called Gasteen, "you're goin' to the jug. Come outa there."

Jubilee, who either liked or disliked a man instantly, grinned at this stranger. The fellow was as softly flexible as an old glove, but his character somehow bit in. "This don't concern you," he said to the newcomer.

"Of course not. But it will when I take a shot at those boys, won't it? The odds seem a bit uneven right now."

"Hawk," rapped out Gasteen, "you want —"

Something happened then. Gasteen quit talking abruptly and wheeled his body defensively. The St. Cloud men broke from a long motionless rank and spread as if faced by a new opposition. The steady "clop" of ponies ran off the prairie, down the small ravine, and into Trail's precincts. A hallo came forward. Gasteen made a flat, dismissing gesture with his hand — and the St. Cloud men gradually faded into shelter. Two riders cantered across Jubilee's vision — LeBœuf and LeBœuf's riding boss; and then a heavy column of LeBœuf hands spread into the square. It looked like the whole ranch crew. Jubilee walked to the porch.

"Been a little argument, but I guess Gasteen's changed his mind."

LeBœuf said slowly: "If he ain't, we'll change it for him."

"There'll be another time," announced Gasteen stiffly.

"Sure. Always is. Where you goin', Jubilee?"

"Broken Stirrup."

"Come along. Townsite, I'm leaving six of the boys here — for your use."

Jubilee turned back, hearing the stranger speak.

"You're Townsite Jackson? I have your letter. My name is James Scarborough."

Townsite said: "I guess you've come a long way to have your ears chawed off. Jubilee, take this man to Broken Stirrup. He's come to see Miss Avery."

LeBœuf escorted Jubilee and Scarborough half across the valley and then turned off. The two men continued on. Deeply curious, Jubilee now and then sized up this Scarborough from the corner of his vision. The fellow rode well enough on the borrowed horse, and he seemed to be at home in these surroundings. A mile from the Broken Stirrup ranch, Jubilee was impelled to say: "If you come here for peace, you sure picked the wrong time."

"Peace? Lord, I wouldn't know what to do with it if I had it."

"You won't like this country."

"You are mistaken. I should like to have been born in it. There is such a thing as being brought up in the wrong environment. There is such a thing as being bred to books and business and polite ways and being utterly ruined thereby. It would have suited me better never to have seen a school or an office or a drawing room. Square peg in a round hole. There's thousands like that, Hawk. Here's one of them."

"With which," thought Jubilee, "we will now gracefully wiggle out of this rush of words before exposin' a total ignorance. But I still like him." He led Scarborough straight to Broken Stirrup's front door and got down, politely waving the stranger ahead of him. His sharp eyes told him something then. Scarborough's manners went smoother and more repressed, but there was a quick play of inner excitement that flickered strongly in the gray eyes. The living room was empty. Jubilee went on into the bedroom and found Dan shored up by pillows, irritably awake.

"The gentleman's name is Scarborough. He's come to see Miss Avery. This is Dan Bellew, of Broken Stirrup, Scarborough. He et something that put him on his back and made him even more damn disagreeable than he usually is."

"Jubilee," said Dan, "on your way out, shut the door."

"Without slamming," drawled Jubilee and obeyed.

Dan twisted his body upright, looked at the standing Scarborough with a long, unsmiling straightness. "You stepped into this, Scarborough."

Scarborough nodded. He said, gently, "Go ahead."

"Jackson showed me your letter. It was my suggestion that caused him to answer it and disclose her whereabouts. Whatever harm comes of it is due to my meddling. That's the first paragraph of the first part. Now then. Nan Avery came here all cut up over something. Putting one and one together, which isn't always good arithmetic, I judged she was running away. After your letter came, it looked to me as if you might be the man she was running from. And that is the second paragraph of the first part. The rest is short and simple. Her business is her business, and I had no right to interfere. But in the short time she's been here I've seen one thing pretty clear — she hasn't been able to shake whatever she ran from. The only medicine is to bring that past right up to the present and do something about it. This is why you're here."

Scarborough's face showed a faint humor. His words were slow, rather wistful: "Mind if I tell you that you have a good head?"

"I hate to see her facin' ghosts," Dan said curtly. "Whatever your part may be in this, you've no right to be proud of it, and you ought to do what you can to straighten it out."

"Why do you suppose I came?"

"At first I thought just to follow her," said Bellew. "I think I had you wrong. You don't look that sort."

"White of you to say so. Now look here. You ought to know the story —"

"Wait a minute. It is none of my business."

"You're quite sure?"

"Why should it be?" grunted Bellew.

Scarborough leaned on the end of the bed, lips wryly crooked. He shook his head. "Give me a little credit for seeing below the surface, too, Bellew. I think you ought to know. Nan and I belonged to the same crowd back in Baltimore. Nice people, all of us —" Scarborough's inflections were ironic — "first families, quite polite and genteel, and pretty dull. Nan's got the spark of life in her. I have always been a man who wore civilized customs with some protest. Well, take two mild rebels such as we were. We liked each other. Always saw the same ridiculousness in certain things and laughed at them. Everything perfectly proper, you understand. But the catch was, I happened to be married."

Dan shifted his weight, scowled. "This is not my business," he repeated.

"My wife instituted a divorce action," went on Scarborough, "and named Nan as co-respondent. The thing was damnable, outrageous. Nan didn't deserve that. There wasn't the least shadow of anything like irregular intimacy between us."

"Of course not."

"But my wife had to cook up some grounds for action — so she took the one that would hit Nan. I'm not blaming anybody but myself. I shouldn't have allowed myself to be even civil to Nan — not in Baltimore, in that set. Nan had to go through the trial, listen to the lawyer suggest a lot of dirty things. Maybe you know what it meant to her." Scarborough's two hands made a futile motion on the bedframe. "It was the sort of grimness she always hated. If you'd seen her come off the witness stand . . . Her friends stuck by her. Why shouldn't they? But she felt it. I think it came near to breaking her heart. That's why she ran away. The reason I'm here is, I feel I've pretty well wrecked her life. I've got to do something about that."

"What?"

Scarborough shook his head. "I had an idea, but it seems no good now. Look here, Bellew, I

234

love Nan. She's about the most gallant lady I've ever seen." Then he added, more quietly, "I came out here to see if she wouldn't marry me. I can see now that it isn't the answer."

Bellew said, "Why?" tonelessly.

Scarborough only shook his head. A horse fiddled into the hard dirt of the yard. Nan's voice, slow and easy, came through the window: "You made a quick trip of it, Jubilee."

They heard Jubilee say, "Dan would like to see you, ma'm." Scarborough straightened. His body went around, and he said wryly: "Well, here's where I take my beating." Nan's fingertips drummed the panels of the door lightly and then she came in, flushed from her ride and a pleased tilt to her straight shoulders. She saw Dan first and started to speak; Scarborough's shift from the wall brought her eyes over to him.

She said nothing for a long-drawn-out pause; nor did she appear greatly surprised. It was a different, more subtle reaction. The fine light faded from her face, and stillness came to it. Bellew, cheerlessly watching, silently cursed himself for his part in this. That which had seemed sound reasoning at the time of the letter looked now like the stumbling, blundering act of a fool. The color died slowly from her cheeks and left her lips formless against the white, even teeth.

Scarborough said, without moving: "Sorry,

Nan. I had to get this straight somehow."

Nan's answer was devoid of expression: "Jamie, you seldom do the wrong thing. But this time you have made a mistake."

"Please go to the living room — both of you," muttered Dan.

The door closed against them, and he heard them walk uncertainly across the room, still held by silence. There was finally one murmured phrase from Scarborough, and after that Nan's voice rose strongly. Dan lifted his bed-stiff knees and tried to find some comfort for his cramped back. It was suddenly dark in the room, a late twilight fading from the window. The creek water made a pleasantly fluid sound across the shadows, and he could hear his crew making a great deal of noise in the kitchen. All this was apart from him; all this only accented his feeling of being thrown back on his own resources.

It was not that he regretted this self-dependence. His own father had taught him to make his own decisions, to shoulder their consequences; and that discipline was his strength. In Bellew was an almost selfless modesty; yet he was candid enough to know that people expected much of him. People placed their faith in him, often made of him a court of last resort. And so, when he felt the inevitable discouragements come to him, he had nowhere to turn; he was — and the thought was ironic — supposed to

be immune from doubt. This was the part he had
to play.

So it was not the making of decisions that
bothered him now; rather it was the error of that
decision which had so touched Nan Avery. As
those voices rose and fell beyond the thin partition, it became more and more clear to him he
had overstepped his judgment. Perhaps for a man
his act might have worked. Men were always
better off when they cleared the back trail, left
nothing behind. They didn't always do it, but it
was a freer world for them when they did. How
could he have been stupid enough to think a
woman's way was a man's way? They hadn't the
same purposes, the same values. Women — and
this was a new and nebulous notion to Dan —
never saw and never wished to see things in
straight black or white. They compromised with
the past; they were supple and wise, knowing that
a definite ending was seldom to be had.

"I've blundered it," he told himself bitterly.
"What comes now is my fault."

The yonder talk dropped off. They were coming back. He was somehow eager to know what
the answer was, but when they came in they were
only shadows against the lesser dark of the doorway, and he had no view of the girl's face.

"Scarborough," he said suddenly, "did you
tell her how you got here?"

Scarborough's answer was on the edge of humor: "I couldn't very well do that."

"She ought to know," Dan muttered. "Nan, he wrote Townsite, asking if you were in the country. I saw you making no headway out there on the ridge — so I told Townsite to let Scarborough know. You can blame me."

Nan's voice was infinitely gentle: "You thought you were helping me, Dan?"

"It wasn't curiosity."

"No — I shouldn't ever accuse you of that."

"That's all. You set out to whip a peculiar sort of problem. I didn't think you were doing it. All I could see was to bring the whole thing to a head, get you started one way or another again."

"Jamie," said Nan, half under her breath, "there is your answer." She turned and slipped away. Scarborough cleared his throat, his outline motionless.

"Light that damned lamp, please," said Bellew.

Scarborough obeyed. His fingers, Bellew noticed, were awkward with the match, and as the lamp wick took hold and spread out an even yellow radiance Scarborough's face appeared tired and old; otherwise there was no expression on it.

"If it is any of my business," Bellew said irritably, "what did that mean?"

"The answer is," Scarborough murmured, "I lose."

"What are you going to do about this?"

"You don't get this. There's nothing to do. The story's written. The ending will be a better one than I could furnish." Then Scarborough said, casually, feelingly: "Thank God."

"What's that?"

Scarborough's glance was momentarily intent, curious. "Let it ride. Do you mind if I stay on for a few days?"

"You'll have to settle that with Nan."

"She won't mind," said Scarborough; and Bellew again caught that accent of wistfulness. "I mean nothing to her one way or another. I'm out of the picture. Her past is out of the picture. It's gone — she's laid it aside, and it doesn't hurt her any more."

"This sudden?"

Scarborough's tired eyes cut across Dan, passed on. "Maybe," he said, "she's found something."

"What would that be?"

Scarborough was swayed by a momentary irritation. "Don't be so confounded obtuse!"

Nan came in with Bellew's supper on a tray and laid it across his lap. Odd quiet settled throughout the room. Jamie Scarborough's glance followed that little scene between the two with a shadowed interest. Nan's slender hands moved in front of Dan with a swift thoughtfulness; her attention crossed to Scarborough, bright and illuminating. Dan's fork lifted and paused. "Listen —"

Neither of the others heard. But Dan's peremptory hail beat across the darkened quarters:

"Jubilee — come here!"

"What is it?" said the girl.

Jubilee came on the run. He reached the bedroom door, started to speak; and then the soft depth of the night was disturbed by a swelling rhythm of sound. Jubilee wheeled, ran toward the kitchen. Dan laid his fork on the tray. "Please put it on the table." Broken Stirrup was caught up in quick motion. Doors slammed to the rear. Shannon's hail sounded through the yard. "Trono — you git inside that stable." Medders and Jubilee were murmuring brief phrases on the porch.

Scarborough showed a livening interest. "If you have an extra gun —"

The far rhythm broke into definite beats and measures. Nan, watching Bellew's face anxiously, saw it firm up. He said, quietly: "Thanks, but the gun's no good right now. I think you're about to see something of interest."

A heavy cavalcade trotted into the packed area. Jubilee's challenge went bluntly out: "Who's that?" Spurs and bridle chains jingled, saddle leather squeaked against shifting bodies; the porch drummed to their advances. A voice said brusquely, "I told you there was another time comin', Hawk. Rest easy. You're in no position to do otherwise." Afterwards the living room filled up with them. Ruel Gasteen bowed his head under the bedroom doorway and came to a stand.

"Bellew," he said in that falsely even voice, "take this whichever way suits you — with protest or without. Makes no difference to me. I've got nineteen men out there."

"St. Cloud's got tired of waitin', I see."

"Never mind."

"Let's have it."

Gasteen tapped his coat. "I've got a warrant here for Jubilee. He's goin' back to the Trail lock-up."

Jubilee shouldered around Gasteen, yellow lamplight cutting deeper and sharper angles across his cheeks. Lorrie slipped past both of them and stood at the head of the bed, stiffly defiant. "I thought so," grunted Jubilee. "Sim Gearin made a pass at me in town, Dan. I pinked him."

"One excuse or another," muttered Dan.

"Well, what's the answer goin' to be?" challenged Gasteen.

Dan's somber stare burned on Gasteen, turned to Jubilee. They seemed to say something to each other across that stifled silence; Jubilee's head fell into a faint nod. "You'd like a play, Gasteen," grunted Dan. "But you won't get one. Jubilee will go."

"Where's your high-and-mighty manner

241

now?" taunted Gasteen.

"In due time. That's all?"

"No." A tight smile slid along the sheriff's mouth — like the creep of acid across dissolving tissue. "Mrs. Wills has got an order from the court directin' me to bring Lorrie back to her. He goes with me now."

"No, you don't!" exclaimed Nan and moved from the wall's shadow.

Gasteen arched his brows. "Well — well!"

"Don't let them do it, Dan!"

Lorrie put a hand against Dan's chest. "I ain't goin'."

Dan's quietness grew into a heavy, ponderable thing. His eyes whipped to Jubilee again. Something in it shook the dangerous rigidity out of Jubilee, settled him more quietly in his tracks. Dan put his arm on Lorrie's stiff shoulder.

"Lorrie, when you're a rider the first thing you do is to follow orders. Understand?"

"Yes, sir."

"All right. You go with this man."

"Dan!" breathed the girl.

But Scarborough, standing near, touched her arm. Lorrie's eyes were on Dan, strangely mature. He said, "Sure," in a muffled tone and went out into the other room. Dan looked grimly at Gasteen. "Anything else Neel St. Cloud wants?"

"That'll be all, this time," growled Gasteen. "When you crack the whip, they jump, don't they?" He stepped aside from the doorway and watched Jubilee pass through it with strict alertness. Then he followed, and his surly order cleared the riders out of the room. Nan turned, running across that room to the porch. There was a fiddling of hoofs, a swift break. Gasteen went off on the dead run. The after silence was like the emptiness following wind.

Scarborough came toward the bed, his eyes wide and interested. "Bellew," he said, "they believe in you."

Bellew pushed the covers aside, slid off the edge of the bed. He stood upright, supporting himself along the wall, swaying a little from that natural vertigo of the bedfast. "Well, the holiday is over," he muttered. "Get my pants out of that closet, will you?" Then he was calling: "Medders — Shannon — come in here!"

Nan stood on the porch and saw them go; saw Lorrie's small body, straight and somehow pathetically courageous, dim into the night. And for as long as the sound of that departing group remained in the evening's air, she stood very silent. Dan's talk crossed the living room, quite brittle. She heard his temper crowding him, she heard him moving. The rest of the men were going into the bedroom. Even Chan came in from the kitchen, his heelless slippers slapping against the floor.

She said: "Not in that woman's hands — not in hers." And then she went quickly down the steps. One of the ranch ponies stood waiting — whose, she didn't know. Nevertheless she seized and threw up the reins and climbed to the saddle. Of one thing she was very certain: What she meant to do now would never meet with Dan's approval, and therefore she had to slip away without it. Gently cruising the length of the poplars, she passed the dim arch of the gate and drifted three or four hundred yards into the night; after that she hauled the pony about, pointed to the black outlines of hills in the northeast, and gave the beast its head.

15. Caught

Nan went rapidly on across the coulees, reached the charred remains of her shanty, and turned into the pass. Beyond the pass she caught the scent of disturbed dust, a sign of recent travel; and a little later, in the deep blackness of trees, she was startled by a muted, arriving sound. Instantly pulling off the road, she heard rather than saw a column run freely by, bound out from the draw. After that she went on, attained the rim of the draw, and saw the few lights of this forbidding habitation pierce the shadows. There she paused, unsure of herself.

The instinctive thought of defending Lorrie lay behind her ride. Now that she faced St. Cloud's quarters, she was at once challenged by her common sense. What could she do? If, as she believed, St. Cloud had pulled Lorrie out of Broken Stirrup to hurt Dan, what could she say to soften the man's temper? To argue Dan's case was obviously hopeless. To argue her own meant a complete reversal of her published attitude toward St. Cloud; and he was too clever a man to miss the opportunism of that. There remained only the welfare of Lorrie himself. But she had no faith in the argument.

"This is — is monstrous!"

She dreaded going down there. All her perceptions warned her against the people living along the gulch — illicit, cruel, unscrupulous people who would have no compunctions regarding her. St. Cloud alone had the outward show of a gentleman; but it was a thin veneer. Behind that flimsy mask was another man, whose ultimate limits of audacity and primitive desires she could only guess at. One thing was very certain: when she entered that black slash in the earth she was entirely at his mercy. Yet with all that considered — within the space of a few foreboding moments — she knew she had to try. And so she urged the horse down the twisting trail, reached the bottom of the draw, and faced the lane leading between the double row of houses.

Here she paused again, struck by a rather curious fact. Smoky Draw seemed empty — or nearly so. She made out one man crossing the far end of the lane, passing from house to house. And after he disappeared there was no sign of life. Most of the houses were dark, the lights of the others were dim, suggestive of vacancy. She was rather careful in checking this thought, watching all those windows for inner movement. The fellow she had observed came out of the lane, went back to his original point, and again vanished. All this while she had heard no murmur of speech.

The idea that came to her then was wild and improbable. She didn't believe in it. Nevertheless it governed her subsequent act, which was to pull her pony back to the farther emptiness of the gulch, dismount, and run lightly toward St. Cloud's house. She climbed the porch steps and halted long enough beside the open door to command a view of a room without occupants; then she stepped in and aside from the lane of light, the breath in her small and quick; an instant later she retreated to the doorway and was prepared to slip out of it.

Somebody moved across the floor above. A woman's huskily unkind voice sounded down the stairs. It was Mrs. Wills's.

"Me, your own mother! Get in that bed and stay there! I know you'd run out of here if you could. That window is locked, and this door will be. You've been spoiled. Mind me from now on or I'll give you a whipping you won't forget in a hurry!"

A door slammed, was audibly locked. Mrs. Wills's feet emerged on the stairs as Nan slid out to the porch and stood in the half-shadows. She heard the woman move aimlessly around the room for a bit. After that another door clicked, and venturing a glance, Nan saw that Mrs. Wills had gone back to the rear of the house. Without considering the next move for what it might do to her, Nan slipped in, rapidly crossed to the stairs, and went up. All that second-story hall was dark; and, poised there, she got the strident echoes of Mrs. Wills now, somewhere outside:

"I don't trust him, Harry. Watch that window. The first time I catch him out of the room . . ."

Across the blackness of the upper hall lay a pencil streak of light, seeping through a keyhole. Nan went swiftly to it, dropped on her knees, breathing: "Lorrie!" A man's voice rolled along the street: "Well, that's your lookout, not mine." She tapped the door panel with her fingertips and called again, more urgently. But there was no answer; unnatural stillness held the room. The light went out, leaving Nan deeply puzzled, deeply fearing. There was afterwards a cautious, grating noise, like a knife chewing across wood. "Lorrie!"

Mrs. Wills's rapid steps beat across the lower floor; the stair steps squeaked. Nan rose and wheeled into the nearest protection she could find, the open entry of a bedroom across the hall. Crouched there, she heard Mrs. Wills come up and try the knob of Lorrie's door. Sudden confusion filled Smoky Draw; echoes fell into it strongly, and one long hail ran from end to end. Mrs. Wills said angrily, "You get to bed or I'll come in there with a strap," and returned to a living room crowded with men. Hearing them — hearing St. Cloud's talk ride curtly above all other speech — Nan felt oddly shocked and weak. She was trapped.

St. Cloud said, with a cutting civility: "Get some coffee for us, Mrs. Wills. And stay away from that boy."

"He's my kid, isn't he?"

"You're a long time remembering it," was St. Cloud's contemptuous observation. "Everybody get out of here but Gasteen and Clubfoot. But don't go to bed. We'll be riding again."

Nan leaned against the doorframe. A faint cross draft of wind touched her, and it occurred to her there must be an open window at the end of the room. But the possibilities of that fact left her indifferent; for after her first violent sweep of fear she knew that she could not run. She had not made this trip merely to retreat in panic; not while Lorrie was a prisoner within the house. So she stood fast, unable to see a way out, yet absorbed by what went on below. Boots scuffed across the living room to the porch. Mrs. Wills spoke angrily and apparently left. There was the clink of glasses. St. Cloud said:

"So you took Jubilee out of Broken Stirrup and sent him to jail?"

It was Gasteen who answered, with a queer admixture of subservience and certainty. Detached as she was from the scene, Nan got that faint arrogance which could not quite rise completely free of fear. St. Cloud, she thought, ruled with the whip. He was the master, compelling obedience.

"Like you told me. Bellew was too wise to fight back. That man plays his cards well. You'll have to watch out for him."

"You're finally learning that?" grunted St. Cloud, full of irony. "It is a wonder you didn't lose your head and make a fight of it there."

"We could of wrecked the place. But you didn't order it done."

"That's the penalty I take for having a bunch of lunkheads. If I let you do your own thinking you immediately proceed to get in a jam. So I have to hold all of you to strict chores. And another opportunity is passed up."

"I don't like to be talked to like that!"

"Shut up. If I had a man, if I had just one man I could depend on to do the right thing at the right time without a set of blueprints, I'd feel better about the next forty-eight hours. Clubfoot, what was south of Trail?"

Clubfoot's voice was flat, without the least modulation of intelligence. "They're about ten miles below the town. I told 'em to wait till I got your word."

A short silence followed. Then St. Cloud said quickly, "I guess we're ready to make the move. We'll never be in better shape. But I wish the next two days were over."

"What you worryin' about?" demanded Clubfoot. "We can lick the valley with both hands tied."

"That's fool talk. You've got no more understanding than a jack rabbit. These people will fight like hell."

"We got more men."

"What kind of men? Border jumpers that love their own skins the best. If things go good they'll stand the gaff. If things get tough. they'll break. That's the nature of a crook every time."

Gasteen said morosely: "A fine thing to say about your own crew."

"Well, they'll have to do. I can't put this off. Now listen very carefully. Take half of the outfit, Clubfoot, and ride down there south of Trail. Pick up that bunch and bring it into the valley by way of LeBœuf's range. You should have all that done no later than noon tomorrow. I'll be watching from the pass with binoculars. When I see you I'll start moving. Understand?"

There was apparently a silent assent, for St. Cloud went on: "As for you, Gasteen, you are to ride to the boys camped on Buck ridge. Stay there till I send you further word by Pete Garcia."

"What's the play to be?"

"Never mind. Get Garcia for me."

Nan distinguished Clubfoot's uneven walk across the lower room. Gasteen said uncertainly: "You're splitting the crew into a lot of pieces, Neel."

"Tactics." More steps sounded in the room. St. Cloud spoke again: "Ride to Trail, Pete. Locate all the boys hanging around town and tell them to drift over to the outfit on Buck ridge."

Something happened before St. Cloud had quite finished his speech. A man came running in. "Say — we've found a pony down at the foot of the draw."

Cold reaction stabbed Nan's body. She stiffened beside the wall, thinking: "I can't stay here."

St. Cloud's challenge was alert and hard. "Branded?"

"Broken Stirrup."

All the men moved below. St. Cloud's call stopped them summarily: "Here — here. No Bellew hand would be that kind of a fool. There's something to this —"

Nan thought dismally, "It was a mistake to hide." Her mind was made up; she had but one alternative. Decided on it, she left the bedroom, hearing Clubfoot explosively speaking. She went along the hall and reached the stairs; and she felt her knees go weak with each descending step. It was not until she was halfway down — the lower room and its occupants spread before her — that she was discovered. Clubfoot's lowering, primitive cheeks whipped around and hit her with something like a physical shock. He yelled exultantly, "There you are!"

St. Cloud wheeled slowly. His nerves, Nan had sufficient presence to observe, were not to be reached by such interruptions as this. His expression remained undisturbed. A lighter, higher flame quickened his glance, and that was the only shift. Yet this man was something else than the St. Cloud of a week ago. The queer chemicals of his body had changed him, even to the outward featuring. Paused at the bottom of the stairs, and feeling the deep antagonism of all those glances, she realized the pose of ease and high, careless humor had gone from him. He was what his own dangerous acts inevitably made him — a still, slim-bodied man with a countenance stained by the somber bitterness of his fertile brain. Cheek and nose were compressed; the slanting light touched up the discontent and the rebellion of his character. All this she saw at a glance, meanwhile feeling weakness pulse through her.

Gasteen started to speak. He said, "Well, we've got —" and was checked by St. Cloud's curt gesture. St. Cloud's question was almost conversational:

"You came on account of the boy?"

"Yes."

"Why did you hide?"

"Why do you suppose?"

"You'd have gotten him away — that's what you were trying to do?"

"Yes," murmured Nan.

253

The unrelenting calm of his manner was broken by a flash of admiration: "You've got spunk. I wish I had more of it on this ranch."

"Don't let her fool you!" cried Clubfoot. And at that moment Mrs. Wills came hurriedly in from the rear. She cried out in strident anger: "What's she doing here? St. Cloud, she's not going to get the kid back!"

"Why not?" Nan asked, all at once filled with energy. "Lorrie doesn't want you, Mrs. Wills! You have no right to him — not even if you are his mother."

"I'd like to slap your face!"

St. Cloud pointed his finger at Mrs. Wills. "Shut up." The room turned still; the doorway filled with curious, immobile faces. "Who is it that wants him?" asked St. Cloud. "You or Bellew?"

"I want him," said Nan. "Mr. St. Cloud — never mind your feelings toward Dan Bellew. It is Lorrie I'm thinking of."

"I am thinking of him," St. Cloud drawled. "At the same time I can't help thinking of you. And since you are so closely associated with Bellew, I am also thinking of him." His voice carried a thin cynicism. "Why bother, Miss Avery? If you want a son, there are other ways of getting one."

Clubfoot tittered. Nan flushed. She divided her glance between St. Cloud and Mrs. Wills. "Oh, be fair! If it will help any I'll *pay* you for the boy. If it is a bargain you want, all right!''

"How much?" demanded Mrs. Wills quickly. But it was not to her Nan looked for a reaction. It was to St. Cloud; and she thought she saw sly shrewdness rise into his speculative eyes. Gasteen broke in:

"Don't let her fool you, Neel. This smells like some of Bellew's politics.''

"How much have you heard?" challenged St. Cloud.

"All that you've said.''

"See?" grunted Gasteen.

St. Cloud shrugged his shoulders. "You walked into it, Miss Avery. I can't let you go back to Broken Stirrup with all this information in your head. You'll have to stay here till I can afford to let you go.''

"When will that be?" Mrs. Wills rasped, knowingly.

"Will nothing induce you to let Lorrie go?" pleaded Nan.

"Nothing," said St. Cloud. "You were a fool to think you could get away with it. You've got yourself tangled up in Bellew's affairs. You should have stayed out of them. Maybe you could pull a man around your fingers back East. It won't work here.''

Nan looked around her, catching the malice in every watching eye. Nothing in all her experience matched this scene with its utter lack of sympathy, its crouched cruelty. Of a sudden her fine courage let go, and she turned swiftly up the stairs, deeply relieved when she reached the upper landing and got out of observation. Paused there, she heard St. Cloud say:

"That kid might be a point in this game. Mrs. Wills, you take him to Trail tomorrow and catch the evening train East." Afterwards the man's tone quickened, fell across the room with a harsh energy: "Get moving, everybody! This business has got to get done in a hurry. Garcia, what are you delayin' for? You should have been gone fifteen minutes ago!"

Pete Garcia set out for Trail, but never reached it that night. For, somewhere along the heights back of the Gunderson ranch and in the deeply timbered stretches of the route, his horse galloped around a bend and met disaster. Pete had no warning of it, could not set himself against it. There in almost pure darkness the pony's forefeet charged into a series of ropes arranged across the trail from tree to tree. The effect of it was to carry the horse out from under himself; he went instantly down on his neck and rump, somersaulting. Pete left a saddle that had become a flying springboard, flailed through the black and landed on his skull yards away. The momentum of the fall rolled him half again that distance, brought him up against a log. There was no more motion left in him then; the light of consciousness died.

A man ran out of the trees and dropped down. Helen Garcia's strained voice came across the small clearing: "Is he badly hurt, Tom?"

"No," said the man, after a moment. "He's just out. I figured the pony would slow down for the bend. It was an easy fall."

"Thank God."

"Now you scatter and leave the rest to me," urged the man. "This ain't a safe trail. I'll tote this boy back into the hills and teach him to play cribbage for a couple of weeks. When things blow over, you let me know."

"He's got to be out of it, Tom."

"He'll be out of it, all right," the man muttered. "Go on, now. Leave everything to me and don't worry."

Helen's "That's swell of you, Tom," came gently on through the dark. "Nothing on him that would give us an idea?"

"Nothin' but cigarette papers. St. Cloud wouldn't make that mistake."

The girl wheeled, reached the trail, and went southward along it at a reckless, slashing pace. She circled down the slope, came out to the valley beyond Gunderson's, and was in town shortly before nine-thirty. Leaving her pony at the stable, she went straight to the jail. The jailer was

Gasteen's man, but he was tractable enough and let her go to the second-story corridor running between the jail cells. There was a lantern hanging in front of Jubilee's cubicle, and when he saw her, dusty, a little pale, and a slight droop to her firm mouth, he showed a quick irritation.

"You've been told often enough, Helen, to draw out of this."

She glanced along the corridor, said in a half-whisper: "I've got Pete roped out of trouble."

"Won't you ever be shut of other people's grief?"

"I wish you were free! I dread what might happen if Gasteen went wild. Or that beast Clubfoot. Don't you know —"

"Now listen," cut in Jubilee, "don't shoulder my sorrows."

"I'm one of the bunch, Jubilee," said Helen quietly. "What kind of a person would I be, not to worry about you? I don't see why Dan doesn't come and knock this darned jail apart."

"Part of the game, kid. Dan figures I'm useful here, so here's where I stay."

"You," said the girl in the same soft manner, "would do anything for him."

"So would you."

"Yes — I guess so. But you're a swell fellow."

"When," asked Jubilee dryly, "did you come to that funny idea?"

"I've had you wrong for a long while. All I saw

258

was a kind of a man that didn't care. Would it hurt your feelings if I said you were like Dan in one thing? — you've got a lot of sympathy and patience in you, mister."

"The congregation will now rise and sing number six hundred. Get on your way."

"Let me stay a little while. You — you're a comfort."

"So's a hammock."

"Don't be tough. You can't swing it."

Jubilee's long fingers closed around the iron rods. "Kid, I can stand a lot of things — but not sisterly kindness from you. You know how I feel."

"I wouldn't fool you, Jubilee. And I wouldn't fool myself. I'm kind of honest that way. Maybe — maybe this isn't so sisterly. I told you I could grow up, didn't I?"

16. Invasion

Nan's absence was noticed at breakfast time. "She went for a ride last night," said Shannon concernedly. "I know it, because my pony was gone. I paid no heed to it, thinkin' she'd turn the brute into the corral when she come home."

"Her bed ain't been slept in," added Link, from the second floor.

Dan said: "When did you miss your horse, Mike?"

"Right after Gasteen pulled out."

"Saddle something and see where her tracks go," ordered Dan. He made a restless turn about the room. "Either she went out for a little air, or she had something on her mind. She knew it was dangerous to ride alone — and she probably would have told me. Unless —"

Jamie Scarborough filled the pause: "Unless it was something she figured you wouldn't approve of."

"Lorrie," said Dan. "That would be it. It made a pretty deep dent in her when Gasteen took him."

He shook his head, went in to eat. For a moment he laid the worry aside and studied the new hands Jubilee had recruited for him. They had drifted in during the night — and here they were, all men he knew very well. Looking along the table, smiling a little, he said:

"Fifteen more homely faces to feed. You'll earn your grub, but I'm glad to see you."

Peach Murtagh grinned. "We got to eat somewhere, Dan."

"All right, listen to these pearls of wisdom. If I'm not around, you'll mind Link Medders. If he's not on hand, Jubilee's the man. Should we be out of sight, you'll take orders from Peach. Think you can handle these saddle bums, Peach?"

"I can lick any one of 'em."

"Further deponent saith not. What comes will come. You're all old enough to know what to expect. Now hark to the articles of indenture, and mark 'em well. No man moves out of this place unless definitely told to do so. No man lifts a gun except by my order or example. No man leaves a job I put him on until it is finished or until his breathin' apparatus ceases to function. I will further add that since most of you look shy of tallow, don't founder yourself on Broken Stirrup's canned peaches."

They were through breakfast and in the yard, idly waiting, when Mike Shannon came back. "No luck," he said, showing worry. "Gasteen's riders made two trails, one straight to town, the other to Smoky Draw. She went one of those ways, following the tracks. There ain't a sign of a single horse elsewhere."

"That means Gasteen took the boy to St. Cloud all right — and sent the rest of his party back to Trail. Well, she's gone to town. Apparently had some scheme."

"Why not after the boy?" queried Scarborough.

"She wouldn't risk getting into St. Cloud's hands again."

"Don't be too sure. Nan would do anything she felt she had to do."

"What's the percentage in her running up against all the odds in Smoky Draw? No, I think the other bet's the best. Trail."

"You're going?" asked Scarborough. And seeing Dan's nod, he added, "If I'm not in the way, I'd like to tag along."

"Mike," ordered Dan, "get Scarborough a horse. All right, everybody rides this morning."

They were soon in the saddle. Shannon presently led out a stringy little beast with calico eyes and a long neck. He said casually, "It's the best I could do, Dan," and handed the reins over to Scarborough. There was then a thoughtful pause. It was one of those inevitable little scenes not to be denied these people who loved a good practical joke. Scarborough stood grave, coolly scanning the semicircle. The point of the thing was, of course, Jamie Scarborough's glaring contrast to the country. All these men were weathered to the bronze shades of the land itself, skins a uniform saddle brown; they were long-membered and heavy-boned, a kind of Indian calm possessed them. By comparison, Jamie Scarborough's well-groomed body was strikingly incongruous. In effect he was a puzzle to be resolved one way or another. Dan caught a subdued glint of understanding in Scarborough's face, and he said lazily: "Beware of an Irishman bearing gifts."

Scarborough chuckled, and what followed was no greenhorn trick. He looped the reins over the pony's head in quick synchronization with his upward spring to the saddle. The horse settled, snorted chestily, and made three tentative crow-hops across the packed dirt; and then halted meekly as the reins snapped a disciplinary pressure along his jaws. There was no more to it than that. Dan's drawl was a little ironical: "Somebody's sold, but I guess it isn't you, Scarborough."

The cavalcade went beating down the poplar-lined ranch road with an easy cohesion, into a valley overcast by a cloud-filtered sunlight the color of burnt amber. The portent of change was in the air, the thick feel of an atmospheric tensity about to burst. Even at this hour the heat was a still, surcharged thing that played dry and electric on the skin. There was no sight of the clear sky; Buck and Squaw ridges were faint streaks beyond a condensing pall.

"You'll see a violent break of weather before night," Dan said to Scarborough.

The course was straight southwest for twenty silent minutes; but at that point Dan swung and made it a southerly ride. Scanning the horizon for explanation, Scarborough noted a forming ball of dust in that direction. Bellew spoke again:

"I should warn you. You're building up a mess of trouble by identifying yourself with me. If I should offer advice, it would be to get a room at the hotel in Trail and take the part of a spectator."

"There's some possibility of action?"

"There's a certainty of it, my friend."

"Lovely — lovely," murmured Scarborough.

"No," countered Bellew with a degree of sharpness, "it isn't."

"I wouldn't wish to be in the way. If I am, say so. But I'd like to assure you I'm no tourist out for a summer's vacation. I can pull my weight in this."

"Why should you want to?"

"When I like a man, Bellew, there are no reservations, equivocations, mental hesitations."

"This isn't your sort of thing."

Scarborough shook his head, quietly indifferent. "My life in the East is closed out. Whatever

264

happens now is of no consequence at all. It is of no importance, of course, but I went up San Juan Hill last year with Teddy. That was my first taste of action. I liked it. I liked this country. Some men are born into the wrong environment and never manage to get out of it. I think I may stay here."

"Without book or bank?"

"Culture and civilized surroundings? Well, I have fed at that spring. It holds no nourishment. When a man is educated away from elementals, he grows anemic. The classics won't help you, Bellew, when you've got to make up your mind to kill or be killed. The strength to meet that issue comes out of the grass roots."

"Idealization."

"Wait and see how it works," said Scarborough calmly.

Dan brought the column to a halt. The distant dust fumarole parted and let a fast-traveling rider through; that rider halted cautiously a half-mile away, then came on. When he rounded in front of Dan the whole group saw the steam-wet flanks of his horse.

"Hello, Luke."

The rider stood restfully in his stirrups. "I was bound your way. LeBœuf tells me to tell you he's sighted somethin' damned funny in the south. Big herd pointed this way. We sight couple thousand critters and about twenty riders. What's it mean we don't nowise know."

Dan shook his head. "That's an odd one." Then his eyes went into the far southern strip ridden by pulsing haze. Scarborough, closely watching, had the illusion of seeing the earth turn to powder before him. Bellew's hazel glance flickered back to the rider. "Tell LeBœuf I'll be in Trail soon. If there's anything new, send me word. If it looks like I'll need him, I'll call. If he needs me, tell him not to delay asking."

The rider wheeled, the Broken Stirrup outfit went on at a quicker pace. "Book or bank wouldn't help you to make a decision like that," mused Scarborough. "Dammit, man, I'd give away all my ancestors to have your beginnings. Didn't I say it? — your learning comes from the grass roots."

But Bellew's mind was elsewhere. The heat became something tangible to push through, that brassy pall grew thicker, distorting the shape of the sun. Sweat seeped beneath Scarborough's hatbrim and left salt in his mouth. They passed a band of cattle standing motionless on the short, crisp grass and reached the valley road. Bellew paralleled it for a hundred yards, glance roving its dusty surface; afterwards they fell into the gentle draw leading to Trail, and so reached town.

The street was quite empty of citizens till Townsite Jackson stepped from the store. Dan, still in the saddle, said:

"Any news?"

"Something's happening in the south."

Dan turned. "Link, take a couple of boys and ride three or four miles that way to see if you can spot anything. This thing is coming to a head. Townsite, is Nan Avery here?"

"Why, no."

"You're sure?" Dan said, sharply.

"She never showed here."

Bellew's eyes went to Scarborough. "You must be right. She went to Smoky Draw, willingly or otherwise. Come on."

He was in motion and as far as the sheriff's office before the rest of the group could follow; Scarborough came along quickly, breath deepening in him, and he reached the office in time to hear Bellew speak to the jailer: "Sorry, Nick. You lose a guest."

These men, Scarborough thought, had an enormous self-composure. Good luck or bad didn't shake them out of a consistently level mood. The jailer got up and reached for his key ring. "I recognize the odds, Dan," he said and walked up the stairs while the small room filled with Broken Stirrup hands. Then he came back, the slim, sorrel-headed Jubilee chuckling behind. That perfect casualness continued. "No charge for the accommodations, Nick?" asked Jubilee cheerfully.

267

"I'm not collectin' the bill," was the jailer's pointed answer. "I just work here."

Jubilee walked to a wall, took down his belt and gun. The satisfaction with which he strapped the belt around him was open; nor did Scarborough miss the extra gesture. Jubilee opened the gun, looked at the shells, replaced it. There was a call from the street, and Broken Stirrup filed out. Link Medders had returned. "I saw that herd, all right. It's way off west, passin' into the valley near LeBœuf's."

"That's our next stop," said Bellew.

Broken Stirrup rose to the saddle again. A lithe, vivid girl Scarborough hadn't seen before came around a corner quickly, signaling. Both Bellew and Jubilee rode across the street. Silently waiting, Jamie Scarborough's analytical mind broke up that three-cornered scene and rearranged it shrewdly. The girl looked at Bellew, speaking carefully and quickly. She was uncommonly pretty. Bellew's head nodded once, and afterwards he turned back. Apparently the scene was over. Yet there was one last act which would have escaped a less observant person than Jamie Scarborough; the girl's hand touched Jubilee's arm, and the sudden smile was so clear, so candid that there could be no mistaking the thought behind it. Jubilee's slanting grin appeared and disappeared; then he returned to his horse.

Broken Stirrup trotted out of Trail, turned west

268

beneath a gathering, blackening ceiling of clouds. Jubilee rode beside Dan; Scarborough fell behind as the pace changed to a steady run and the murmured talk of the ranks ceased. There was something in the wind. Bellew's clipped words drifted to the rear: "This is probably it, Jubilee. He's makin' his bid now."

"What the hell? He ain't got a shred of right."

"Certainly not. Who is to enforce the law against him?"

"I know, but there's a limit even he don't dare monkey with."

"I've told you we're dealing with a man who has a fertile imagination."

"Look ahead."

They were paralleling low buttes; and now, in the intermediate distance, a gray, sinuous line broke out of those buttes and advanced sluggishly into the valley. Dust rolled up like smoke; riders shot from the line, circling in the foreground. Even Scarborough knew what it was. All this talk about cattle coming up from the south now stood materially yonder; a herd was pushing into the valley. Bellew's "That's it" was very flat. Link Medders, altogether silent during this ride, abruptly bent down, drew his rifle out of its boot, and passed it to Scarborough. "Shoulda oughta hadda short gun on you," he grunted. "But this'll help."

"They spot us," called Jubilee.

The line of cattle passed endlessly out of the hidden ground, moved farther into the cloudy valley; but the riders of that outfit were swinging off, making a compact arrangement. All this was now a matter of a mile. Bellew kept the pace; his body swung in the saddle.

"Keep your shirts on," he warned the crew.

"Heavy bunch," grunted Medders. "Wise, too. They're comin' this way so as not to stampede the beef."

Bellew said, "Easy," and slackened the gait. That opposite crowd made a wider and thinner barrier while one man advanced a little to the front of it. There was, Scarborough saw, some unwritten sagebrush tactics involved here; for he was picked up in a like movement of the Broken Stirrup ranks. They were drifting. The long Broken Stirrup column described a straggling arc, lost all shape, and regained it again surprisingly. When the thing was done, Scarborough found himself in a motionless half-circle, looking across the yellow earth to a group motionless as statues. The man in the foreground sat askew, one short leg half thrown across the saddle, two gleaming eyes staring out of a heavy head. Dull black hair straggled across his brow, leading Scarborough to reflect he never had seen features so dully animal, so sullenly sly.

"Clubfoot," called Bellew, "what've we got here?"

"What's it look like to you?"

"I don't judge you people by looks."

"Well," grunted Clubfoot, "what you see is what you see."

"Bound across the valley for Smoky Draw?"

Clubfoot stared, let the silence remain momentarily. The burning heat suddenly began to blister Scarborough's skin. When he touched the metal of the rifle before him it stung his fingers. That grotesque figure took up the talk with a kind of dogged reluctance. "We ain't goin' to Smoky Draw. We're spreadin' the beef in the valley."

"On whose range?" drawled Bellew.

"What difference does that make? Yours or LeBœuf's or Gunderson's."

"So that's it?"

"That's it," mocked Clubfoot. He stirred, put his malformed foot into a shortened stirrup; he flashed a swift glance behind him, as if reassuring himself of solid support. "I wouldn't try it if I was you, Bellew. We got enough boys here to catch anything you want to pitch."

"I notice that," said Bellew. "Twenty-five strangers. By any chance did you buy this beef? Or did those boys find it?"

Clubfoot's answer was again sardonic: "What difference does that make?" He caught Bellew's lift of head, and he put in another quick thought:

"Don't expect LeBœuf to be here in a hurry. He's got lots to think about at home. So've you." Clubfoot's false grin made a smear across his lips. "Look up the valley and you'll see some more."

Scarborough turned, and at that instant he said to himself: "This St. Cloud is a fellow to watch." Long spires of dust raveled high in that northern area where lay the pass; cattle were coming out of there — another herd entering the valley. His interest shifted, and he laid his attention on Bellew, who sat erect and calm in the saddle. He had only a profile view; but that was enough to give him Bellew's fined-down features. The adjoining Jubilee's cheeks were awash with violence; and ill-repressed temper formed yellow points of light in his eyes as he kept them on Bellew. The grouped Broken Stirrup hands were immobile. "Make up your mind," muttered Clubfoot, strain riding his talk. "Take it or leave it."

Bellew only said, "Come on, boys," and put his pony half around. The outfit fed in behind, two and two again, racing away. Scarborough thought: "That's strategy," and looked around to see the opposite bunch still rooted. Jubilee's erupting words were cataclysmically vivid. They rose and they fell like brandished war clubs. Medders's expression was utterly stolid, as if the man refused himself the right to think. "A good first sergeant," Scarborough observed.

Distances were deceptive. One moment that advancing cloud had been far off; within a mile it was close at hand, another compact string of riders suddenly racing on ahead of the cattle. Jubilee went silent again — some low word from Dan effecting that change. If there had been defensiveness and slight uncertainty on the part of that other lawless bunch, this one showed none of it. They all streaked forward, gear metal slicing bright blades of light into the oppressive murk; and their course was head-on. Dan spoke again:

"Keep cool."

That advancing outfit deployed on the gallop, came against the Broken Stirrup group in a kind of blanketing movement, and halted with a suddenness that lifted rapid whorls of dust. One man paced ahead — one restless man with features of cameo sharpness. Everything about him was alert, restless, arrogant.

"This is it, St. Cloud?" called Dan.

"Your answer should be interesting," the restless man said.

There was an outward idleness to him, Scarborough noted; but it was only a mask covering an inner intensity, a lightning nervous energy.

"My answer can wait."

"It has before," said St. Cloud cynically.

"It can again. My compliments for a play well worked. You intend to make us fight for our own range."

273

"I wouldn't put it that way," St. Cloud drawled. "I'd just say I am now moving into the valley, lock, stock, and barrel. The wanderer returns to his first home."

"Of which you don't own a legal inch. It's pretty raw even for you to try."

"I told you I'd come back."

Bellew bent forward. "Supposing the valley doesn't do anything in reply? Supposing we sit tight and just wait?"

St. Cloud's manner of negligence left him. His answer was impatient: "You can't afford to. There's room here for just so much beef. Mine or yours, but not both."

"Still," pointed out Bellew, "your scheme won't work unless we get together and hack at you. Maybe we could better afford to sit by. How long can you support your riders? They're eatin' you up in pay right now."

"You won't sit by," challenged St. Cloud angrily.

"Why not?"

"Because I won't let you, you fool!"

"That's what I was waiting for," said Bellew. "All right, boys."

Scarborough was caught up in the forward rush. Broken Stirrup passed across the front of St. Cloud's line, kicked up the yellow soil. The silent Link Medders reached over and took back the rifle; Jubilee's talk ceased. The tall ranch trees lifted ahead of them, and at three o'clock of that insufferable afternoon they were home again. Nan had not returned.

Bellew called a council in the living room. Jubilee and Medders and Peach Murtagh came in. Scarborough offered to leave but was told to sit still. "There's no question of it now. Miss Avery's at Smoky Draw. I wanted to pump St. Cloud on that, but felt I'd get nowhere. There's the chance he's holding her as bait — figuring I'll attack that place. If so, he'd of course have a trap set for me."

"I'll eat turkey," offered Jubilee. "You passed up two fights, and I thought you did it wrong. But that fellow has deliberately placed his strength at different points so that the valley can't make a solid party. What he wants is to tackle us one at a time."

"You've got it."

"You're goin' to try to get together with Gunderson and LeBœuf anyhow?"

"I don't know yet. One thing is still unexplained. Presumably that lower outfit is to cover LeBœuf. And presumably St. Cloud's own immediate party is to watch me. Which leaves Gunderson. Who is covering him? Did you notice that Gasteen wasn't in either party?"

"Back in Smoky Draw, maybe."

"St. Cloud leans on him too much to leave him there, out of the play."

"Well?"

275

"Take a man and cross Buck ridge. Scout it for anything you can find hiding around Gunderson's. You know the hideouts in that district best."

Jubilee got up. "Be back an hour after dark," he said.

"How about my going with you?" suggested Scarborough.

There was a pause. Jubilee happened to be rolling a cigarette, and he kept his eyes on it throughout the operation. When he lifted them they were quietly humorous. "Come along."

They were soon away. After that the afternoon dragged through its stifling peak. The crew ate a delayed dinner, sat under the locusts. Looking down the valley, Bellew watched St. Cloud's contingent drifting gradually with the cattle, keeping his attention there all through the remaining light. The man would, he knew, put himself at the head of the party most likely to be useful; and if that were so, then those shapes thinning out in first dusk would soon strike. "For it's me he's after, and it's me he'll come for. He's got too much fat in the fire to delay. This is his ace in the hole, and he'll play it without delay. Probably I can expect the ball to open tonight. Or does he expect me to open it?"

Dusk fell into dark — an early, lowering dark. A rider came down off Squaw ridge and through the back yard, a LeBœuf hand looking tired. He never got off his horse.

"LeBœuf says if you've got anything figured, not to count on him now. It looks like he's goin' to have a fight on his hands tonight. He can't risk movin' out."

"So that end of the sack is puckered up," decided Bellew. "All right. Tell him to play it that way. We'll make out here." Afterwards he called into the shadows: "Everybody ride."

It was then nine o'clock, and Jubilee had not returned with Scarborough. Bellew warned Chan: "If you hear anything coming, get back into the canyon and stay there. Take Trono's family with you." Then he led the outfit down the poplars and into the open. The moon was an exact half-circle and very dim; a congested fog shifted with the dark, thickening the shadows. Nothing stood in silhouette; nothing suggested yonder movement. For a little while he idled straight eastward across toward Buck ridge, tentatively expecting to intercept Jubilee. Yet after half an hour of this he straightened around to the southwest and quickened the pace.

"We'll try for Gunderson's," he told Medders.

Hard on the heels of his statement one lone report rolled faintly across the night and seemed to die at their feet. Halted and acutely listening, Bellew at last heard the echoes cracking again, more and more frequent. Somewhere down the valley, apparently originating from Gunderson's, a steady fire opened and was maintained. The column came up around him, waiting. Bellew's mind closed suddenly down. "St. Cloud has got Gunderson blocked off, too. If his men are spread out that thin, he can't have anybody left in Smoky Draw. I don't give a damn where he hits. I know where I'm going to hit."

Wheeling through the dark, he settled into a fast gallop, bound for Smoky Draw. Behind, the firing seemed to increase. A heavy drop of rain spat against his hatbrim.

17. The Flame Signal

The smell of the ridge was overpoweringly aromatic; a resinous scent of pine blended heavily with the pungent, suddenly dampened dust. Water sluiced off bent boughs, and the rising wind shook flat sheets of it into Scarborough's face, thoroughly soaking him. All in the space of a half-hour this had happened, filling the parched and oppressive air with the gusty makings of storm; he had the illusion of a thirsty earth swelling. Meanwhile he tailed patiently and silently after Jubilee Hawk, quite lost in a world without order. The trail bent interminably across arroyo and flat, insinuated itself into blacker depths. Through the trees all things were formless, and in the occasional open area a few blurred outlines lent a ghostly impression. He lost the sense of time completely.

Jubilee's subdued murmur fell back: "Always like this. Never no sufficiency of anything. Either she burns or she floods. It's goin' to be one hell of a night." Afterwards the man's shadow vanished. Scarborough gave his pony free rein and drifted around a tricky turn to collide with Jubilee, halted on the margin of another open space. Jubilee said: "Know where you are?"

"Not the faintest idea."

"On the heights back of Buck ridge — one mile from Gunderson's. Wait here."

Jubilee's horse remained; Jubilee's body slid on, leaving no wake of sound. Scarborough was strangely stirred by the sudden feel of isolation, and his introspective mind played with the thought of having intruded upon a wilder world whose inhabitants resented him. Below the rush and slap of the wind the voice of the night creatures came strongly. The deep brush churned out echoes that were like water falling off the heights. Jubilee returned, spoke before Scarborough could register the man's presence: "Follow close." They turned off the trail, ponies' shod hoofs clacking briskly against rougher surfaces. They rose steadily, stopped again. Jubilee said: "Smell anything?"

"Pines — some sage — wet ground."

"That's all?"

"Horses."

"No smoke?"

Scarborough keened the air again. "I get that. Pretty faint."

"Good boy! Wait." Jubilee was gone once more, but this time for only a small interval. When he returned he was breathing harder, and his shadow made restless motions from side to side. He talked in quick, suppressed phrases: "Dan was right. They're just beyond, in a canyon. A small fire burnin' under a ledge."

"Who?"

"Put here to pull something on Gunderson. We stumbled onto 'em — that's luck. Now we got to do some figurin', old boy."

"You're sure it wouldn't be Gunderson's men hiding down there?"

"What for? If he meant to make a play, it would be out on the prairie. The point is, he's got to be warned. But we can't afford to go tell him and risk losin' touch of these fellows. You got any answers?"

"It's your party."

"And a damn wet one," said Jubilee. A coyote's dismal yammer fled before the filling wind. "You're up to your neck in something," muttered Jubilee.

"If I didn't like it I'd say so."

"Good boy! Pull your rifle from the boot. Leave the horse as is."

Scarborough obeyed. Jubilee's added explanation was very terse: "We settle down on the edge of that canyon and we get busy. When Gunderson hears the racket he'll know somebody's on his back doorstep. It may be fun, mister, or it may not be."

Scarborough followed Jubilee's bobbing shadow up a quicker slope, along a slight barrier of broken rock, and out to a kind of shelf. Jubilee went to his stomach, sibilantly cursing the water. Following suit, Scarborough saw the vague slash of the canyon directly below. He was, he discovered, posted on the extreme edge of a wall that went at least sixty feet straight down. The fire he saw instantly — a thin and whipping blaze sheltered by an overhang of the canyon wall. He could make out no figures around it; beyond the radius of firelight lay a solid blackness. Jubilee's talk was almost conversation: "Aim at the fire. Don't hurry — we'll be here for a while."

His bolt clicked and made a clean, hungry echo against the throaty rumor of the storm. Scarborough, feeling an odd calm go through him, waited for the shot; but the sound of it was greater than he expected and seemed to tear a hole through the night, echoes bounding away before the wind. One red eye of flame leaped from the body of the fire and fell aside. He saw movement then. A faintly visible body circled that lower light. His down-trained gun tried to follow. After his shot, the mushrooming points of a replying fusillade spotted the dark depths. There was no question of the number involved after that; the volleyed echoes raced away, down the slopes of the ridge.

Dan crouched on the higher edge of Smoky Draw and looked into a street apparently empty. One light showed out of the end house — St.

Cloud's house; otherwise the long row of buildings huddled darkly beneath the beating rain. Link Medders crawled from the thick brush and slapped his wet chest. "Went all along the back of the buildin's. Didn't see nothin' — didn't hear nothin'." The rising wind began to pound at the trees, began to boil through the draw. Curdled blackness lay all around.

"They'd be mighty still," said Dan.

"I don't doubt we'll run into somebody."

"That light is a snare and a delusion. We'll leave it strictly alone. What we're going to do is start at this end of the street and walk along the edge of the walls — on the east side. Get up closer to me." His voice had risen against the boiling accents of the storm; and he stopped speaking until all the hands had made a small circle about him. "They can't see into this any better than we can. If it's a big party here, I'm guessin' poor. Link leads off. Everybody else follow him. Straight down, toward the big house. Flat against the walls. Don't get exposed in front of any doors or windows. I am going across to the opposite side and fire a shot somewhere near the mouth of the canyon. That ought to draw something. If it does, you'll locate the source."

Link said, "This gettin' separated is dubious," but Bellew was moving away then. He put one quick reminder across his shoulder, into the teeth of the wind: "Trono stays back to hold the horses." The group, when he turned ten yards away to look, was somewhere behind a screen of darkness that seemed to thicken and thin with each fresh assault of driven air. He went down the incline rapidly. He crossed the level bottom, got against the far slope. But instead of pursuing his way to the rim of the draw, he swung and walked along that narrow way existing between the canyon wall and the back ends of the buildings. He had no particular need, he saw, to be careful, for the rain drummed heavily on the roofs, and the sound rushing through the draw was like the dashing of a wild current. At each corridor between buildings he paused, saw nothing. Five full minutes later he had reached the foot of the draw — where the main road came down — without locating the least sign of defense. The thought of elapsing time troubled him, knowing as he did that it was quite likely St. Cloud might attack Broken Stirrup, find it empty, and come back to the hills. Lifting his gun, he let the hammer fall on one shot; that shot whipped into the high air and fled away in raveling echoes.

There was no immediate answer; nor did Bellew wait for one. The sense of needed haste pushed him across the street to the side of St. Cloud's house. Pulling himself to a window, he looked in once and ducked back from the lane of light shining out. In so far as he had been able to see, nobody held the lower room; and with this judgment he hurried to the rear of the place, came to the door there and shoved it in front of him. As he did so a cross current reached the lamp standing on the table and snuffed out the flame. Darkness seized the room.

Bellew stepped in, closed the door, and shifted aside, shoulder blades to the wall. All the outside rumors filled the house, upstairs and down, with uneasy echoes that blurred his focused attention. Yet the air of emptiness possessed the place. He felt it, he grew sure of it; and acting on that impression, he moved toward the lamp and reached for a match. The porch boards squeaked. The front door came open, slammed against the inner wall. He said, "Medders," sharply and stood still until his foreman's voice, very calm, came back: "Listen, Dan, I think this joint's deserted."

"So do I." His match touched the lamp wick, the yellow light made fan-shaped shafts across the room. Medders came in with an alert side twist of his body, followed by a part of the crew. He had no need to indicate what should be done. Medders was across the room instantly, opening that inner door leading to the kitchen; the others blocked off the front and rear silently. Dan went up the stairs three at a time, wheeled into a bedroom. He tried another match, whipped it out; and then Medders came on up, bearing the lamp.

It was only a moment's exploration that netted nothing but the sure fact of this house's utter vacancy. In one room he saw a lot of women's clothes thrown carelessly on the bed.

"I sent the men back to try all the houses," grunted Medders. "But we'll find nothin'. Minute I hit this street I knew we'd have no party."

They went down to the living room and waited while the hands drifted in from the search. Dan looked at his watch, stared over at Medders. Medders said casually: "God bless this rain, Dan. We can do what we wouldn't otherwise dare to do."

"She must have been here earlier. There were just two places she would have gone, here or Trail. She didn't go to Trail. Therefore we've got to figure that either she started for Trail and was caught or came here and was caught. Only one answer. St. Cloud's got her hidden."

"Yeah," agreed Medders. "He moved her and Lorrie out of your reach."

Dan shook his head. "We're wasting time. Well, St. Cloud will never come back to the draw." Walking to a corner of the room, he dropped the lamp. The flame went purple and then flashed brilliantly into the spilling oil. All the men stood there soberly for a little while, watching the flame catch hold of the wallpaper. Dan ripped down a curtain, laid it on the spreading fire; he capsized a chair atop it and afterwards stepped back. Medders spoke. "These houses will burn like powder, but the timber's too wet to catch. God bless the rain." And, watching the cloud gather across Bellew's hazel eyes, he added quietly: "Don't worry. The man's too busy to do any harm."

"Let's get out of here."

They went to the porch, and Medders sent a man back for the horses. A little later they had to move into the street, pushed out by the quickening heat of the fire. Medders slipped quietly away and didn't reappear until the horses came down; then they all filed out of the draw. Paused a moment on the rim, Dan watched long fingers of flame lick through St. Cloud's doorway.

"I built little bonfires in some of the other joints," said Medders. "Just to be sure."

"Wherever he is," grunted Bellew, "he'll soon see the signal risin' out of the hills. We're coming toward the end of this business, Link, but I don't see any certain conclusions."

They filed into the black stretch through the timber, overwhelmed by the slash and crack of the heavy branches above. A fine spray of pine needles fell down, sharply stinging the flesh. Medders came abreast Bellew. "It's likely he'll do the same to Broken Stirrup. You'd thought about that, Dan?"

"It's part of the risk. I came to Smoky Draw to

ruin whatever outfit he'd left there, and to get that girl out of trouble. Neither's happened. Now we've got to look another place. We're dealing with a man we can't depend on to do the usual thing."

"Where next?"

"Gunderson's."

"Eighteen men ain't much should we meet that yellow-haired devil out there."

"It will do."

"Which I was about to add," put in Link. "No, by Jupiter, he ain't touched Broken Stirrup!"

The cavalcade came into the pass and went through. All the valley lay dark, and no streak of flame broke the western edge where Bellew's ranch stood. They passed the site of Nan's former cabin, ran down the easing grade by Mitchell's, and straightened into the flat road, bound for Gunderson's. Dan let his pony go, more and more obsessed by unexpected disaster in the offing. He said something of that to Medders, shouting it through the bite of the heavy rain: "He refused to do what we thought he might do. The man's got a mind like a razor!"

Something else was alive in his head, displacing all other considerations. This thing had gone on through three years, growing unenduringly bitter, spreading fear over the valley, touching everybody with that premonition of a reckoning one day to come. The day was here. No doubt of that now. And the reckoning lay somewhere on the flats in the dark of this tempestuous night. The burning of Smoky Draw was only a gesture, a minor act, in the struggle between himself and St. Cloud. Whatever else was clouded and uncertain, one thing was as inevitable as the rising and the setting of the sun: nothing would be final, and no answer would rise out of this play now going into its bloody, bitter stage until he and St. Cloud met face to face and one of them died. Let Smoky Draw burn, let all the man's crew desert him, St. Cloud was not to be beaten until a bullet got him. That, Bellew told himself as he breasted the thick and driving substance of the night, was the murderous issue of this fight. That was it — the two of them facing each other down the length of their gun barrels.

Medders said: "I pick up the shooting."

Attenuated echoes whipped past with a javelin thinness — many reports that lifted and fell, sometimes spaced, sometimes crowded in sudden, snarled bursts. Beyond doubt the fight was heavy and drawn out — and at Gunderson's ranch. Dan played his pony for the last measure of speed, bothered by the tricky visions of the night. Barriers of cloud seemed to float across the road and pass away, leaving definite shadows due ahead; and then they plunged into a pocket of darkness. A moment afterwards he knew something lay off there, barring the route. Those outlines came up so swiftly that he had to wrench his horse out of the steady run and veer aside.

"Cattle!" yelled Medders. "What in hell they doin' here —"

The beef was moving toward them in a collected mass, drifting with the wind. Dan turned, skirted an almost solid edge of stock. That pressure stopped the cattle, pushed them slowly back. Dan called out: "We'll go around this bunch —"

"Wait!" yelled Medders. "Wait!"

Dan reared up in the saddle, hearing the abrupt beginning of a new sound on the right, out toward the open valley. It was too unmistakable to be missed; one moment there had been no such rumor, the next moment a collecting, rushing noise drove at him. A great cry sailed forward:

"Straight ahead — that's them!"

"St. Cloud!" yelled Medders.

Dan halted. "Hold it!" he cried and knew then he was in a fight. A long, ragged line broke through the darkness — wide enough to smother his own party completely and wide enough to tell him he was definitely outnumbered. This was St. Cloud's long-delayed and long-maneuvered play.

18. A Matter of Viewpoint

The room to which Nan went after the scene with St. Cloud was the same one in which she had hidden; and such was her fear of the man that she ranged from one dark wall to the other, expecting anything, expecting everything. Perhaps five minutes afterwards Mrs. Wills came up, drew the door shut and locked it, her acid voice coming through the panels. "You fool — you crazy fool!" Nan, at once very weary, sank full length on the bed.

It was low ebb for her. She had been, she realized, mistaken. Not so much in making the trip — for she might have been successful in it — but in going away from Broken Stirrup without leaving an explanatory note. What hurt most was that another burden had been placed on Dan's broad shoulders. So thinking, she turned and tossed on the bed, believing she would never sleep, determined not to sleep. Yet sleep came; and when she woke, stiff and cold, a sultry daylight was shining through her window and the door was open.

She went into the hall, conscious of an outer

quietness. Nothing moved along the street, and the house itself carried only a faint sound of activity. She descended the stairs reluctantly and found Mrs. Wills rocking in a chair. Mrs. Wills's eyes filled with the old hardness; lines sprang around her petulant mouth.

"You can go to the kitchen and wash. There'll be some breakfast for you on the table."

Nan went on through the long dining room and into the kitchen, meeting the curious inspection of the cook. She felt a little ridiculous before him as she scrubbed off the dust of last night's trip, and was glad to finish and get back to the dining room where her meal had been placed. This one mark of consideration seemed odd — the more so when Mrs. Wills came in and stood without speech at the far corner. It was a grudging gesture, and Nan had the notion that this meal might not have been kept for her unless St. Cloud had ordered it so. She ate little, soon walked out to the porch. It was around ten, the air heavy and oppressive, the sun obscured by a thickening haze. A few men sat in front of a barn toward the head of the canyon, a few horses were tied at a rack, a dog skulked across the deep yellow dust. She could not conceive of a more dismal habitation for people; this little canyon was a dreary pocket gouged out of the surrounding hills, made the more unbeautiful by the flimsy houses strung along it. Turning impatiently back, she discovered Mrs. Wills standing in an attitude of watchfulness, crouched unfriendliness mirrored in the slattern eyes.

"What am I supposed to do?" asked Nan.

"Nothing."

"Where — where is Lorrie?"

"Where you won't see him," snapped Mrs. Wills. "You've got nerve interfering with my child."

"It is an unpleasant thought — that he is your child."

"Yes?" exclaimed the woman. "Well, wait awhile and you'll make a few mistakes in life, too. If you ain't made some already."

Nan shrugged her shoulders. "I don't want to fight with you. I'll apologize for the remark. Would money interest you at all?"

She noticed, as before, cupidity appear in the woman's face at the mention of money. Mrs. Wills straightened, and one hand played across the frowsy yellow hair. Then the manner was replaced by morose resignation. "Don't talk about it. St. Cloud would kill me."

"I thought you said he was your boy?" challenged Nan.

"You don't know St. Cloud."

"I think I do."

"Then you shouldn't have to ask such a question."

"What is he going to do?"

Mrs. Wills showed her contempt. "How do

you suppose I know? But if I'm any judge of the man, he's trying to find out if Dan Bellew is going to come after you tonight."

"Dan —" began the girl and severely checked herself. Mrs. Wills, alert again, said, "What's that?" But Nan shook her head. She had made many mistakes; she would not make this one. To conceal what that hard-eyed woman might read, she walked to the bookcase and opened it. The volumes were all old, catholic of content. A history of the Jews rubbed shoulders with a life of Senator Benton; somebody had shown a taste for reading, but it was not Neel St. Cloud. For as she idly lifted the books she saw the dust caked on the page tops. This little library was another outer surface of the man — plausible but meaningless. What he really was lay behind all the show of manners; a man unscrupulous, overleaping, treacherous.

She thought of that again when, beyond four o'clock of a day that dragged across her nerves almost unbearably, St. Cloud rode into the draw with a long file of riders behind him and came to the house.

He had no immediate word for her, his former gallantry was thrown aside. He spoke to one of the men in an edged manner somehow quite savage. Strain drew the smooth face into thin lines, made it openly malicious and bitter. His eyes, red with sun and dust, burned a path around the room and halted on Mrs. Wills.

"Get your things together. Get the kid."

"Why?"

"Do what I tell you!"

Mrs. Wills went up the stairs quickly, saying no more. Nan came toward St. Cloud, full of fear. "Please let me —"

He had the air of seeing her for the first time; and that air was unforbearing and arrogant. "The information will do you no good — and Bellew no good. When the big man of the valley comes dusting up here tonight to get you, he won't find Lorrie. He'll find you, but not the kid. The kid is going out of the country on the night train east. I'd put you in hiding, too, except that you're bait to draw the sucker."

"How," said Nan quietly, "do you know he's coming here tonight?"

St. Cloud's eyes were alive with grim interest. "What makes you think he won't come?"

She said nothing, and St. Cloud, coolly measuring her, finally said: "You women are all alike, trying to play a high game. A little of this and a little of that — a little of anything it takes to win your point. Let me tell you something you won't like: There is no woman born that hasn't got her price. Every last one of you is crooked somewhere."

"That's the kind of women you know," murmured Nan.

"An outcast has no chance to know another kind," muttered St. Cloud. "If there is another kind, which I don't believe. Women are the same as men. No man is any better than he ought to be. Even your beloved Bellew —"

"Is big enough to whip you!" cried Nan. "You're rotten!"

"Soon know about that," St. Cloud snapped. He turned on Mrs. Wills, who came down the stairs with no other luggage than a bundle wrapped in paper; and he walked to the porch with her and spoke some swift word that seemed to find a sensitive point in the woman. She looked up and said, "Neel," in a begging voice. His answer was to push her to the steps. Nan thought, "You're a scoundrel, to boot," and watched Mrs. Wills climb to a waiting saddle. After a moment Lorrie, already mounted, came up from another part of the street. He looked directly ahead of him, and so never saw Nan. For her part, she knew the futility of a scene and stood where she was. Heavy-hearted, really desperate at the thought of his being carried beyond her, she watched the pair pass out of the draw. St. Cloud shouted an order through the muggy heat and returned to the room.

"You're not through with me," he said to Nan, levelly. "I am meeting Bellew tonight. After that, I'll be back."

He unbuckled his gun belt, threw it aside, and

took another down from a peg beside the mantel of the fireplace, striding to the street. Going as far as the door, she watched him swing up at the head of his men and follow Mrs. Wills into the timber. For some reason or other she counted that group. There were twenty-two of them; and after they had faded from sight she looked to the other end of the street and discovered five hands left behind, near the barn. The cook came across the room, staring over Nan's shoulder at the departing outfit. Turning away from him, Nan noticed uncertainty creeping into his fixed vision. He murmured some brief word under his breath and walked out to the small group remaining.

There was nothing she could do. She walked aimlessly about the room, at loose ends, depressed by a stifling atmosphere. Blue vapor settled heavily along the canyon, the cooked smell of boards and earth swelled through the heat. So close was this late-afternoon air that the kicked-up dust in the street made stationary layers on it. Once more looking out toward the barn, she observed the men there to be risen and engaged in an absorbed conversation; the cook was returning, and rather than meet him Nan went back to her sweltering room and dropped full length to the bed.

"If I could only get away from here," she thought and clenched her fists beneath her head. To be helpless like this produced a slow ache as real as physical hurt. She could not lie still, she could not relax. One thought kept turning and turning through her mind: St. Cloud believed Dan would come to Smoky Draw this night. If he believed so, he would come back and wait in the shadows. Would Bellew come? If he came, would he watch for just such an ambush? "If," she groaned, "I could only get away!"

Twilight arrived, and a faint electrical pulsing in the air. The men were below, eating supper. One of them came to the stairway and called up, his tone neither kind nor unkind. She tried to make her answer casual: "No, thanks. I'd rather not eat." After that darkness covered the canyon rapidly, prematurely. The surcharged air began to revolve before the faint pressure of wind. Boots dragged along the lower floor, and an intermittent conversation crept up the stairway. At first she paid it little attention; later the greater irritation of the words pulled her from her own dark reflections. They were, it was plain, quarreling amongst themselves. Out of the endless murmur small phrases were distinguishable. She heard St. Cloud's name mentioned; Bellew's, and her own. One chesty voice kept riding into all others, insistent and stubborn. There was an explosive interchange of sentences, the falling of a chair, a freighted silence. In that interval of silence she heard the first rain skirmish across the roof.

She was abruptly startled to realize her name was being peremptorily called. Going to the hall, she found a man at the foot of the stairs, striking the flat of his fist against the banister.

"Come on down," he grunted. "Don't be so slow."

She descended, feeling an unusual strain in her knees. The cook, who had called her, backed away to a side of the room and so placed himself as to watch five others arranged near by. The cook's cigarette threw thin smoke over a set, dogged face. All the rest appeared heckled and jumpy; and they looked at her with an irritable dislike. The cook said:

"Well, it's decided?"

One of the others made a flat, futile gesture. "You decided it."

"Then it is," announced the cook. "Ma'm, your horse is standin' at the porch."

"Well?" breathed Nan.

"Get on it and go."

"Free?" Nan murmured unbelievingly.

"This is bad enough," growled the cook, "without you to be here and make it worse."

Nan came alive; an instant haste got hold of her, for a moment swept her self-possession away. She turned to the stairs, remembering her hat in the bedroom, but on the verge of going up she abruptly wheeled toward the door. The cook said:

"Go where you please. But you better stay away from Broken Stirrup. You figured to ride there?"

"Yes!"

"Don't. Bellew won't be there. St. Cloud will be."

Nan's eyes fell to the center table, saw St. Cloud's discarded gun and belt. "May I take that?"

One of the hands said, "No," curtly. The cook contradicted him "Entitled to some protection, ain't she? Sure, take it."

Nan seized the belt, went to the door. She turned, staring at the cook, wonder in her mind. "If I ever see you again, I'll thank you."

The cook shook his head, gone grim. "You'll never see me or any of these boys again. We're fadin'."

Nan cried, "Thank you!" and ran across the porch to the shadow of the horse waiting at the steps. She climbed up, hung the belt over the saddle horn. Rain came slanting out of a pitch-black sky, stinging her cheeks. Her only protection against the elements was her riding breeches and a thin hickory shirt, and she was soon wet; yet she felt no cold and no discomfort as she put the horse up the canyon's slope and ran freely through the dismal trees. And her mind was settled. Whatever the value of the cook's warning, she meant to ignore it and run straight for

Broken Stirrup — to warn Dan if it were not too late.

Yet when she reached the pass her eyes went instantly to the west, to the place where Bellew's ranch lights should be cutting bright points through the darkness, and found no lights there. Nothing but shadow and uncertainty. Some sustaining hope went out of her then, a leaden fear took its place. She halted, trying to use her reason and finding it of little account. Only one thing came out of all the confusion — she could not help Dan. The long-delayed fight was moving toward its conclusion. Somewhere in this miserable black he rode; somewhere Neel St. Cloud waited. She could do nothing. So only one thing remained.

She went forward, alive to the passing of time, on down the slope into the flats. A far-off fissure of lightning appeared, left a pale glow in the memory. There was a wind rushing out of the south, gathering momentum over the treeless valley, blasting the rain before it, throwing Nan's breath back into her lungs. Caught and shaken by that force, she bowed a bare, dripping head and kicked the horse on. Somewhere — she could guess nothing of the distances — faint shots leaped up and were tossed across the flats. The farther she went the stronger they grew; and when she raised Gunderson's ranch lights to the east she thought she knew where the fight lay. It prompted her to pull off the road. A great circle took her about Gunderson's; downwind she lost all rumor of firing. After that her course was pure speculation, and she put her faith in the laboring horse; and when, immeasurably later, she sighted Trail's glow, she was surprised at her luck.

The town huddled beneath the heavy fury of the elements. Water sluiced down porch corners, fogged the bright windows, lay ankle deep on the forming mud. One man's face she saw staring out of the saloon; elsewhere was silence, desolation. Past the sheriff's office, she turned against the railroad station house and went in. Somewhere the long blast of a train whistle rose and was flung forward; the agent came quickly out of his office, headed for the door. "Wait," said Nan. "Did a woman come in here this evening with a boy?"

"No," said the agent. "Better get some dry clothes on."

"Has there been a train either way in the last few hours?"

"No. Excuse me — that's the eastbound."

Nan leaned against the wall, mind ragging away at this affair. Then St. Cloud had lied to her — as she ought to have expected. Lorrie had been taken elsewhere. And in all the length and breadth of this savage land, where was she to look? Unconsciously she clenched her hands. She was, she discovered, numb from the beating of the wind; her soaked clothes dragged against her skin. There seemed no answer — no clear way — and more or less in despair she walked back into the furious night. A headlight's cold beam washed across her, and the engine went clanking by, firebox guttering, drivers pushing the weight of the train to a deliberate halt. The conductor stepped down, lantern idling against the shadows of the station runway. Nobody got off. She heard the agent saying, "Siding at Red City for Twenty-two," and started for her horse. Somebody stumbled in the shadows, and somebody came running through the dark, toward the line of cars. Idly posted, Nan saw it to be a pair hurrying past the engine; and then, as the diagonally placed gleam of the firebox hit them, she pulled herself erect and ran forward — at Mrs. Wills, whose one hand held and pulled a reluctant Lorrie.

"Wait a minute," said Nan. "Wait!"

Mrs. Wills stopped, dragging the boy beside her. The engine's light slid across one half of a face haggard with temper and exertion. Her hat was so much loose pulp on her head, and she ripped it off in passionate haste, the yellow hair falling down.

"You're not going to stop me!" she yelled. "Where — where did you come from?"

"You'll not take him!" challenged Nan.

The fireman bent far out of his cab; the agent and conductor walked up, the conductor saying impatiently, "If you people are going to get aboard —"

"Listen!" screamed Mrs. Wills. "Let me alone or I'll mark that face of yours till you'll never look in a glass!"

"Lorrie — do you want to go with her?"

"No, ma'm!"

"Let him go," said Nan.

Mrs. Wills started on. Nan stepped in front of her, raised her clenched hand, struck the woman an outraged blow across the face. The breath spilled out of Mrs. Wills, her shrill scream was half-mad. "I'll kill you —"

"Mrs. Wills, I've got a gun hanging on that horse! If you don't let him go I'll use it!"

Mrs. Wills's shoulders drooped. She was, Nan thought distantly, a sorry figure there; a spent, unstable creature jerked mercilessly about by fear and rage. But there was no rage left. It dropped away, leaving her stupidly settled.

"You lost him long ago," Nan said in a gentler voice. "Get on the train yourself."

"What else can I do?" moaned the woman. "I'd never dare go back to Neel. Oh, God, my life's a mess!"

The conductor swung his lantern in a short circle; the engine's bell rang metallically through the riot of wind. Mrs. Wills dropped Lorrie's arm, her face in the shadows. She said, "Good-bye, kid," and went after the conductor. Lorrie walked over to Nan, putting his shoulder against her as the cars slid past. Mrs. Wills vanished inside.

"We hid in a barn on the edge of town for an hour," said Lorrie.

"Lorrie, that was your mother. Don't think badly of her. Don't ever do that."

"Let's go home."

"Home?"

"Our home's Broken Stirrup, ain't it?" asked Lorrie, a little anxious.

"Yes."

He said nothing more for a little while. Presently she felt his hand grope into hers. "Well, you're wet. Maybe you want to stay in town. Whatever you say."

"No — we'll go home. I'm anxious about it, son."

He turned off, calling back: "I'll meet you at the square. Those horses are in that barn yet."

The agent came out of his office, carrying a coat, and got to Nan as she swung into her saddle. "Here," he said, "put this on before you're washed away. I never saw anything like that before."

Nan thanked him, slung the coat around her shoulders. "You're kind," she said, thinking all the while of Bellew. It made her words seem distant, and she realized it, adding, "very kind." Then she went on down the street. Lorrie was already there; and together, quite silent, they galloped out of Trail into the desert. She spoke only once.

"You'll have to be the guide, Lorrie. Stay well away from Gunderson's."

It was after this, a good hour afterwards, that Jubilee Hawk came gaiting into Trail holding Jamie Scarborough in his arms. Jamie's hat was off, and the lights of town struck a pale face that seemed to sleep. Jubilee wheeled at the square, cantered across a sidewalk, and dropped to the mud, bringing Scarborough down after him. He carried Scarborough like a baby, Scarborough faintly smiling as if the jest were on him; Jubilee kicked at a house door and groped it open, intruding into Doc Nelson's front room and into a comfortable family circle.

"The first shot," said Jubilee bitterly. "It simply broke his lower leg into sections. He's lost a bucket of blood."

"On the sofa," said Nelson, matter-of-fact.

Jubilee spread Scarborough along the couch with a strange gentleness. Scarborough was still smiling. Nelson came out of another room with a tray of instruments and laid it on the floor; his gray glance scanned Scarborough's face, read it for what it held. This scene was old to him; he could not remember the number of men who, borne hurriedly out of a troubled night, had lain on that sofa. And as his knife slashed back a

306

trouser leg, he was thinking of another thing.

"It's started, Jubilee?"

"Yeah. How does it look?"

"I guess we'll straighten him out." Doc Nelson was like that. "You can't kill these small, meek-looking men. The big ones die quick; the little ones survive, to get shot again. Where's Bellew?"

"I wish to God I knew," said Jubilee morosely. "Well, if it's not too bad —"

Jamie said quietly: "Go on back. Sorry you had to lug me in."

"They weren't headin' for Gunderson's," stated Jubilee. "Probably a wide-open contest right now. Somebody was on our trail all the way to town." Jubilee walked to the door, paused there. "You're a game guy, Scarborough."

"I wish I were in the rest of it. Doc, if you hear me squeal, pay no attention."

"Get out of that lighted doorway," said Nelson sharply.

Jubilee went back to his horse, rode along the street and across the square to Townsite's. Going in there, he found an empty store. "Old codger's heard of this and probably is on the road to Gunderson's now. Damn funny how fast the smell of blood travels." He went around, got a box of .44 cartridges, filled the loops of his belt. And hurried as he was, ingrained honesty halted him long enough to take the counter pencil and write on a piece of paper: "Hawk — bx .44's." Impatience boosted him out of the store, into the rain-laced street. He circled the hitch rack, reached for the reins, and cast one oblique glance at the saloon. Nobody stood there; and afterwards the old habit of inspection turned his head toward Cleary's hotel. Nobody there, either. Gripping the horn, he started his upward swing. What struck him then, he didn't know. It was some kind of a force that literally repelled him from the seat, an odd premonition telegraphed through the murk to record on his nerves. His glance flashed back to Cleary's, back to the saloon. Ruel Gasteen stood just outside the saloon doors, those doors still swinging from his outward passage; and Gasteen's body was a fair, motionless shape against the broken background of light.

Jubilee's right hand still hung to the horn. He thought, "That's who followed me," and then he added, "It's eighty-five feet as I once paced it." There could be no question of Gasteen's purpose. This was war and no quarter to any man; other than that, Gasteen's rigidity was a signal plain as day. Men stood so when they thought of killing or being killed. Gasteen's lips moved. Some sound was plucked away by the racing wind, and some word was framed on his long lips and lost identity behind the silvering screen of rain. Jubilee said conversationally, "It might as well be now," and let his hand drop from the saddle horn. It plunged on down, struck the gun butt and recoiled with it. Gasteen's body broke at the middle, his own arm raced backward. Saloon light raced fragmentarily along the dark metal barrel of his gun, and it was his first shot that beat the wind and the rain apart and sent a cracking echo across the four sides of the square. Clotted mud slashed Jubilee's leg, a fact only dimly recorded as his eyes took a long sight. His answering fire broke the steady roar coming out of the sky, and his slug made a clean breach of that taut figure across the square. It shook Gasteen, it blasted the life out of Gasteen. The man was dead even as he made a half-turn and collapsed on the dark walk.

Two people ran out of the stable, one leaping for the hotel porch. Jubilee held his gun cocked against the sky. "If there's more of 'em," he said coolly, "I'll wait right here," and he watched with a close-eyed interest until a small figure raced into the edge of his vision and sloshed across the muddy pools. Helen Garcia's voice beat into the wind:

"Jubilee — Jubilee!"

Those men he at last recognized and dismissed. Helen's hand gripped his arm with a fierce pressure. "Jubilee, I was afraid —"

"Listen, Buffalo Bill, don't talk to me like that unless you mean it."

Helen's body swayed with the whirling drafts;

her sharp face pointed up to him, full of quick emotion. "Why do you suppose I ran — why do you suppose?"

"If that's an answer," said the man, "I'll be back to hear it. I'll be back."

"It's come to that, Jubilee?"

"The ball's rollin'," grunted Jubilee, climbing to the leather. "So long, kid."

Helen lifted a hand, her bare arm wet with rain, water streaking down from her eyes. "All I can do is wait, Jubilee! If I could follow, I would!"

Jubilee spurred away and was absorbed by the darkness. A later flicker of lightning outlined him fugitively at the head of the gentle grade; then deeper night came down with a pealed-out crash of thunder.

19. What's to Be Will Be

All St. Cloud's guns were alive, flat detonations beating through the wailing wind. Stock-still — his men equally motionless behind him at that moment — Dan Bellew's mind hurled itself savagely at the barrier ahead, only to realize a sure defeat as the odds stood. Lightning licked across the sky, and beyond the heavy crystal screen of rain he viewed St. Cloud's men as a camera would catch them, that instant of pale glow freezing them into postures. They were then in the act of spreading, each rider and each horse vividly outlined; afterwards the ensuing darkness released them from the illusion of being transfixed, and the flickering muzzle lights danced wanly along a ragged line.

Bellew wheeled full about, shouting at the solid shapes of his people. "Get behind the cattle! The cattle between us!" He raced away, feeling the edges of the herd shift and recede. Jubilee Hawk's voice lifted a long and resonant wolf cry indescribably affecting. One man — Dan never knew which — clung doggedly beside him, turning as he turned, matching pace for pace; there

311

was, then, an irregular corner to this mass of stock, and Dan turned it and ran dead on. When the next knifing, electric-blue streak split the shadows he saw the St. Cloud party across a sea of solid cattle backs.

"Turn!" he bellowed. "Keep together — and turn! Push this beef against 'em,"

Link Medders's call was downwind, very faint: "That's it — break 'em up!"

"Keep together!" roared Dan.

He shoved his pony against the swiftening current of the herd, and fired point-blank at the leaders. Sudden volleys cracked out to either side of him; very dim were the yonder guns of the Smoky Draw crowd, whipped away by the torrential rush of the storm. Sage stems pricked his skin, and water roped down hatbrim and shoulder. But the beef was breaking. He could feel panic take hold of that mass and go shuddering through it. After that, the pressure fell off, and he was rushing behind a stampede.

"Keep together!"

Link Medders's wolf howl reëchoed, and the signal caught hold of the thigh-and-thigh Broken Stirrup riders, lifting weird answers into a world gone mad. Link Medders, cold as ice in a thing like this, had fashioned an identifying signal out of the moment's needs. Thereafter it rose and fell, continuous and intermittent. The herd had broken. Dan passed stray cows rolling off on other tangents, he galloped into a widening breach, catching the deep pound of hoofs on either hand. The muzzle flashes to the fore lay suddenly wide apart, and at the next shuttering glow he saw one group of St. Cloud's men huddled compactly in front. They were not more than a hundred feet away, faced toward him. In the foreground was a figure at once recognizable from the torso so heavily seated in the saddle; it was Clubfoot Johnson, his eyes stretched wide by the lightning. Darkness squeezed in. Dan said aloud: "St. Cloud drew Clubfoot's men away from LeBœuf! I'm fighting most of his outfit!" His voice lifted massively: "Keep together — straight ahead!"

Broken Stirrup bayed. One thin and turning shape slid across Bellew's path, and he drove a bullet at it, seeing nothing afterwards. He was, suddenly, jammed into that recoiling group, leg squeezed against another saddle's side. Powder's heat breathed along his cheek, his eardrums rang from the close report; he fired again and saw the fellow fall. The horse bucked away. A howling figure came up from behind and passed on, yelling, "Bellew — Bellew — Bellew!" Broken Stirrup struck with a heavy shock. Somebody went down, horse collapsing at Dan's feet. Dan's pony reared up and over and on — and then all cohesion was lost in the bitter man-to-man combat under heavens rolling out long fanfaronades of thunder.

The lightning made guttering flashes, illuminating a scene of strewn havoc. Cattle ran down the valley in scattered lines; rider wheeled in front of rider, a figure sprawled quite dead below Dan. That stampede, he saw, had ruined St. Cloud's ordered charge; the outlaw's ranks, caught in the frenzied flood of livestock, were so many fragments thrown off in every direction. Riderless beasts careened aimlessly across the eerie earth, men afoot were running blind. He saw one other thing before the black closed down; he saw something like solid opposition forming up to the east — the nucleus of another attack. Instantly wheeling that way, he lifted his call. Answers came hallooing back, but he was alone as he charged the spot where he last had seen the arranging St. Cloud line, alone and identified by the previous flash of lightning. He realized that when he heard the pony wince in a manner almost human and felt the beast tremble throughout. He was out of the saddle before the animal fell, out of it and warned by an onlunging shadow ahead. Sure as he was of that man's politics, he hallooed to be certain; the answer he got was a streaming crimson slash against the gloom. A boot, too, clipped his shoulder in passing, and at that broadside figure he drove a bullet, wheeling as the man went by and dropped from the horse. But it was not a hit. The man was up, running forward and just visible. For one long moment quite still, Dan caught the crush of other riders traveling by, the consequent belch of fury just beyond. Broken Stirrup and Smoky Draw were engaged again; again the tremendous yelling played into the rearing reports of the elements. Somebody cried, "Bellew — Bellew!" But Bellew, drawn into himself, smashed two shots at the figure crouched now near him and let an empty gun hang at the end of his arm.

"Bellew — God forever damn you!" It was a spending blasphemy, full of ancient hatred, and it wailed thinly away. There was a long burst of cold light out of the sky, but Bellew knew without the light who died there fifteen feet away. Clubfoot Johnson's grotesque body rolled over on the black earth and stopped face down. Bellew said "Good!" in a grinding voice, eyes following a single rider who was racing on away from this field altogether. It was all he saw, just a man and horse turning fugitive; after that, blind murk was rent by ricocheting roll of titanic thunder. He stood there, something growing in his head. "He was traveling straight northwest. That's to Broken Stirrup." A long yell kept beating at him from one quarter and another, carrying his name insistently forward. "Who would be going there?" he asked himself. "Who'd have any reason to do that?" Then his tone lifted stridently: "Medders! Shannon! Murtagh!"

The circling horsemen drove instantly inward. "Bellew!"

"Shannon? I want your horse!"

Shannon sprang down, thrust his reins into Bellew's fist. "Why didn't you call sooner? We got this licked — by God, we got it licked!"

"St. Cloud's runnin', Mike, and his crew will be scattered in a minute. Keep together!"

He sprang up and spurred off, Mike's strong yell in his ears. The wind came with him, the bite of the rain was at his back. But the firing made milder sallies across the prairie. It was weaker, more ragged, spaced out. And, scratching the horse with his spurs, he knew the story out there was nearly told. St. Cloud was no coward. He would not run unless he felt the game going wrong. And in running he would take the direction where his own dark talents might still find use. That was Neel St. Cloud: versatile mind finding one more thing to do. He meant to burn Broken Stirrup, then pass on. Bellew understood the man's tricky nature well enough to realize that St. Cloud was consigning his followers to whatever end awaited them. They could die or they could run. Neither alternative meant anything to him; St. Cloud had no regard, no loyalty, no compassion.

Broken Stirrup's light broke into the slanting rain, making star-shaped points across the black; and at intervals he saw St. Cloud's horse pass through that beam. The man was not far away; he could not, Bellew calculated, much more than put his feet on the ranch porch before he, Bellew, would be on top of him. Thinking of that, Bellew let the reins lie slack and awkwardly thumbed fresh loads into the cylinder of his gun. The fight, it occurred to him, had taken place rather near to Broken Stirrup, for he still heard an occasional report whip by him on the wings of the wind.

The house lights brightened, the silhouettes of the poplars appeared. He saw St. Cloud drop at the porch and pause there; but that was momentary, for the man heard pursuit pounding up behind, and he wrenched himself around to meet it. Bellew reined in, dropped to the earth a hundred yards away.

"St. Cloud."

St. Cloud pivoted, ran along the face of the house, turned into the yard. Bellew wondered about that, was puzzled by it. Racing forward, he cut wide of the corner and caught St. Cloud's bulk pass the kitchen lights, still retreating. Somewhere beyond, the man loosed a bullet that went aside. Then a shotgun boomed hollowly from some part of the house — and Bellew understood St. Cloud's avoiding tactics. The man fired again, farther away.

"St. Cloud!"

The man's voice came back, labored and venomous: "Come on!"

Bellew would have lost him altogether, but a second bullet left its muzzle wake high against the shadows. That was from the canyon trail. Reaching the foot of the slope, Bellew groped from one rock to another, rising with the quick grade. He slid around the pine butts, assailed by the crying of the gale in the tree tops, by the deep reverberation of trapped air in the canyon beside him; St. Cloud's voice was very thin:

"Come on!"

The ending, one way or another, was a certainty, a thing of short moments waiting somewhere in this small area that ended at the rim of the gorge just above. Bellew said to himself, "He plays his chances right down to the bitter end" and halted at the base of another tree. He could see nothing in the shadow-ridden region. But he knew approximately where St. Cloud had to be; somewhere, not more than eight feet off, level with him, backed by a chasm affording no more retreat. Thinking of that, Bellew coldly admired the man. If St. Cloud had planned a setting, there could not have been a better one. Advance and retreat stopped here. All that remained was a final stand.

"St. Cloud —"

The man's voice was irregular, taunting: "Come and get me!"

"How far," muttered Bellew, "do I have to follow you? Your game's up."

"You're askin' for a surrender?" rasped St. Cloud.

"You know better. I don't want that."

A shot lashed at him, unexpectedly, hungrily. Bellew marked the point of light, held his fire.

"You'll never get it!" shouted St. Cloud.

"I told you once —"

St. Cloud fired again. The bullet bit at the pine's bark with a small squealing sound. Bellew's gun, trained on the last flash, kicked roaringly back. "I told you once we'd get in each other's way. You're through."

The thin, sardonic answer failed to come. Bellew picked up a strange sibilance in the roiling currents of the hillside — a kind of rasp that had no counterpart in his experience. "Another trick?" he challenged.

The man fired twice, headlong. Bellew's mind was relentlessly tallying those shots. There had been six; it was problematical whether or not St. Cloud had had time to reload. It was, he repeated mentally, problematical. There was no mercy in him, no softness; he wanted to crush and destroy that yonder figure. Stepping away from the tree, he walked slowly forward. He put a shot into the black; he placed two more rakingly after it. St. Cloud's voice was quite near and quite slow: "No man is quick enough to match me! You're not!"

Bellew placed him. Bellew charged. But that vague shape wheeled before his eyes, staggered on. Bellew yelled, "You fool —" and sucked back the rest of the warning. St. Cloud had plunged on into that narrow fissure whose bottom lay sixty feet below.

"You fool," Bellew, repeated, all the animus fading from his voice. "There's no escape that way."

Some sound came crying up the slopes, rousing him. He turned, unutterably weary, lax with the passage of a strain that had been with him, sleeping and waking, for so long. He was, at that moment, like a house abandoned after long tenantry; and as he went loose-muscled down the grade toward a brightly glowing door, he kept thinking: "He didn't know the pool was drained dry. He meant to escape that way. It's all done — it's over — tomorrow is another day." It absorbed him, as would some bright novelty; and he went across the yard toward the door with his eyes fastened on a figure there and not recognizing it until a voice, running violently down all the notes of relief, said:

"My dear — thank God!"

It cleared his mind, it lifted him freely and fully. Nan Avery's supple form swayed out, and her hand drew him on into the enveloping warmth of the kitchen. Lorrie stood stiffly by, eyes glowing like fire.

"We came home, Dan," said the girl gently.

"That's the way it is, Nan? You're sure?"

"Yes."

Lorrie turned swiftly, went out of the room,

face showing acute embarrassment. Sharp-struck echoes rose in the yard, and a call imperatively hailed the house: "Bellew!" On the heels of it, Jubilee Hawk, adrip from hat to boots, came striding through the living room. He paused on the threshold of the kitchen door, heavy-angled face severe. He said, "St. Cloud's outfit is a complete wreck scattered all the way from here to the state line. Where's St. Cloud?"

Bellew looked down at her. He said again: "You're sure, Nan?"

"Here," she said abruptly and lifted her arms. "Here I am."

Jubilee Hawk made a funny noise through his nose, wheeled back to the living room. "Me," he advised himself, "I've got to track clear back through this damn weather to get my welcome, whilst his is right on the premises. Things always come out just right for that guy."

Ernest Haycox during his lifetime was considered the dean among authors of Western fiction. When the Western Writers of America was first organized in 1953, what became the Golden Spur Award for outstanding achievement in writing Western fiction was first going to be called the "Erny" in homage to Haycox. He was born in Portland, Oregon and, while still an undergraduate at the University of Oregon in Eugene, sold his first short story to the OVERLAND MONTHLY. His name soon became established in all the leading pulp magazines of the day, including Street and Smith's WESTERN STORY MAGAZINE and Doubleday's WEST MAGAZINE. His first novel, FREE GRASS, was published in book form in 1929. In 1931 he broke into the pages of COLLIER'S and from that time on was regularly featured in this magazine, either with a short story or a serial that was later published as a novel. In the 1940s his serials began appearing in THE SATURDAY EVENING POST and it was there that modern classics such as BUGLES IN THE AFTERNOON (1944) and CANYON PASSAGE (1945) were first published. Both of these novels were also made into major motion pictures although, perhaps, the film most loved and remembered is STAGECOACH (United Artists, 1939) directed by John Ford and starring John Wayne, based on Haycox's short story "Stage to Lordsburg." No history of the Western story in the 20th Century would be possible without reference to Haycox's fiction and his tremendous influence on other writers of stature, such as Peter Dawson, Norman A. Fox, Wayne D. Overholser, and Luke Short, among many. During his last years, before his premature death from abdominal carcinoma, he set himself the task of writing historical fiction which he felt would provide a fitting legacy and the consummation of his life's work. He almost always has an involving story to tell and one in which there is something not so readily definable that raises it above its time, an image possibly, a turn of phrase, or even a sensation, the smell of dust after rain or the solitude of an Arizona night. Haycox was an author whose Western fiction has made an abiding contribution to world literature.